The Coven

The Coven

Chrissy Lessey

Tenacious Books Publishing

Published by Tenacious Books Publishing

Copyright © 2017 Chrissy Lessey

Published in 2017 by Tenacious Books Publishing
tenaciousbooks@gmail.com

This book is a work of fiction. Names, characters, places, and incidents are either the product of the author's imagination or are used fictitiously.

Library of Congress Cataloging-in-Publication Data
The Coven / Chrissy Lessey
ISBN 978-0-9989518-0-5 (e-book)
ISBN 978-0-9989518-1-2 (print)

Cover Image: © iStock
Cover Design: Anita B. Carroll www.race-point.com
Book Design: Erin Rhew www.erinrhewbooks.com

Printed in the United States of America

www.tenaciousbookspublishing.com

For Jeff

prologue

June 1718

Lucia perched on a long piece of driftwood, gripping the smooth, pear-shaped amethyst that hung from her neck. Splintered pictures of her worst fears raced through her mind. Angry mobs. Screaming women. Crying children.

Executions.

She closed her eyes. That couldn't happen. Not again.

A child's joyous squeal jarred her from her thoughts. She opened her eyes to see the youngest generation of her people running about in the sand, their gleeful giggles rising above the roar of the crashing waves. Their mothers looked on with contented smiles, blissful in their ignorance of the coming danger.

They enjoyed a simple life here. With only their own kind on the island, they were free to live as they pleased. They danced and sang and honed their skills in the open, without fear of discovery. Lucia let her gaze drift to the cottages and shacks that stood in the grassy area beyond the beach. To the captains of passing ships, the settlement would appear to be nothing more than a fishing village.

In truth, it was all that remained of Lucia's kingdom.

She called to one of the nearby women. "Grace, fetch my daughter. Hannah and Catherine too." She let her hands fall to her lap and hung her head. This wasn't what she wanted to do. It was what she had to do.

The queens who'd come before her had made great sacrifices to protect their people. She blinked, recalling the details of the vision that would force her to divide her group. Her own mother, in Salem Village, had suffered far worse to keep their secret hidden. Still, Lucia knew the pain of this day would haunt her forever.

She glanced at a woman who walked along the shore. "Abigail, gather the children and their mothers. Go hide in the brush by the freshwater pond."

Abigail's mouth fell open, but she did not hesitate to do as Lucia instructed. She ushered the little ones away from the beach.

Lucia had sent the men and older boys to fish on the other side of the island early that morning. Now that the women and children had left the shore, she had just one remaining task.

She sighed when she caught sight of Charlotte, Hannah, and Catherine walking toward her. It was almost time. Discovery and persecution would soon arrive on the horizon.

Tucking a stray graying hair behind her ear, she rose to greet them. These three women would ensure the survival of her people. Hannah, fierce and strong, could withstand the challenges to come. Catherine, still a teenager, was the youngest among them, but her unique gift would serve them well.

And then there was Charlotte, Lucia's only daughter. The future queen.

When they stopped before her, she told them of her visions, both of that day and in the long years to come.

Rebellious tendrils from Charlotte's auburn braid whipped in the wind. "But mother, we are ready to fight!"

Lucia shook her head. "No, we are not."

"Surely we can beat them with our magic." Hannah crossed her arms. "They are mere men."

"Yes, but to what end? There are far too many of them, and their behavior exceeds the ignorance-fueled violence our people have faced before." Lucia pursed her lips. "Cruelty is a way of life for these pirates. If we fight, there *will* be bloodshed." She stopped short of explaining that there could be no enemy survivors. If any of the invaders left the island after learning of their magic, they would tell others and more would come to hunt her people.

Catherine faced her with a defeated frown. "Then there is no other way…"

"I don't understand how this could happen." Charlotte heaved a great sigh. "How do they know about us?"

Unable to meet her daughter's gaze, Lucia studied the waves as they broke on the shore. "I can only assume that someone on a passing ship saw something they shouldn't have. Whatever the source, these men would not come if it were only a guess."

"We were too careless here." Hannah dropped her arms to her sides and hung her head.

Lucia nodded. "We were." She paused, gathering her thoughts, and then faced the young women once more. "The pirate captain will not leave empty-handed. It's a matter of pride. He collects beautiful women just as he does any other treasure. You will go with him as a distraction to keep him from seeking out the rest of the villagers."

Catherine's lip quivered. "Why us?"

"Do not despair. You each possess qualities that are essential for the success of this endeavor." She cupped Catherine's cheek. "Your unusual gift will ensure your safety in the new village. Listen in on the thoughts of those around you so you will know if anyone ever suspects our secret. You can warn Hannah and Charlotte if a threat arises."

She turned to Hannah. "Your resilience will see you through the hard times ahead, and your powerful magic will be a great asset in your new life."

Lucia reached for Charlotte's hands. Looking into her eyes, she saw the young woman her daughter had become, but she still remembered the child Charlotte had been not so long ago. Her heart sank. She'd trade places with her in a second if only she could. "He will not want me. You must go in my place and lead our people."

Charlotte's delicate features pinched in agony. "What will happen to you?"

"I will stand with you until the end." Lucia forced a weak smile and squeezed her daughter's hands before releasing them.

Catherine pointed to the sea. "They're coming!"

Lucia turned to the water. During their discussion, a large ship, accompanied by three smaller sloops, had appeared on the horizon.

"It is time." She held her voice steady but hastened to share all that she knew. "You will settle in a new village. I have seen it in my visions." She paused. "I do not know how you get there. I only know that you will."

"Can't we return here to our island?" Catherine's voice quaked.

"No, my dear, do not come back. It is clear now that we are too vulnerable here. I must evacuate the others and find another home among the colonists, but we'll stay near the ocean where our powers are the strongest. Like you, we will integrate into another community and hide in plain sight." Lucia drew in a deep breath and reminded herself again that she had no other choice. Her people depended on her. "We will have to separate, but it ensures the greatest chance for our survival."

Lucia faced Charlotte and spoke for all to hear. "Daughter, as of today, you are the true queen of our people. Your descendants will lead future generations." She removed her amethyst necklace and placed it around Charlotte's neck. "Hide it."

Breathless, Charlotte covered the pendant with her hand. It began to flicker and then faded away until it was no longer visible. She lowered her hand and looked to her mother for approval.

"Well done." Lucia could not bring herself to smile. Instead, she wrapped her arms around her daughter, remembering how she'd felt when she received the amulet decades earlier. "You *are* ready for this."

Lucia pulled away and watched the boats approach the island. The pirates would come ashore soon. And by the time they left, she'll have lost her title, her home, and her only child.

It's the only way.

She spotted the flag on the largest vessel. On its black background, a white skeleton with horns held an hourglass in one hand and a spear in the other. A pierced and bleeding heart lay below the sharp tip of the spear, a symbol of a violent and torturous death. Her stomach clenched at the vile sight.

She raised her chin and turned back to the witches who awaited the fate she'd orchestrated for them. "Remember, no matter what happens, we cannot reveal our magic to them. When they leave here today, they must believe that their information was false."

The young women nodded.

Lucia embraced Charlotte once more as the pirate ships drew near, sealing an unavoidable fate. "Do not be afraid."

Chapter One

Present Day

Vanessa

The woman in black had raced to the Los Angeles airport as soon as the call had come in. Unwilling to waste any time, she'd not bothered to return to her oceanfront house to pack a suitcase. With no baggage to check, she purchased a one-way ticket to Raleigh-Durham International Airport and proceeded farther into the bustling concourse.

She pressed her phone to her ear as she walked. "Have the car waiting for me when I arrive." Her jaw tightened as she listened to the response from the other end of the call. "I don't care how you get it, just do it!" She disconnected and shoved the phone back into her leather handbag.

At the security gate, she placed her stilettos, along with her bag, into the plastic tray and waited for her turn to pass through the metal detector. Though she was certainly the most dangerous passenger the security agents would ever encounter, the exercise was a waste of time. An airport security check could not expose the weapons she possessed.

Her black dress fit like a second skin, leaving nothing to the imagination. She knew she had already caught the attention of the agents at the gate. One, in particular, lacked the stealth most of her admirers had. He stared straight at the low neckline of her dress, allowing the trays he was supposed to inspect to roll past him unchecked.

Ignoring the agent's hungry gaze would have been the polite thing to do. Instead, the woman in black bent forward, just a bit, to meet his eye level, and she raised one of her well-sculpted eyebrows. The man's face flushed a bright red when he realized she'd caught him staring at her. He cleared his throat and resumed his work.

She was accustomed to the attention, though it had become tiresome and predictable. With long coal black hair and emerald green eyes, she knew she was an unusual beauty. And she knew how to use it to get what she wanted.

The woman in black passed through the metal detector without incident, proceeded to her gate, and waited for first class to begin boarding. Struggling to hide her contempt for her fellow passengers, she cast a wary glance toward a young mother with an infant and a toddler in tow. Children were nasty little creatures, always sticky, drippy, or crying. Why anyone would choose to assume the care of one, much less two, she could not imagine. She looked away, comforted by her certainty that the pesky little monsters would be flying in coach.

She turned her attention to a flat-screen television that hung on the wall. The muted Weather Channel showed a radar picture of the Atlantic Ocean. A pretty meteorologist pointed to a new tropical depression that had just developed off the coast of Africa. With any luck, the woman in black would be well on her way back to Los Angeles before the storm neared the coast.

When the time came to board the plane, she found her seat on the aisle. She settled in and took a moment to observe the other passengers around her. As usual, there were several businessmen to consider.

One was quite attractive and in his mid-thirties, not much older than she. As he loaded his briefcase into the overhead compartment, she noticed his bare ring finger. No wedding band.

That's too bad. All the good ones are single.

She fastened her seatbelt and waited for takeoff. Having flown many times in the last twelve years, she could recite the flight attendants' safety spiel from memory. The only thing that seemed to change from one trip to the next was her alias.

Until today, her travels had always been without purpose. She'd seen the world, or at least the parts of it she had interest in seeing, and since she could work anywhere, she'd had no reason to tether herself to any one place.

At the thought of her job, she scanned the men on the plane again. She didn't *have* to work anymore. In fact, she could retire anytime she wanted. Even with her expensive tastes, it would take several lifetimes to drain all of her bank accounts.

While her work was often tedious, it provided an income and relief from boredom. And one element of it made it worth her time— the look on her target's face when she broke the news to him. She stretched. It would be a long flight, and she was already bored. Time to find her mark and get to it, perhaps for the last time if everything in North Carolina went as she hoped.

When the plane leveled out, she unbuckled her seatbelt. Across the aisle, a silver-haired man in a designer navy suit met her gaze. He smiled and then returned his attention to a short stack of documents resting on the tray in front of him.

The woman in black motioned for the flight attendant. "I'll have a merlot."

"Certainly, Ms. Colby." The perky attendant hurried away to fetch the wine.

This would be her last day as Ms. Colby. She pursed her lips in a self-satisfied smirk. After twelve long years under assumed names, she looked forward to using her birth name when she reached her destination.

The attendant hummed a cheerful tune as she delivered the red wine. Then, she turned to speak to the silver-haired man on the other side of the aisle. "Would you like anything from the bar, Mr. Sampson?"

"Yes. Bourbon, please." He stole another glance at the woman in black as he replied.

Like shooting fish in a barrel. She retrieved her phone from her hand-bag and connected to the plane's Wi-Fi service. A simple Internet search revealed everything she needed to know about Mr. Sampson. He was the CEO of an enormous pharmaceutical corporation. He was also someone's husband. In other words, he was perfect.

The flight attendant strode down the aisle with Mr. Sampson's bourbon. She didn't notice Ms. Colby's gaze fall to her feet, nor did she catch the slight nod that followed.

An instant later, she stumbled. She managed to avoid falling, but not before a splash of bourbon spilled onto Mr. Sampson's sleeve. Her smile vanished.

"I'm terribly sorry!" Her face flushed bright red. "I'll get a towel." She hurried back down the aisle.

The woman in black caught Mr. Sampson's aggravated glare, and she leaned toward him. "I have some spot cleaner in my purse. Come with me to the restroom, and I can clean that right up for you." She narrowed her eyes and tilted her head, hinting at something else, something *extra*.

A broad grin stretched across Mr. Sampson's face as all traces of his irritation slipped away.

Simpleminded fool.

The woman in black eased out of her seat and made her way to the restroom in the front of the plane. He followed her without hesitation. She could feel his eyes on her, indulging in the view her curve-hugging dress provided.

She slipped into the tiny room and placed her bag beside the sink. Her phone rested on top of it with the video camera set to record. He entered the room only a second later and pulled the narrow door closed, his breath already ragged with anticipation. Without a word, the woman in black took control and inducted yet another member into the Mile High Club.

When they were finished, she smoothed her dress back into place, reached into her bag, and handed him a piece of paper with a long series of numbers on it.

"What's this?" Mr. Sampson frowned.

"A bank account. Transfer three hundred thousand dollars to it before this plane lands."

He gave her "the look." They always did. First, their jaws dropped in shock, as if they could not believe that she had any motive other than finding them irresistible. Men and their egos—it was almost too easy. Shock then shifted to anger when they realized she was blackmailing them.

"No." He zipped up his pants with a firm yank.

She showed him her phone, rewinding the video to a particularly damning scene. "You are worth millions. I'm sure you won't even notice a few hundred thousand dollars missing."

"Go to hell!" He pivoted and reached for the door.

"I'm curious, Mr. Sampson. How much will your wife get in the divorce?" Though she spoke without urgency or emotion, she still managed to stop the man in his tracks. "It's your choice. You can either pay me now or pay her after this airs on the news."

He turned to face her, his lips pressed into a thin line, and glared at her for a long moment. "You bitch!"

"Close enough." She winked and pushed past him to let herself out of the restroom.

There was no shortage of people who would take issue with her chosen profession, but she had no reservations about her work. She was always in control, from selecting her mark to determining her fee. No one could ever mistake her as the victim in these encounters. Without a doubt, she was the predator, preying on the powerful. And she was not ashamed of it. She grinned as she returned to her seat, pleased with her accomplishment.

Mr. Sampson emerged from the lavatory a moment later, three hundred thousand dollars poorer, his sleeve still stained with bourbon.

chapter two

Stevie

Stevie Lewis had lived near the water her entire life, but the sight of dolphins still filled her with joy. She watched the pod swim gracefully into Taylor's Creek, their movements a secret symphony, in harmony with a song known only to them. From her perch on Carrot Island's sandy shore, she had a clear view of their sleek, gray forms as they danced around each other.

A bottlenose broke through the glassy surface of the water. His four companions skimmed just beneath him as he leaped into the air, arced, and dove back down. The pod continued their carefree parade through the narrow inlet, treating Stevie to an enthusiastic show of playful splashes and jumps.

"Charlie, look! The dolphins are jumping!"

Stevie's smile faded as she looked down at her five-year-old son, and the familiar pain jabbed her heart. She wanted to share this experience with him and see his cherubic face light up in sheer delight. She wanted to hear his giggle again. Stevie wanted a lot of things—all of them entirely out of reach.

She watched as Charlie scooped a handful of sand and let it sift through his fingers. Golden ringlets fell around his face, hiding his pale blue eyes. Just a few years ago, those eyes had sparkled with bright curiosity. Now, a need for routine and a lack of connection to the world clouded them. His furrowed brow overshadowed his dimpled cheeks, evidence of the countless fears and worries tormenting his young mind.

She ached for the days when he'd been a happy baby and a spirited toddler. He'd walked and talked just like other children until shortly before his second birthday. Then, without warning, he seemed to forget the words he already knew. He'd begun to shy away from Stevie's hugs. The inexplicable meltdowns started around the same time. Soon after that, he'd stopped talking altogether. Charlie's regression had lasted several months, and, by the end, he'd emerged as a different child. He was trapped in the prison of autism, and Stevie was trapped in a prison of pain.

But she still remembered his sweet, lost voice.

"Wuv you, Mama!" He used to proclaim the words at random moments, delighting her with his enthusiasm.

She would give anything to hear him speak again.

Stevie took a deep breath and released it with a sharp exhale. Picking up her Nikon, she shifted back toward the water to search for the lively pod of dolphins. She was too late; they were already gone.

"When I was your age, I loved to watch dolphins play," Stevie said as her son continued his solitary ritual of sifting sand through his fingers. Though he could not reply, she knew he both heard and understood her words.

"I guess the sand is pretty cool too." She forced herself to smile. She'd grown accustomed to their one-sided conversations.

Camera still in hand, Stevie snapped a few shots of Charlie. He would never look toward the lens and smile, so she didn't bother to ask. His smiles were rare and fleeting. With a sigh, she thought of her friends who had all accumulated huge photo collections of their grinning children looking straight at the camera—some with birthday cake smeared on their faces, others beaming as they displayed an art project or held up the first fish they'd caught. Those mothers captured happy times and joyful faces, a luxury Stevie could no longer enjoy.

Back to work. She resisted the urge to wallow in self-pity and instead looked across the wide expanse of water to her hometown of Beaufort. She'd come to Carrot Island to get pictures of the town's historic waterfront. With tourist season winding down, she'd need to capture extra special shots to garner the interest of the locals, who had access to these views year round. Keeping that in mind, she glanced around for a unique perspective that would bring Beaufort natives into her small shop on Front Street. Lexi, her friend and business partner, had already upped the ante by starting a collection of abstract Crystal Coast paintings.

Stevie shifted her gaze a couple of blocks west to the Maritime Museum, which housed artifacts from the many local shipwrecks. With the number of pirate ships, Civil War vessels, and German U-boats congregated on the sandy sea bottom, it was no wonder that the treacherous area off the coast of North Carolina had long been known as the "Graveyard of the Atlantic." As she studied the land she knew like the back of her hand, her heart swelled with gratitude and pride. Not everyone had the benefit of living in a place with such a colorful history.

Several news vans crowded the museum's parking lot, leaving Stevie to wonder if they had uncovered another sunken ship. The last time a discovery of an old shipwreck made the news, it turned out to be the *Queen Anne's Revenge*, Blackbeard's flagship. She had been in elementary school at the time, but she still remembered the excitement of the find. Historians, treasure hunters, and tourists alike had descended on the town in response to the revelation.

Stevie made a mental note to find out what was going on at the museum. If there was going to be another influx of tourists this late in the season, she needed to get busy snapping pictures.

She bit her lip. She needed to come up with a new way to share her vision of the Crystal Coast. Variety kept the customers happy and her mind busy. She'd already amassed an enormous collection featuring the pristine beaches and abundant life on the surrounding barrier islands. From hermit crabs to wild mustangs to lighthouses, she'd covered it all. Though she'd taken a hundred similar pictures before, she spun around and snapped a quick shot of a sea grass covered dune. One more wouldn't hurt.

She turned back toward the town and adjusted the zoom on her camera, focusing on the small strip of shops and restaurants that stretched along the waterfront. She centered on Clawson's Restaurant and took the shot. Lowering her camera, she scanned the waterfront for another subject and spotted an enormous yacht at the town docks. Its modern shape stood in sharp contrast to the historic homes and buildings that lined the street. She sighed. The boats at the docks may have become sleeker over the years, but the rest of Beaufort had changed little since the eighteenth century.

Stevie began to feel the heat from the late summer sun, so she tucked her Nikon inside her bag and tied her hair back into a ponytail. She kicked off her flip-flops and sat down on the oversized towel next to Charlie. Digging her toes into the warm sand, she took a sip from her water bottle.

"Are you thirsty, Charlie?" Stevie asked as if she expected him to answer. She always spoke to him that way because she believed that he would answer—someday.

Without looking up, he let the sand finish falling through the fingers of his right hand while he reached for the water bottle with his left. His expression remained unchanged, far too serious for such a young boy.

After Stevie stretched her legs in front of her, she rolled up the hem on her denim shorts. She closed her eyes and let her head fall back, allowing her face to soak up more of the sun's rays.

Life was good here. They had the island all to themselves. There was no one around to cast a judgmental glare or laugh at her son's unusual behavior. She found solace in the salty breeze coming off the water while Charlie found comfort in the endless grains of sand running through his fingers. Stevie watched as he scooped as much as he could hold into his small hand. He seemed to like the weight of it in his palm, as if the pressure comforted him somehow. He tilted his hand, allowing the grains to slip from his grasp. She wondered what he experienced as the spilling sand brushed against his soft skin. Why did he enjoy it so much?

All of a sudden, Charlie abandoned his silent sifting and turned to the east. Two wild mustangs, a mare and her foal, rounded a sand dune and stopped to snack on sea grass about twenty yards from where they sat. Stevie retrieved her camera from the bag, controlling her movements to avoid startling the animals.

She adjusted the focus of the lens and tried to capture the majesty of the horses. Tourists purchased these pictures by the droves, and they loved it when she told them the stories of how the animals had swum ashore hundreds of years ago from shipwrecked vessels. People came from all over the world to catch a glimpse of these creatures who'd not only survived but flourished on the barrier islands. And they often took home one of her prints as a souvenir.

Both horses had honey-brown coats with blond manes and tails. Stevie snapped their pictures. Even without words, the mare still taught her foal everything she needed to know in order to thrive. Stevie wished her own life were so simple.

The mustangs moved back to the east. When they were out of sight, Charlie's gaze flicked to the boat waiting nearby.

"Ready to go home?" Stevie tucked her camera into its waterproof case.

She shook the sand out of her towel and placed it in her beach bag. They crossed the narrow beach to the boat, and she rested her bag on one of the seats. Charlie tensed and stopped in his tracks, still several feet away from the skiff.

"Don't worry. I haven't forgotten." She reached into the bow of the boat, produced the object of Charlie's concern—noise-canceling headphones—and placed them over his ears. With the headphones to shield him from the sound of the motor, he relaxed his shoulders. He climbed on board, donned his life vest, and took a seat. Stevie pushed the boat away from the beach before jumping on board. After two forceful pulls, the motor revved to life, and they were on their way across the creek.

Stevie approached the western end of the waterfront, piloting her skiff toward her private dock. After she secured her boat, she turned to help Charlie step out. Without a reminder, he'd already placed his headphones and life vest under the seat. Stevie took his hand, and together, they crossed Front Street and headed toward the home that Stevie had inherited from her grandmother.

She grinned with pride as she took in the sight of her waterfront home. In keeping with the rules of an old town ordinance, the house was painted white with black shutters and doors. A quirky up-and-down picket fence encased the small but meticulously manicured lawn. Wicker rockers adorned the full porches of both the first and second floors. Though the five-bedroom home was much too expansive for just the two of them, Stevie enjoyed living there. It had sheltered generations of her family, and someday, it would belong to Charlie.

"All right, let's get you cleaned up." Stevie guided her son through the front door. The old wooden floorboards creaked as they crossed the foyer.

Charlie paused on his way to the stairs, glancing at a painting of three beautiful young women. It had hung in that spot for as long as Stevie could remember, and she barely noticed it anymore. She'd never seen Charlie take an interest in it before this moment.

"That's a portrait of Charlotte, Hannah, and Catherine. They were some of the earliest residents of Beaufort. Charlotte is one of our ancestors." Stevie laughed, surprised to hear herself uttering the same words her grandmother had used many years ago to describe the artwork to her.

She remembered standing before the painting as a child. Her Grandma Rose had smiled and promised that she would someday tell Stevie all about these three women and their very special secret. With a heaviness in her chest, Stevie realized that promise had never been fulfilled. Since Charlie had shown an interest in the portrait, she decided to see if her mother could fill them in on the women's story.

Charlie continued to gaze at the painting, and Stevie wondered what had triggered his sudden fascination with it.

"We can look at this more later. Right now, it's bath time." She nudged him in the direction of the stairs. "We have to get all that sand off of you."

While the warm water filled the claw-foot tub, she helped Charlie get undressed and climb in. She washed him, being extra careful not to let any water drip down onto his face.

When he was younger, an unexpected drop of water would have triggered an epic meltdown. Though he'd recently outgrown that particular sensitivity, and had even begun to enjoy swimming, Stevie still kept her guard up.

She ran her hands through his hair, remembering the little blond cherub he'd once been, full of giggles and grins and questions. Back then, she'd had such hopes for him. She'd dreamed of watching him play soccer, sharing laughs over a playful pod of dolphins, and guiding him from a curious little boy to a successful man. But since his diagnosis, autism had consumed her focus. Instead of shopping for cleats and shin guards, she researched supplements and consulted with specialists, remaining in constant pursuit of the next milestone in his development.

As she washed the suds off his back, she tried to force herself back to the present. To the progress, not the pain. As he'd gotten older, the once-frequent meltdowns had become rare occurrences, and for him—for them—it meant huge progress.

"All clean!" Stevie announced as she lifted him out of the tub. She dried him off and dressed him in his favorite dinosaur shirt and knit, pull-on shorts.

She watched Charlie walk into his bedroom. He drifted to the long table on the back wall to play with his Lincoln Logs. She studied him for a moment, wondering once again what her child was thinking. He lived in a world of his own, but she would give anything to bring him back to hers.

The doorbell rang, startling Stevie from her thoughts. She left Charlie to play in his room while she ran downstairs to answer the door.

Chapter three

Susan

Like so many times before, Susan Moore sat in the corner of the day room in eastern North Carolina's largest psychiatric hospital. She stared through the bars of the nearest window, watching the bright sunlight trickle through the leaves of an old oak tree in the courtyard.

With a heavy sigh, she turned away from the view. Not even the beauty of the outside world could brighten the monotony of her everyday life inside this place. In twelve years, nothing had changed. She slept, she ate, she took her medications, and she stared out the window.

Even her fellow residents remained the same. No one ever left, for this floor housed the people who had not entered the facility of their own volition. None of them would recover from their mental illnesses. Unwelcome in the outside world, they were locked away to protect the general public from their tormented minds and tortured souls.

To ease the pain of her miserable existence, Susan always swallowed the pills the nurses gave her three times a day. She never raised a fuss about taking them like some of the other patients did. She welcomed the tiny, round passports to her extended mental vacation. Without them, Susan figured she might actually go insane.

But on this day, everything *had* changed.

Several hours earlier, the television, which was always on in the day room, had blared the Friday morning news. Susan had paid no attention to the meteorologist because the weather inside the hospital remained consistent. Not even reports of the latest tropical depression in the Atlantic had given her pause. It was not until the next segment, when the anchorwoman announced a certain historic discovery, that Susan had turned her head to follow the report.

By the time the two-minute feature story had completed, she'd developed a newfound sense of purpose. She knew she needed a plan but found it difficult to concentrate. The fuzzy, overmedicated mind that once made her existence bearable had now become a liability.

But she knew how to fix that.

As the day wore on, Susan's perceptive dullness had begun to recede. Though it would take a while for all of the medications to clear her system, her reality had already grown sharper. Her thoughts moved with more clarity than they had in years, so she concentrated on developing her plan.

A nurse approached her with a familiar paper cup in hand. "Time for your meds." She shook the cup for emphasis.

Susan turned to face her. She crinkled her nose at the sight of the nurse's audacious scrubs, which would only be appropriate for a ward populated with colorblind clowns.

Susan accepted the pills and put them in her mouth as she always did. As soon as the nurse turned to deliver medication to another patient, Susan made her way down the hall. She resisted the urge to grimace, even as the bitter drugs began to dissolve under her tongue.

Finally, she made it to the bathroom, where she spit the pills into the sink. Just as she had that morning, she turned on the faucet, sending the chemical comfort she'd enjoyed for far too long down the drain.

She glanced around the expanse of the large room. There were currently eighteen patients in the ward, most of whom were present now. Each pursued a leisure activity, or at least an odd approximation of one. A handful of patients sat on the worn, outdated couches focusing their blank stares at the television screen as cartoon characters performed a variety of silly antics for their viewing pleasure. At a nearby table, two women worked together on a puzzle that had almost all of its pieces. Others, under the close supervision of orderlies, completed simple craft projects using safety scissors designed for small children.

Susan scowled as her psychiatrist entered the room. Dr. Max, as he insisted his patients call him, strolled toward her. He smiled as he looked around the room, as if it were perfectly natural for adults to watch cartoons and require supervision when using dull scissors. She returned her attention to the window and awaited the inevitable.

"Susan?" he called as he approached her.

With reluctance, she glanced his way. She knew what he wanted, and she intended to comply because, for now, she had no other option. But soon, she'd never have to see his smug face again. Before long, she would possess the one item that would change the trajectory of her life forever...and maybe Dr. Max's too. She started to smile but clamped down on it, reminding herself to play the part of the drugged up patient until her help arrived.

"It's time for your evaluation." He gestured for her to follow him. "Please come with me."

Susan rose from her chair and followed the doctor to his office. They'd been through this process many times before. He would ask her questions, and she would answer them. She always tried to say as little as possible in order to avoid giving away any more information than was necessary. Since she had so little control over what came out of her mouth, she had given up hope of ever passing the evaluation. She pursed her lips together in frustration. If only she could pick and choose what to say. Susan shook her head to rid it of the thought. No use dwelling on it. She'd just have to make do with her limitations, for now.

Trailing behind the doctor, she crossed the threshold into his office. Like all of the other rooms in the state-funded hospital, no one had redecorated it in several decades. Dark wood paneling covered the walls, and a metal desk with rust spots occupied the center of the small room. Susan settled into one of the orange vinyl armchairs in front of the desk and waited for him to begin the routine evaluation.

Dr. Max sat in a faux leather chair behind the desk and opened Susan's thick file. He skimmed through the notes the hospital staff had added since his last review.

"You've been compliant with your medications," he mumbled as he read. "Still no visitors though."

Since it was not required, Susan did not offer a response. Instead, she studied the sparse strands atop the doctor's balding head.

He looked up from the file with his eyebrows raised. "You made a phone call this afternoon. You've never done that before."

Susan replied with a cold stare.

"Aren't you going to answer me?"

"Answer what? I didn't hear a question." Given her particular situation, the distinction between a question and a statement held great significance. She did not have to answer a statement. A question, however, required a response. A truthful one.

Susan suspected that Dr. Max had practiced the serene smile that he wore now. It telegraphed his inner calm as well as his unceasing willingness to listen to the troubles of his patients.

What an asshole.

The doctor closed her file and leaned forward. "How are you feeling today, Susan?"

She did not bother to look at him. "I feel like I want to leave this place." She'd provided the same answer in all of her previous evaluations.

"Is that frustrating for you?" Dr. Max asked.

"What do you think?" She glared at him. Though she wanted to stop there, she felt an overwhelming compulsion to answer his question fully. "Yes."

With the exception of the day she arrived at the hospital against her will, this was the first time she had shown any anger toward the doctor. The pharmaceutical calm had dulled her emotions, leaving her without tears or smiles, and certainly no anger. As her fury returned, she noticed that she no longer slurred her words.

Susan shifted uncomfortably under Dr. Max's studious gaze. She wondered if he planned to increase her medication. Perhaps tomorrow she would have an additional pill to wash down the drain. She stared at the threadbare carpet beneath her feet.

After a long pause, Dr. Max spoke again. "Do you know why you are a patient in this hospital?"

"Of course I know!" Susan threw her head back and groaned. Then she lowered her chin and glared at the doctor. "Do we really have to do this again?"

"I have to ask these questions." He reopened her file, clicked his pen, and scribbled a quick note. Then he looked back at Susan. "Do you still believe that you're a witch?"

"Yes," she answered through clenched teeth.

Susan knew that her admission of being a witch was not enough to require inpatient psychiatric care. To the uninitiated, it was merely an eccentric idea, not a symptom of insanity. It was the rest of her story, the part she could not help but admit to, that forced the authorities to keep her locked up.

"Susan, what would you do if you were discharged from this hospital?"

Her knuckles grew white as she tightened her fists. She grimaced, knowing her next statement would once again confirm the doctor's diagnosis and justify her confinement. She bit her lip, as if that alone would be enough to stop the words from exiting her mouth. It wasn't.

The words tumbled, unbidden, from her lips. "I'd go right back to Beaufort and kill them all."

"Who?" Dr. Max asked, as if he'd not already heard the answer countless times before.

"The coven! The witches who did this to me!" Her shoulders slumped in resignation, and she fell back against the chair.

Dr. Max jotted down another note. When he was finished, he clicked his pen and placed it on top of her file. The evaluation was complete. The corners of his mouth turned up in another plastic smile as he looked at her.

Susan clenched her jaw at the sight of his smug smirk. She would not forget his role in her imprisonment.

A new idea occurred to her. She straightened her shoulders and leaned forward in her chair, focusing her sharp glare on the doctor.

He raised an eyebrow and tilted his head. "Do you have something else you would like to say?"

Susan nodded. "There *has* been a change to my plan."

"Oh?"

"Yes." She grinned. This truth she was happy to share. "When I get out of here, I'm going to kill *you* too."

Susan stood and left his office. As she made her way down the hall, she heard the unmistakable click of the doctor's pen.

chapter four

Stevie

Stevie answered her door and found Sam waiting on her porch. "Hey."

He stood just beyond her welcome mat with his hands crammed deep inside the pockets of his jeans. His smile did not quite reach his eyes. "Hey."

Their relationship was amicable, but there were still plenty of awkward moments, like this one. She knew Sam hated ringing the doorbell of the house that had once been his. "Come on in." With a wide sweep of her arm, she ushered him inside. Maybe her graciousness would somehow ease his tension. With any luck, hers as well.

Sam followed her to the kitchen at the back of the house. "How's it going?"

"Not bad. Charlie's having a good day. We just got back from Carrot Island. I got some great shots while we were there."

"It was a good day for it." Sam relaxed his hands by his sides. "Can't beat this weather."

"Yep. Warm and sunny all day."

The weather. Perhaps the safest possible subject for a divorced couple to discuss. But Stevie had nothing more to add to the matter. She glanced to the floor in search of inspiration and came up empty as an awkward silence filled the room.

"Oh, I remember what I wanted to ask you!" She looked up at him, relieved to have another safe topic to tackle. "Do you know what's going on at the Maritime Museum? I saw news vans out front. Did you happen to hear anything about it while you were at your water taxi outpost?" The words babbled out of her mouth in quick succession. She'd never had trouble talking to him while they'd been married, but now… Her cheeks grew warm with embarrassment.

"Yeah, some divers found Blackbeard's treasure near the wreckage of the *Queen Anne's Revenge*. Pretty cool, huh?" His bright blue eyes sparkled. "That old son-of-a-gun left something behind after all."

"Are you serious?" Stevie raised her eyebrows. "People have been searching these waters for that treasure forever. Crazy that it would turn up after all this time."

"They think the hurricane last month stirred things up on the sea floor and made the chest visible. Can you believe it? Hidden down there for three hundred years…" Sam shook his head, and his shaggy blond hair fell over his eyes. He pushed it out of the way and smiled.

"I wonder what they'll do with it." Stevie imagined a chest full of shiny gold coins and jewelry. Probably worth more money than she'd ever earn in her lifetime.

Sam scratched his head. "I reckon it will take a while to get it all cleaned up and catalogued, but after that, they'll probably just display it with the *Queen Anne's Revenge* exhibit at the museum."

Stevie nodded. "Maybe it will bring in more tourists." Already, she'd begun to envision a photo set she could take of the treasure. And maybe she could convince her old friend from high school, who now worked at the museum, to give her an exclusive photographic tour.

"That will be a good thing," Sam said. "We could sure use the extra business."

Silence fell once more. Stevie's thoughts drifted to the reason for Sam's visit—Charlie's first weekend stay with his father. She stepped toward her kitchen counter and began to load bottles of dietary supplements into a plastic bag. She worked in silence as she mulled over her concerns.

Sam leaned against the counter, watching her.

She pursed her lips as she tried to decide how to voice her concerns without starting a fight. "I'm still not sure about this." She loaded the last of the bottles into the bag and zipped it closed. "Charlie's never been away from home before."

He's never been away from me.

Sam crossed his arms. "Hey, I'm not the one who wanted the divorce. This is part of the deal that you agreed to."

Stevie caught the sharp edge of his tone. If she didn't choose her next words carefully, they would wind up arguing. *Again.*

"I guess I thought it would be a while before he went to stay with you on the weekends." She shrugged and gulped. "I thought things were going pretty well the way they were."

Sam let his arms fall to his sides. "I'll still visit him here during the week sometimes. But I need more time with him, just the two of us. I'm not going to be like my father." His eyes grew dark.

Stevie knew the pain of his father's abandonment still stung. "You're a good dad, Sam." Her reassuring smile lasted only a second before her apprehension took over once more. "It's just that I can't imagine a whole weekend without Charlie." She sighed and zipped the seal on the plastic bag. "But…" She dragged out the word. "I guess I'll have to get used to it."

"Please tell me I don't have to give him all of those pills." Sam eyed the bag of supplement bottles.

Stay calm. Stevie forced herself to look at him. This same old argument had grown tiresome long before their divorce. "Yes, you *absolutely* have to give him these. They help. They really do."

"Didn't the doctor tell you not to believe what you read on the Internet?"

Stevie narrowed her eyes. "All of these supplements were prescribed by one of his doctors."

"You mean that 'all-natural' doc who doesn't even accept health insurance, right?" Sam shook his head and looked away.

"Don't start this again," she warned him through gritted teeth. This was one argument she was not willing to lose.

Sam faced her once more. "I'm just saying that it's a hard way for a kid to live. That's all."

Stevie's face grew hot with anger. "You want to know what's hard? Autism. That's a hard way to live."

"You've already got him on that crazy diet. Now you want to pump him full of pills?" Sam raised his voice.

It was true that Stevie had first discovered information about the gluten-free, casein-free diet online, but the results were undeniable. Though the supplements were a new addition to Charlie's treatment plan, she was sure they were helping as well.

Her entire body tensed. *She* was the one who did all of the research. *She* was the one who met with all of the doctors, specialists, and therapists. To have him question these interventions singed her frayed nerves.

She'd devoted her life to helping Charlie get better, spending countless hours researching every possible treatment to find the safest and most suitable options. If Sam thought a healthier diet and a few harmless supplements were drastic, he would really hate some of the other treatment options she'd read about.

"These are all-natural supplements. You just open the capsules and empty the contents into his juice. He doesn't even know he's taking them." Stevie's jaw tightened with the all-too-familiar frustration of discussing this issue with Sam. "And even *you* have to admit that the diet has helped him."

It was the same fight they'd had a hundred times before. Sam wanted to follow the directions of Charlie's doctors and specialists, which often consisted of doing nothing, with the sole exception of speech therapy. One had suggested that Charlie might grow out of it, and another had recommended they simply pray for him. She'd left each of those appointments in tears, refusing to accept that she was powerless to help her son. Sam, on the other hand, had taken the advice of those doctors without question.

She studied the man who'd once shared her life, her home, and her bed. He looked like the same boy she'd fallen in love with, but too many years and too much pain had turned them into strangers. They'd been a happy couple once, but that had changed when autism crashed into their lives. Before long, they fought every day. Sam blamed Stevie's obsession with researching treatment options, and Stevie blamed Sam's unwillingness to seek answers. She hadn't wanted Charlie to grow up with parents who argued all the time, so she'd asked Sam to move out. He'd obliged. They'd both thought they would work things out at some point, but that day had never come.

"I need to know that you're going to do this." She held out a piece of paper outlining Charlie's daily supplement schedule. The sheet shook in her trembling hand as she fought to keep her temper under control.

Sam was quiet for a moment. Finally, he took in a deep breath and accepted the paper from her. "Let me see." Though his anger had diminished, he frowned as he skimmed over the lengthy list of supplement names.

She pointed to an item on the list. "That one is very important. It helps keep him calm." She softened her voice. "Just follow the schedule, okay?"

Stevie wondered what might have happened if they'd mastered the skill of avoiding all-out war while they were still married. A small stab of regret pricked her heart, but she pushed the thought from her mind. It was too late now.

"I'll do it…for you." Sam's smile returned.

"Do it for Charlie."

"Yes, ma'am." He saluted.

Stevie struggled to suppress a smile. "Not funny."

Sam chuckled. "Okay, where is he?"

"Upstairs." She grabbed the bag of supplements from the counter.

As Stevie followed him out of the kitchen, she allowed her gaze to linger on his broad shoulders longer than she should have. When he glanced back at her, she blushed and looked away. There were a few things she missed about being married to Sam.

Stevie and Sam entered Charlie's bedroom. She expected to find her son standing at the long table, where he worked on his many Lincoln Log creations, but he was not there. She glanced around the room, which she had painted blue for him after reading an article online that claimed it was a soothing color. As it turned out, Charlie did not seem to care what color his walls were. His main concern was having an ample supply of logs to play with.

"Charlie?" Sam called. There was no sign of the little boy.

"Check the hideout. He's been in there a lot lately." Stevie stuffed the bag of supplements into Charlie's red backpack.

Sam walked over and pressed the tiny switch inside one of the paneling grooves, unlocking a secret door. A section of the wall opened to reveal a five-by-five closet.

Stevie smiled, as she often did when she recalled playing in that same hideout as a child. Her Grandma Rose had filled her head with stories of women and children hiding from pirates and of colonists using the secret room to store their treasures.

Now, it housed a different kind of treasure—Charlie. Unlike Stevie, and the others who'd played in the hideout as children, he used the dark, quiet room as a sanctuary from the sensory input that unsettled him. Especially when Stevie pulled out the vacuum cleaner. The mere word "vacuum" sent Charlie bolting for the hidden closet.

"There you are." Sam opened the secret door wider. "Can Daddy have a hug?"

Charlie stood up and hugged his father. Sam's eyes glittered with joy as he accepted his son's embrace.

Hugs were a new achievement for Charlie. Stevie bit her tongue, resisting the urge to point out that that particular improvement had come *after* she started giving Charlie the dietary supplements.

Sam patted his son's shoulder. "We're going to have a fun weekend together, buddy."

Charlie crossed the room to the nightstand. He picked up his tablet and began to type.

Stevie grinned. She had a feeling she knew what he was going to say.

He almost never used the tablet when he was with her. She was good at guessing what he wanted or what was bothering him at any given moment. His dad, however, needed help sometimes.

Charlie finished typing and showed the screen to Sam.

"Name Charlie," Sam read the words on the screen. "I'm sorry. 'Buddy' is just a nickname. You don't like it?"

Charlie pointed to the screen again, driving his point home.

"Got it." Sam nodded. "I won't call you that again."

Sam picked up the backpack and led Charlie out of the room. As Stevie followed them down the stairs, an empty sensation gnawed at the pit of her stomach. She hoped she could get through saying goodbye without getting emotional. The last thing she wanted was for Charlie to see her upset.

"I'll see you on Sunday." She ruffled Charlie's blond curls and planted a kiss on his forehead. "I love you."

"I'll take good care of him." Sam gave her arm a sympathetic stroke.

She forced a smile. "I know you will."

Stevie watched them walk toward Sam's old blue pickup truck. She let out a long, slow breath and wondered what she was supposed to do with herself during her first weekend alone since Charlie was born.

chapter five

Dylan

Dylan Kent sat behind the massive mahogany desk in his London office. Across from him, two car company executives waited while he reviewed the final paperwork for his purchase of their corporation. He always insisted on meeting the sellers in person before signing off on a deal, and this occasion was no different.

They watched him with eager anticipation, but he took his time reviewing the file, unhurried by their zeal. He studied the legal documents in silence, allowing his gaze to skim over wordy addendums and agreements, and skipped past all of the flagged lines that required his signature. His gold pen rested on his desk, unused.

After several long moments, he looked up from the papers and met the restless stares of his guests. "Before I can sign the agreement, I have a question for you."

The younger executive stole a fleeting glance at his senior counterpart before turning back to Dylan. "We are happy to answer any questions you may have, Mr. Kent." He nodded, his face tight with apprehension.

The young man has every right to be uneasy.

Dylan folded his hands, the picture of calm against the business-men's storm. For years, he'd bought and sold international corporations and had never fallen prey to a bad deal. A few corporate giants had tried to cheat him over the years, but he'd always managed to sniff out deception and avoid potential pitfalls. This deal would be no exception.

I wonder if the London tabloids will hear about this one. The relentless paparazzi stalked him just as they pursued their celebrity and royal targets. If he cut his hair, the story made front-page news. In a recent story, one of the rags had indulged in speculation as to whether or not his square jaw was a result of genetics or surgery. The shutterbugs' interest in him had become an unavoidable annoyance, which left him with little tolerance for any other irritations—as his guests would soon discover.

"As you are aware, gentlemen, my purchase offer is quite generous." Dylan leaned forward.

The two men nodded in agreement. "It is, sir," the older one replied.

"Then you'll understand that I want to be sure my investment is safe." He glanced from one representative to the other. "Are there any issues within the company that I should be aware of?"

The younger one stiffened. "Certainly not. Our cars exceed all safety requirements, and our manufacturing practices feature state-of-the-art technology."

"I see." Dylan paused as he glanced at the purchase contract resting on his desk. "Are you sure that there are no safety issues among the existing models?"

"I assure you, Mr. Kent, there is nothing for you to be concerned about." The older man nodded, his head bobbing up and down like a fishing lure. "You can complete this purchase knowing that the transition will be seamless. You will have no regrets."

"Thank you very much for meeting with me today." Dylan smoothed his silk tie as he stood up from his chair. "But I'm sorry to say that I won't be purchasing your company."

The older representative's mouth fell open, but he did not speak.

"But, sir." The younger man popped up from his seat. After a brief pause, he slumped back in the chair, fell quiet once more, and hung his head.

The older one regained his composure first. "What can we do to change your mind?"

"At this point, there is nothing you could do to make me want to buy your company." Dylan stepped from behind his desk, escorted the men out of his office, and closed the door behind them.

As he began to return to his chair, a sharp knock rattled his door.

"Come in."

His assistant, Maggie, entered the office. "That young one looked like he might start sobbing at any moment." She tilted her head. "I take it the deal fell through."

"You're correct." The moment they'd stepped out of his office, he'd all but forgotten the encounter. Before the meeting, he'd hoped they'd tell the truth about the safety issue, but he'd suspected they wouldn't. And as with any failed deal, he pressed onward and upward.

"Don't tell me they tried to pull a fast one on the human lie detector." Maggie flashed him a knowing grin.

"I'm afraid so." He settled into his leather desk chair. "Please call our contacts at the news networks. Let them know that there are currently twenty thousand sedans with faulty brakes on the streets of the United States." He closed the file and moved it to the far corner of his desk. "Feel free to share the contact information of those gentlemen. I'm sure they'll appreciate the call." He smirked, certain the attention of the press would solve the problem faster than any government intervention could.

"How did you manage to uncover that?" Maggie raised an eyebrow in suspicion.

Dylan smiled. "You know I cannot divulge my trade secrets."

Maggie stepped closer to his desk. "You received a phone call from Patricia Guthrie while you were in the meeting." She handed him a small piece of paper with a phone number written on it. "She said you would know what it's in reference to."

"Thank you, Maggie."

Dylan reached for the telephone as his assistant stepped out of the office and closed the door behind her. After all these years, Patricia would only contact him for one reason, and he was ready for it. He dialed the number listed on the paper and waited for her to pick up.

After the usual pleasantries, he asked the one question he'd been waiting the whole time to ask. "Is she back?"

"Randy says she's on her way." Patricia's familiar southern accent dripped like honey through the receiver.

"Then so am I." He tightened his jaw. "I'll see you soon."

Dylan disconnected the call and walked out of his office, stopping at Maggie's desk. "Please call the pilot. I need my jet ready immediately."

"Right away, Mr. Kent." Maggie picked up the phone but paused before dialing. "Where are you off to this time?"

"Home."

chapter six

Vanessa

After an overnight layover in Atlanta, the woman in black arrived at Raleigh-Durham International Airport on Saturday morning. She walked alone, bypassing the flurry of welcoming hugs and kisses her fellow travelers enjoyed. No one waited to embrace her.

A twinge of regret coursed through her, but she held her head high. She'd done what she had to do to survive—living a solitary existence of necessity, spending her ample free time honing her skills, and preparing for an occasion such as this. She raised her chin and dismissed those pesky feelings. Soon, she would face those who had forced her into hiding. And it would not end well for them.

She exited through the main door and found what she was looking for—a sleek, black BMW convertible waiting for her next to the curb. It was the exact model she had ordered the day before. A young man in a charcoal-gray suit stood beside the car, scanning the crowd for its new owner.

"Ms. Vanessa Moore?" he asked as soon as he saw her.

Her pulse quickened. She had not heard that name in years, and it gave her a thrill to have it back. She could be herself now, not Ms. Colby or any of the other aliases she had hidden behind for so long.

No more hiding. When she reached her destination, she would move about freely, confident in the knowledge that her previous activities there had remained a well-guarded secret. Only a few people were aware of her true nature, and she knew they would try to stop her. But soon, she would have what she needed to get rid of them. All of them.

The young man stepped toward her and handed over the car keys. "Ms. Moore, the security guard is heading over here again. He'll want you to move the car out of the drop-off zone right away."

Vanessa rolled her eyes. "It won't be a problem. I'm leaving now." She slipped a few large bills into the young man's hand and made her way to her new car. She eased into the black leather seat, brought the powerful engine to a roar, and zipped away from the airport.

Vanessa turned on the satellite radio system and began scanning the stations. She bypassed the twangy country tunes and the bass-infused pop songs in favor of classic rock. Settling on a song she recognized, she turned up the volume.

Eager to unleash the BMW's full potential, she pressed the accelerator all the way to the floor. She sped down the interstate, heading east, not at all concerned about getting a speeding ticket. If a cop somehow managed to stop her, she would have no trouble taking care of him. She laughed at the angry motorists honking and shaking their fists as she flew past them.

If they only knew.

Vanessa stared across the length of the day room, searching for her mother. The last time they were together, Vanessa had been a teenager, fresh out of high school. Now, she was a grown woman. A lump formed in her throat. They'd lost a lot of years.

She found Susan sitting across the room in a battered armchair, staring through a window. Her mother had withered during her time here, becoming pale and thin instead of the wild and vibrant woman Vanessa remembered. Susan's once black hair had faded to a dull gray. She now looked at least a decade older than her fifty-two years.

They'd both lost so much, but Vanessa intended to fix that.

She squared her shoulders and made her way toward Susan. "Mother."

Susan turned her head and rose from her chair. After twelve long years apart, Vanessa stretched out her arms to embrace her mother.

Ignoring the invitation for a hug, Susan brushed past her daughter without pause. "Follow me. We need privacy."

Vanessa swallowed hard as she let her arms fall to her sides. "Of course, Mother."

A smiling nurse stopped them in the hallway as they exited the day room. "It's time to take your medicine." She offered Susan a pleated paper cup that held a single pill.

"I'm not due for anything right now."

"This is a new one." The nurse's cheerful grin did not falter. "Dr. Max ordered it for you yesterday, and it just came in."

Susan accepted the medication without asking any additional questions. She popped the pill into her mouth and jerked her head back as though she were downing a shot of tequila. She handed the empty cup back to the nurse and continued the rest of the way to her room. Vanessa followed two steps behind.

They entered the private room, and Susan closed the door. Vanessa had forgotten how austere the hospital quarters were. It was nothing at all like the luxury she enjoyed in her own home or during her frequent vacations. She wondered how her mother had managed to survive in this dismal setting for so long.

Peeling seafoam green paint coated the bare walls. Next to the narrow bed sat the nightstand where Vanessa had tucked away a copy of her phone number just before she went into hiding. Her mother had used that number for the first time yesterday, to call her back home.

Susan spit the pill she had feigned swallowing into a tissue and tossed it into the metal trashcan beside the door. "The nurses stopped checking to make sure I was actually swallowing those things after the first couple of years. Up until yesterday, I took the pills willingly the entire time I have been here. They help make this place somewhat tolerable." She sat on the edge of her bed. "Now that there's work to be done, I'm skipping the drugs. I need a clear head."

"Why don't you just let me get you out of here, Mother? It wouldn't be difficult at all." Vanessa struggled to keep her voice steady. She'd made the same offer twelve years ago but had been rejected.

"I'm safer here, at least until I can defend myself. If the coven were to find out I had escaped, they would hunt me down. And this time, there's no telling what they would do to me."

"I can protect you." When the coven bound her mother's powers, she'd braced herself for the same punishment. But it had never happened. Surely they had tried—and failed.

Susan shook her head. "No. I can't risk it."

Vanessa stared at the bars on the window. The coven. Those self-righteous witches had forced her to go into hiding and stolen Susan's powers. Why should they get to live in freedom while her mother endured this hellhole?

Susan rose, shoulders straight and chin high. In Vanessa's eyes, her mother was now a queen holding court with her one and only subject. Vindication was finally within reach, and the time had come to make plans.

"You've seen the news reports?" Susan rubbed her hands together.

"Yes, and I'm ready."

"Good. Wait a few days for some of the excitement to die down. Then go get the necklace," Susan instructed. "Bring it to me as soon as you have it. It will make me whole again. Then I can finally leave this awful place."

"Anything else?" An expectant grin crept across Vanessa's face. A surge of magic tingled in her fingertips, and she itched to unleash it.

Susan looked into her eyes. "You'll need to take care of the others, of course."

Vanessa nodded. "I've had a private detective watching them for years. Did you know that Patricia has a young grandson now?"

"No, I didn't." Susan's cold eyes lit up. "That's good. Start with him."

chapter seven

Stevie

Lexi Pollock clapped her hands together and grinned. "I know exactly what you should do!"

"Somehow I knew you would." Stevie rolled her eyes. She had a feeling she would not want to take part in whatever adventure her friend had in mind.

"You're going to Backstreet with me. There's a great band playing tonight." Lexi flitted around their shop. She moved with the grace of a dancer in spite of her high heels and form-fitting blue gingham sundress. Her petite frame and short, spiked bleached-blond hair reminded Stevie of a pixie. "It'll be fun! Just like the good old days."

Though Stevie and Lexi had been best friends their entire lives, their ideas of fun had diverged around the time of Charlie's birth.

Stevie sighed and glanced around the shop to avoid answering. Instead, she took in the view of all that they had built together. Decorated with driftwood, hurricane lanterns, and one very old wooden ship's wheel from a long-ago sunken vessel, Coastal Visions was an homage to the local culture. Stevie's framed photography and Lexi's watercolor paintings lined the walls.

After several years of running the shop themselves, they now enjoyed the luxury of having an employee manage it for them most days, which allowed them ample time to pursue their photography and painting interests. Both women had a flair for capturing the natural beauty of the area in their art, but that's where their similarities ended. And nothing about Stevie's art or lifestyle said "take me to Backstreet to see a great band."

"Well? What do you think?" Lexi clasped her hands and tucked them under her chin like a little girl begging for candy. "We haven't had a girls' night out in forever."

"I don't think so, Lex. That's not really my thing anymore. I was planning to, you know, just hang out at home. Besides, I have some new pictures to print." Stevie's gaze fell to the floor.

"So, you're finally unburdened for a weekend, and you're going to spend it working?"

She snapped her head back up and glared at Lexi. "Charlie's not a burden!"

"That's not what I meant." Lexi frowned for a moment. "I just want to see you have a good time. Let your hair down for a bit." Her smile returned, and she gave Stevie's ponytail a playful tug.

Stevie could not deny the loneliness she'd endured after Charlie left with Sam the night before. She'd cooked herself a nice dinner but had no appetite. She'd tried to work on her latest prints, only to find it difficult to concentrate. When she'd settled in to watch television, she couldn't shake the void created by Charlie's absence. Faced with the possibility of another night like that, she reconsidered Lexi's offer.

Stevie bit her lip, still reluctant. "It would probably be good for me to listen to music that isn't performed by cartoon characters." She looked at her best friend, who awaited her reply with an undeniable hopefulness. "All right, I'll go."

"Fantastic!" Lexi bounced up and down. "Yay!"

Stevie wagged her finger. "Don't get too excited. I'm leaving if I don't like it."

"Understood." Lexi attempted to give a solemn nod but could not manage to hide her smile.

The chime on the front door rang and both of them looked to see who was coming into the shop. Summer was almost over, so the tourist season was winding down. Most of the store traffic consisted of locals during this time of year.

"Hi, Mom," they said in unison.

Two women entered the store, looking like a pair of aging hippies. Lexi's mother, Deborah, wore an ankle-length batik dress. Her long, graying hair hung loose, forming a wiry cascade that stretched almost to the center of her back while Stevie's mother, Patricia, allowed her unruly auburn curls to fall to her shoulders. Her gauzy white broomstick skirt swished across the tops of her sandals as she approached her daughter.

Patricia rested her hand on Stevie's shoulder. "How are you, dear?"

She shrugged. "I'm okay. It's just a little weird. Last night was hard, not having him at home."

Patricia never missed an opportunity to offer unsolicited commentary regarding her daughter's life. "It's good for him to spend time with Sam—"

"I know, Mom. It just takes some getting used to." She turned from her mother, hoping to signal the end of conversation before it turned into a lecture.

"Don't worry, Patricia. I am all over this. We're having a girls' night out tonight. She'll be fine once she loosens up a bit." Lexi nudged Stevie with her elbow.

"Where are you girls going?" Deborah asked.

"Backstreet Pub," Lexi replied.

Deborah arched an eyebrow. "Don't do anything I wouldn't do."

Stevie covered her mouth to hide the snort of laughter threatening to escape. Not doing anything Deborah wouldn't do did little to limit their options. The Pollock women lived life to the fullest, even if that meant having their moral fortitude questioned. Lexi was already well on her way to exceeding her mother's legendary status in the little town. She did not need any additional encouragement.

Patricia glanced at Stevie. "Have you noticed any activity at the Kent house?"

The question caught Stevie off-guard. She hadn't seen Dylan Kent in twelve years. While his house was next door to hers, it had remained empty since he and his father left town soon after the accident that killed Dylan's mother, Rebecca.

The memory of that awful night rushed to the forefront of Stevie's mind. Rebecca had rammed through the guardrail of the drawbridge, crashing into the water below. It had been a clear night, and there had been no evidence of drugs or alcohol in her system, no obvious explanation for why she'd lost control of her car. On that same night, Stevie's grandmother had suffered a fatal stroke. In the days following the tragedies, she and Dylan had grieved their unexpected losses together.

Stevie looked to her mother, baffled by the question. "I really haven't paid much attention to it, Mom. Why do you ask?"

"I heard a rumor that Dylan was coming back to town." Patricia waved her hand as if to dismiss the idea.

A lightness rose in Stevie's chest at the thought of Dylan's return. Though she had long since outgrown the secret crush she'd had on him in high school, she couldn't deny that she looked forward to seeing him again. "I'll keep an eye out for him."

"Please do. And keep me posted." Patricia cast a sideways glance at Deborah. "The Historic Society would like to welcome him back to Beaufort."

"Definitely." Deborah smiled.

Stevie tilted her head. She could not help but notice the unspoken exchange between her mother and Deborah. What weren't they telling her about Dylan's possible return?

Before she had a chance to ask, Patricia changed the subject. "Speaking of the Historic Society...Lexi, will you be able to join us for the meeting next week?"

Lexi gave a thumbs-up. "Wouldn't miss it."

Patricia looked at Stevie but did not speak.

Knowing that someday she would have to become involved with the Historic Society, Stevie bristled under the weight of her mother's gaze. The women of her family had presided over the group for generations. With Patricia as the current president, Stevie was certain that her presence would soon be required at the meetings in order to learn the ropes.

But she was not interested in joining, much less running, the Historic Society. She cringed at the thought of taking on the responsibility of telling people what shade of white to paint their fences. Perhaps Patricia would pass the torch to Lexi, since she actually seemed to enjoy participating in the group.

Lexi glanced at her watch. "Time to close up shop."

Patricia gave Stevie a quick hug. "Stop by and see us soon. Maybe dinner tomorrow?"

"Sure, Mom." Stevie nodded. "Sounds good."

When their mothers left the shop, Lexi turned off the lights and locked the front door. Stevie stored the cash register drawer in the safe and activated the security system.

As they left, Lexi checked the lock on the back door and then linked her arm through Stevie's. "I'll go home with you and help you get ready."

"No." Stevie held up her hand in protest. "You're welcome to come with me, but I'm perfectly able to dress myself."

Lexi raised her eyebrows and giggled. "We'll just see about that."

Chapter eight

Stevie

Stevie fell back on her bed with a loud groan. "Oh come on, Lexi! It's just Backstreet Pub. I don't see why I have to wear a dress. I'm fine in this." She pointed to her standard attire of a t-shirt and shorts.

"Don't you have *any* dresses?" Lexi's exasperated call came from deep inside Stevie's closet.

"Nope."

Stevie listened to the sound of hangers sliding back and forth along the rack inside her closet. She grinned, knowing Lexi would only wind up disappointed with anything she found in there. Maybe then her friend would give up on this silly waste of time.

"Ah, here we go." Lexi emerged from the closet carrying a red sundress. "This is perfect!"

"Where did you find that?" Stevie gestured toward the dress. "It's not mine."

"It was in your closet, hidden behind a ridiculous number of faded blue jeans." Lexi shrugged.

Stevie crossed her arms. "I think I know my own clothes. I've never bought anything like that."

"Maybe it belonged to your grandmother." Lexi tilted her head and held up the dress as she studied it. "You know how you're always finding her stuff around the house."

"I highly doubt that." Stevie eyed the dress' narrow waist and short hemline. She was certain that Lexi had smuggled it in and then simply *pretended* to find it in her closet. It wouldn't be the first time her best friend had tried to trick her, though she never understood why Lexi went to such ridiculous lengths to get her way.

"Well, then, I guess you bought it and forgot about it." Lexi glanced from the dress to Stevie and back again. "You're going to look gorgeous in this!"

Already tired of discussing it, Stevie sighed and resigned herself to play along. She adored Lexi, but there were times when Stevie just did not have the energy to keep up with her.

"Whatever. You can't make me wear heels though. I'm sticking with the flip-flops." Stevie threw a playful glare at her best friend. "I mean it."

With a smug grin, Lexi laid the cotton dress on Stevie's bed. She paused and fiddled with the white eyelet bedspread before glancing around the room. "Have you ever considered updating your bedroom? Maybe a more contemporary style?"

With few exceptions, Steve hadn't changed the décor since she inherited the home. "I kind of like it the way it is." The look might be outdated to *some* people, but Stevie enjoyed the connection she felt to her family history in this house.

"The furniture isn't so bad." Lexi gestured to the antique four-poster bed and matching armoire. "But this…" She tapped the coverlet on the bed. "This really isn't your style, is it?"

Stevie placed her hand on her chest in mock horror. "Is a board member of the Beaufort Historic Society suggesting that I modernize my house? I'm pretty sure you'll get the pillory for that." She giggled.

"Besides, isn't it a little late to be concerned about my personal style?" She jerked her head toward the dress that Lexi had selected for her.

Lexi rolled her eyes in a flamboyant display of annoyance. "I'm only trying to help you lighten up a little. You're always so serious."

Muttering more mock-angry protests under her breath, Stevie slipped into the red dress and Lexi proceeded to primp and style her. Lipstick, mascara, and hairspray…so much hairspray. Stevie covered her mouth and nose, trying to avoid inhaling the toxic cloud that surrounded her.

"Am I thoroughly unrecognizable yet?" She tugged at the hem of her dress, already beginning to regret accepting Lexi's invitation for a girls' night out.

"You look beautiful." Lexi stepped back to admire her own work even more, her eyes twinkling in smug satisfaction. "Really, Stevie, if you'd just put a little effort into it, you'd find a guy in no time."

Stevie grimaced. "I don't *need* a guy. I'm doing fine on my own."

Lexi gave her a once-over. "You don't seem fine to me."

"I really don't have time for a relationship. Charlie keeps me very busy," Stevie said.

"I'm not suggesting that you start up a *relationship*." Lexi dragged out the last word to emphasize her distaste for that institution. "I'm just saying that you've got to stop making excuses and live a little. It'll be good for you."

Stevie set her jaw. "If you think I'm going to go home from the bar tonight with some random stranger, you're out of your mind."

"It's Beaufort, hon; there are no strangers here." Lexi smirked.

"Let's just get this over with." Stevie walked toward the doorway. Her flip-flops slapped the bottoms of her feet with each step. She stopped and glanced back at Lexi, whose amused giggle had brought her to a halt.

"Fine! I'll wear the damn heels." Stevie slumped against the wall in defeat.

"Fantastic." Lexi beamed and skipped back to the closet to find more appropriate shoes. She emerged carrying a pair of strappy red sandals with two-inch heels.

"Okay, seriously." Stevie shifted her weight to one leg and propped her hand on her hip. "Did you bring all of this with you, or is there some kind of alternate universe in the back of my closet? Those are *not* my shoes."

"Sure they are. I was with you when you bought them," Lexi assured her.

Stevie drew her brows in tight. "Really? I don't remember—"

"See? This is exactly why you need to loosen up and get out more. You're getting forgetful already." She wagged her finger. "You've got to keep those brain cells stimulated with fun, new experiences to help stave off dementia."

"Dementia? Don't be ridiculous!" Stevie blinked. "I'm only thirty!"

"That's my point. You're far too young to be so forgetful. We need to stop it in its tracks." Lexi hurried to grab her purse from the top of the dresser. Then she spun around to face Stevie. "Now, are you ready to go?"

"I guess so." Stevie shrugged and followed her friend out the door.

As they made the short walk to Backstreet Pub, Stevie realized she hadn't visited the bar in years. In fact, she couldn't recall having much fun at all since Charlie's diagnosis. An odd mix of apprehension and excitement gnawed at the pit of her stomach as she accompanied Lexi into the two-story brick building.

As a legendary fixture in the town, the pub was already crowded with Saturday night revelers. Stevie spotted fishermen, business owners, and a few boat dwellers she recognized. They were all clad in attire ranging from stained t-shirts and faded shorts to spotless polos and pressed khakis. She glanced down at the red abomination that Lexi had insisted she wear and realized she was overdressed. She felt her cheeks grow warm as several men she knew from town greeted her with enthusiasm.

"Geez." She leaned in closer to Lexi. "They act like I've come back from the dead."

"It *has* been quite a while since you were here." Lexi continued to scan the crowd.

"Yeah, but I see most of them around town all the time."

"Did you even look at yourself in the mirror?" Lexi looked her up and down. "You're hot, Stevie."

"I'm not sure how to respond to that." She released an uneasy giggle.

"You can start by thanking your super-awesome very best friend." Lexi batted her eyelashes.

"Thanks." Stevie shook her head and tried to hide her grin.

Lexi ordered two chardonnays from the bar and passed one to Stevie. They sipped from the disposable plastic cups and scanned the room, acknowledging friends and acquaintances with smiles and waves. The usual stiffness in Stevie's shoulders began to let go. Before long, she realized she was smiling for no particular reason.

Upstairs, the band began to play. The drummer's steady beat throbbed through both floors of the pub and out into the rear courtyard. Stevie looked up at the ceiling, knowing a crowd of people danced upstairs. She used to be one of them, but she'd not let loose like that in years.

It does feel good to be back here.

Stevie tapped her foot to the fast beat of the song. "You want to go upstairs?"

Lexi nodded. "Yeah! Let's dance!"

They went outside to the fenced-in courtyard and climbed the wooden steps to the upper deck. The door hung wide open, so they watched for a moment as the band covered an old Rolling Stones song. The small dance floor was packed, and Stevie recognized most of the faces. They came from a diverse range of backgrounds, from the kid who operated the register at the bookstore to the gray-haired attorney who owned the most prestigious law firm in the county—a perfect microcosm of Beaufort.

Stevie and Lexi stepped into the crowd and danced through two songs before the band stopped for a break.

"More wine?" Lexi waggled her eyebrows.

Stevie shook her head. "I should probably slow down. I'm already feeling it."

"You've only had one. You can't possibly be drunk yet." Lexi fished a few bills from her purse. "I think the strange sensation you are experiencing is called *relaxation*."

"I guess you're right." Stevie sighed. "Thanks for dragging me out here tonight. I still don't think this ridiculous dress was necessary, but I am having fun."

Lexi threw her arm around Stevie's shoulders and gave her a gentle squeeze. "Good."

"Hello, ladies," a deep voice called from behind them.

Stevie had not heard that voice in years, but she recognized it right away. She was already smiling when she turned to greet her old friend Dylan Kent.

"Dylan!" Lexi squealed and tackled him with a welcoming hug. "You're back!"

Stevie's breath caught in her throat. When he was a teenager, Dylan's deep brown eyes had shown a compassion that seemed well beyond his years, and she remembered the butterflies that had taken flight in her stomach every time he'd smiled at her. She forced herself to take a breath, hoping to slow her racing heartbeat. Maybe she'd been wrong to assume her adolescent crush had faded.

"Stevie." Dylan flashed the same bright smile she remembered with such fondness. "It's great to see you again."

She stepped forward into his embrace. Resting her head on his broad chest, she inhaled the warm scent of his cologne. With reluctance, she pulled away, hoping the dim lighting of the pub hid the blush that burned her cheeks.

"How have you been?" Dylan stroked her bare arm.

She could hardly remember her own name at that moment, much less sum up the events of the last twelve years. She ran her hand through her hair as she tried to form a coherent thought. "We certainly have a lot to catch up on. It's been too long."

Lexi leaned toward Dylan. "Did your dad come back with you?"

"No." He shook his head. "Dad stayed in London. He's moved on now."

Curious, Stevie raised her eyebrows. "Oh, has he remarried?"

"Yes. She's a great lady. Honestly, I am happy for him. He had a really hard time after my mom died."

"I'm so glad to hear it." Stevie glanced at his ring finger and noticed it was bare. She bit down on her lip in an attempt to hide her relief. She glanced up to Dylan's face once more, only to find him looking right at her, smiling.

She scolded herself. She hadn't been divorced for long. Plus, she had her hands full with Charlie. She looked away. Dylan should remain off-limits.

"You're not the only one from our graduating class to show up in town today." Lexi raised an eyebrow. "I heard that Vanessa Moore was seen on the waterfront this afternoon."

"Well, that's quite a coincidence." Dylan's smile faltered. "I'll be sure to look her up while I'm here."

"I think it's time for another round." Lexi locked her arm around Dylan's. "Why don't you come with me to the bar?"

"Sure." He nodded. As they walked away, he turned back to Stevie and winked. "Back in a minute."

The local band returned from their break. Led by the guitarist's steady strums, the drummer unleashed a thick beat. Stevie moved away from the dance floor to a spot on the outside deck where she, Lexi, and Dylan could talk. It was a warm night, but the oppressive humidity of summer had already diminished. It would be autumn soon, her favorite time of the year.

Dylan and Lexi returned with the drinks. Dylan handed Stevie a chardonnay and then took a long pull on his beer. "So, Stevie, what have you been up to since I saw you last?"

"Well, Lexi and I opened a shop on Front Street." She took a quick sip of her wine for courage. "And I have a five-year-old son. His name is Charlie."

Lexi jerked her thumb at Stevie. "She got married *and* divorced while you were away!"

Dylan chuckled. Stevie resisted the urge to elbow Lexi in the ribs.

The three friends nursed their drinks as they caught each other up on the details of their lives. Dylan showed no surprise to hear that Beaufort had not changed much since he'd left for London. Lexi tossed in a few bits of the juiciest gossip from the town, and Stevie shared some of her favorite stories about Charlie.

Dylan finished his beer. "I should get home. I still have some unpacking to do."

"Why don't you walk Stevie back to her place? You guys are next door neighbors now." Lexi winked at Stevie.

Dylan looked at Lexi. "What about you?"

"My apartment is just across the alley. I'll be fine. Besides, I'm not done here yet." She eyed a muscular man who stood on the other side of the deck. "I'll catch up with you two tomorrow." She threw a friendly wave over her shoulder as she abandoned her old friends.

"Whoa, looks like that guy spends a lot of time in the gym." Stevie glanced at Lexi's new companion with wide eyes. "His biceps are bigger than my head."

"I guess Lexi is the same as ever." Dylan chuckled.

Stevie laughed. "Oh, no. She's *much* worse now."

"Come on." He smiled. "I'll walk you home."

The old, familiar butterflies took up residence in Stevie's stomach once again as Dylan touched the small of her back and led her away from the pub.

Chapter Nine

Stevie

Stevie stretched as the late morning sun beamed through her bedroom window. She had not slept this late in years, not since before Charlie was born. She picked up her phone from the nightstand and dialed Sam's number.

"How is he?" She croaked out the question, her voice still thick with sleep.

"Geez, Stevie, you sound rough." Sam chuckled. "Just waking up?"

"Yeah, I slept in this morning." She sat up in her bed. "How is Charlie?"

"He's having a great time."

She twisted the coverlet around her finger. "What's he doing now?"

"He's watching cartoons and flapping his hands like he always does when he's happy."

She smiled at the joy in Sam's voice. "Okay. So everything's going all right?" She wanted to ask if he'd followed the supplement schedule and stuck to Charlie's dietary restrictions, but she held back.

"I promise you he's doing fine. Don't worry so much."

He'd said those words a hundred times. The familiarity both warmed and pained her. Stevie let out the breath she had been holding in. "That's like telling a fish not to swim."

He laughed. "I know. Believe me, I know."

"I'll be at my parents' place this afternoon. Can you drop Charlie off there? I know they'd love to see him."

"No problem. I'll see you there."

As soon as she disconnected the call, her phone rang. She answered it right away.

"Well? What happened?" Lexi's gossipy drawl crawled through the phone line.

"Ugh." Stevie groaned. *Lexi has such a one-track mind.* "Nothing happened. Dylan walked me to my door and then went to his own house. That's all."

"That's *it*?" Lexi sighed. "Always a gentleman." She said it like a condemnation instead of a compliment.

"I don't see that as a bad thing."

In fact, I considerf it a very good thing. The butterflies in her stomach resumed their incessant fluttering.

"He's still cute." Lexi giggled like they were still teenagers gushing over a boy.

"Yep." Stevie kept her voice flat. She had no interest in pursuing girl talk with Lexi, certainly not before fortifying herself with coffee.

"Do you think you'll see him today?"

"He's right next door. I'm sure we'll cross paths at some point." Stevie glanced out the window, already hopeful but not willing to let Lexi know it.

"Well?" Lexi paused, leaving nothing but dead air between them.

Stevie rolled her eyes. "Well what?"

"You didn't ask about my night." Lexi's pout traveled across the line. "Aren't you curious?"

Stevie snorted. "Not really. I'm pretty sure I know what happened after I left."

"Give me a little credit. Maybe I've changed."

"Have you?" Stevie sat up straighter.

"Well, no." Lexi giggled.

Stevie shook her head and smiled. "Then I guess there's really nothing for me to ask about."

When their call concluded, Stevie went downstairs to start a pot of strong coffee. She hoped the caffeine would dull the headache she'd earned from having one too many glasses of wine at Backstreet the night before.

As she looked through the kitchen window while filling the coffee pot with water, she found she had an unobstructed view of Dylan sitting on his back deck, reading a book. She studied his stunning profile—the straight line of his jaw, his broad shoulders, and his thick crown of dark brown hair—but she let her attention linger on his lips. Caught up in the moment, she considered the possibilities. Her body flushed hot and then cold.

When Dylan smiled suddenly, Stevie jumped. She glanced away and focused on filling the coffee pot. For a moment, she was certain that he had caught her staring at him. But he hadn't looked her way at all; there was no way he could have seen her.

Must be a good book.

Since it was another beautiful, sunny day, Stevie decided to walk the few blocks to her parents' home on Ann Street. She enjoyed the shade of the live oak trees that lined the sidewalk and the brush of the warm breeze on her skin.

In spite of her efforts otherwise, her thoughts kept returning to Dylan. More than a decade had passed since she'd last seen him, and her immediate attraction to him now took her by surprise. Though she was convinced that she was too old for this type of infatuation, she could not deny that it was happening. There was a certain lightness in her step today, which left her feeling more like a carefree teenager than a thirty-year-old single mother. She didn't mind that sensation at all.

She bit her bottom lip to keep from grinning like a fool.

As Stevie neared the front door of her parents' house, she heard a familiar Fleetwood Mac tune blasting from her mother's stereo.

She let herself into the house and found Patricia dancing in the kitchen. "Hey, Mom."

As her mother twirled around the room, the ankle-length sundress she wore swished along with her. She waved at Stevie without missing a single beat.

"Where's Dad?" Stevie had to shout to be heard over the music.

"He's in the 'man cave' watching the game." Patricia used air quotes and rolled her eyes.

Stevie left her mother in the kitchen and headed to the den in the back of the house.

"Hey, Dad." She offered him a warm smile as she entered the room.

Her father reclined in his favorite leather chair watching the Panthers game on his oversized flat-screen television. Since he wore large wireless headphones, no doubt to drown out her mother's thundering music, he hadn't noticed Stevie's arrival. She shook her head at the spectacle her parents made, but at the same time, she adored their eccentricity.

Stevie stepped closer to her father and touched his arm to get his attention. "Hey, Dad."

He removed his headphones as he stood to greet her. "Stephanie."

She resisted the urge to correct him. They'd had the same "Stephanie versus Stevie" argument her whole life, and neither one of them had backed down yet. She curled the side of her nose to show him she didn't appreciate the use of her full name.

With a grin, he opened his arms for a hug.

"Got this idea from Charlie. He's a smart kid." He waved the headphones. "These things really work to drown out your mother's music."

Good thing her father had never liked Fleetwood Mac like her mother did. Otherwise, Stevie may have been named something terrible like "Rhiannon" instead of the generic "Stephanie." She shuddered at the thought. Though she hated when her father used her full name, at least it wasn't a wacky one from her mother's eclectic musical tastes. "How's it going, Dad?"

"Oh, I'm doin' all right. Season's starting to slow down now, which I don't mind one bit." He ran his hand through what remained of his hair. "I think Sam and I set a record this summer for the number of trips out to Shackleford and back. It'll wear you out."

"You've got a while to rest up before next summer." Stevie patted his chest.

"Yes. And football season's just getting started." He returned to his place in the leather recliner.

"I can take a hint." Stevie grinned but rolled her eyes. "I'll go help Mom with dinner. Can I bring you anything? Do you want another beer?"

"Not yet, sweetie." He held up a half-full beer beside his seat. "But you could ask your mom to turn down that racket so I can hear the game."

"Will do."

Stevie ambled back to the kitchen and stood by the old oak table. "Dad would like to be able hear the game."

"Fine." Patricia turned the volume down. "Fleetwood Mac's music transcends time. It's as good today as it was in the seventies. Don't you think?"

Stevie snorted. "Do you really want me to answer that?"

"To each her own, I suppose. I respect your right to have the wrong opinion." Patricia raised an eyebrow and smirked. "Now tell me about last night. Did you girls have fun?"

"Surprisingly, yes."

"I don't see why you're surprised. You and Lexi always have a great time together. I'm glad you got out and enjoyed yourself. Did you dance?" Patricia set a pot of water on the stovetop and turned the burner up to high heat.

"Yes, I did." Stevie fiddled with the tablecloth. "By the way, Dylan Kent is back in town now."

"That's great! I will stop by to see him tomorrow." She pulled a long-handled spoon from a drawer and placed it next to the stove. "Is Thomas with him?"

"No." Stevie shook her head. "His dad stayed in London. Dylan said he got married again."

"Good for him!" Patricia turned to face Stevie. "I was so worried about them after Rebecca died. It was such an awful time."

"Dylan seems to be doing all right now too." *More than all right if you ask me.*

"Glad to hear it." Patricia pulled a cutting board from one of the lower cabinets and placed in on the counter. "Can you help me make the salad?"

"Sure." Stevie walked toward the refrigerator, opened the door, and looked in the crisper. "You're out of lettuce. Do you want me to run up to the grocery store for some?"

"I'm certain I bought some. Look again just to be sure." Patricia nodded her chin toward the crisper.

Stevie turned back to the open refrigerator. "Oh, yeah, here it is. Don't know how I could have missed it." She lifted the head of lettuce out of the drawer and stepped over to the sink to rinse it.

Patricia placed a large salad bowl on the counter next to Stevie. "How's Charlie enjoying his weekend with Sam?"

"It's going well. Sam will drop him off here this afternoon." Stevie patted the lettuce leaves dry. Then she tore them into bite-size pieces and dropped them into the bowl.

"Wonderful! Do you think Sam would like to stay for dinner? It would be great to have us all together again." Patricia kept her voice light, like she hadn't just made an absurd request.

Stevie cringed. "I'm sure he'd just love to have dinner with his ex-wife and his former in-laws."

"You guys get along fine, and it's good for Charlie that you do." Patricia tapped Stevie on the hand with a spoon. "It doesn't *have* to be difficult, you know. Sam and your father make it work at the water taxi business. So, don't think of it as a dinner with former in-laws, think of it as a business partners' meeting." The water on the stovetop came to a boil, so she turned off the heat. She placed several teabags into the pot and then poured a heaping cup of sugar into an empty pitcher.

"We're both moving on with our lives now, Mom. It's just not… appropriate." Stevie sliced a tomato with more aggression than it deserved.

"Oh, are you dating someone?" Patricia raised an eyebrow.

"No."

"Is he dating someone?"

Stevie put the knife down and frowned at her mother. "No."

"Well, then, I don't see what the problem is." She shrugged. "He's still your father's business partner, so it makes sense to invite him for dinner."

Stevie sighed in defeat. "It only makes sense to you, Mom."

The doorbell rang.

"I'll get it." Patricia called back to the den before sailing toward the door—as if there were any chance her husband would pull himself away from the game to answer it.

69

Eager to see Charlie, Stevie pushed aside worries about sharing a family dinner with her ex-husband and followed her mother to the door.

"Give Grandma a big hug!" Patricia bent down and opened her arms as Charlie entered the house. "I've missed you so much."

Stevie waited her turn and then knelt to embrace her son. "Did you have fun?"

Charlie remained silent, but a quick smile danced across his face. Sam, who hovered in half-in and half-out of the doorway, beamed. Their faces told a happy story, and Stevie's whole body relaxed.

"Charlie, it looks like you're the most popular guy in the room." Sam passed their son's backpack to Stevie.

"Oh, come here, silly. You know we love you too." Patricia grabbed Sam's shoulders and pulled him in for a hug. "Jim is watching the game in the den, if you'd like to see him."

Sam glanced at Stevie and raised his eyebrows. She dropped her gaze and nodded.

"Great. Come on, Charlie." Sam headed toward the den. "Let's go see Grandpa."

Patricia turned to Stevie. "Will you set the table in the dining room? We'll need *five* place settings."

Stevie left Charlie's backpack by the front door and entered the small but formal dining room. She flipped the switch to turn on the chandelier. Its light reflected off the polished cherry wood Queen Anne-style dining table, which sat in the center of the room.

When she opened the middle drawer of the buffet, she gasped as she caught sight of an enormous amethyst pendant lying on top of a stack of soup spoons. She lifted it out of the drawer by its long, thick gold chain and cupped the purple stone in her hand, feeling the weight of it. She'd never seen her mother wear it.

Stevie's heartbeat quickened. She'd never had much interest in jewelry, but this crystal created a swirl of excitement within her that she could not explain.

A vision of four women on an island suddenly played out in her mind. Three of them looked familiar, though she could not quite place who they were. The oldest among them had gray hair and wore the necklace Stevie now held in her hand.

The image was as vivid as any of her own memories, but she had no knowledge of the event that haunted her now. A rush of grief engulfed her. She leaned against the dining table to steady herself.

With the same abruptness with which it had arrived, the image receded from her mind.

Stevie's hands shook as she struggled to make sense of what had just happened to her. She wasn't sure if she'd just witnessed a vision of the past or a glimpse of the future. The women had been dressed in white linen shifts, which offered no indication of a specific period. With no cars, landmarks, or buildings to reference, the scene had been timeless.

She rubbed her eyes and shook her head. Perhaps it had been nothing more than her overactive imagination.

But it seemed so real.

Maybe her mother could shed some light on the strange piece of jewelry, or maybe she'd just laugh and tell Stevie not to drink so much next time at Backstreet. Stevie sighed, pressed her fingers against her forehead, and squeezed her eyes shut. She was unsure whether she should mention the strange vision at all.

"Stevie, are you ready in there?" Patricia's call floated in from the kitchen.

Startled, Stevie gripped the large amethyst tighter to avoid dropping it. The lights in the chandelier flickered, causing her to jump.

"Almost!" She answered louder than was necessary before shoving the necklace back into the drawer as fast as she could and gathering the silverware for the table.

Jim, Sam, and Charlie joined her in the dining room, carrying dishes from the kitchen. They took their places at the table.

"You boys must be hungry." Stevie forced a casual smile as she attempted to push the odd vision from her thoughts. She tried to keep her hands steady, but the stack of plates rattled in her hands.

"It's halftime." Jim scooted his chair closer to the table.

Sam laughed.

"Of course it is." Patricia entered the room. "It's not my first day on the job, you know." She placed the salad bowl on the table.

"You planned dinner around the football game?" Stevie grimaced as she stared at her mother.

"It was no trouble." Patricia gave her husband a quick kiss on the cheek.

Stevie tilted her head to the side as she watched her parents' interaction, their genuine affection for one another. When she'd left home, she'd worried they might be bored without her to entertain them, but they'd embraced their empty nest with more enthusiasm than most. Sometimes they acted more like newlyweds than the long-married couple that they were.

Patricia glanced at Stevie. "Honey, are you feeling all right? You look a little pale."

"I'm...uh, I'm fine." First she'd manifested some bizarre vision and now she sat all zombie-like at the table, enough to garner the notice of her mother's hawk eye. *Snap out of it, Stevie. And no more girls' nights at bars.*

Patricia nodded without saying anything else. Stevie blew out a deep breath and tried to focus on something, anything but what had happened with the jewel.

"This looks delicious." Jim gave his wife an appreciative pat on her hand.

"Go ahead and dig in." Patricia filled their glasses with sweet iced tea and then took her place at the table. Her gaze fell on Stevie again, but she didn't say anything.

Stevie prepared Charlie's plate, skipping the bread, croutons, and butter in order to keep his diet free of gluten and casein. She glanced at her mother, expecting to hear her usual comment about how "a young boy needs to eat those things in order to grow up big and strong." But Patricia just smiled at her with an unmistakable gleam in her eye. She looked proud, but Stevie had no idea what she had done to bring such delight to her mother. Her accomplishments on this day consisted only of making a salad and setting the table.

She passed the plate to Charlie, happy to have a small slice of normalcy in this odd evening. Between Sam's attendance at the family dinner, her mother's incessant grin, and that very strange vision, Stevie could barely stomach the idea of eating. She glanced at her watch, ready to return to the quiet predictability of her own house.

Sam piled food on his plate. "Thanks for inviting me, Patricia. This is great." He selected a warm dinner roll from the breadbasket. "I can't remember the last time I had a home-cooked meal."

"Is that so?" Patricia raised her eyebrows. "Well, you just feel free to come by anytime, Sam. You're always welcome here."

Stevie coughed, nearly choking on a crouton. "Mom, I'm sure he stays very busy these days. Don't you, Sam?" She glared at him.

"No, not really." He met Stevie's glower with a broad grin, as if to challenge her.

Stevie pursed her lips and returned her attention to her food. She and Charlie ate in silence while the rest of the family discussed the Panthers game. Sam was completely at ease at the family dinner, but Stevie was still uncomfortable with it. She poked at her salad. Sometimes she wished they were one of those miserable divorced couples who could not stand to be around each other. At least, in some ways, it would make things easier. She glanced at Charlie's unreadable expression and hoped he didn't feel as confused by Sam's presence as she did.

"Can you stay for coffee, Sam?" Patricia pointed at him with her roll.

"No, thanks. I really should get going. I have to make another run out to Shackleford tonight." He flicked his gaze toward Stevie. "Got a couple of newlywed campers heading out there."

"It's a nice night for it." Patricia looked at Stevie. "I remember how much you two used to enjoy camping on the island."

The heat of embarrassment crept up Stevie's cheeks. Though it seemed like another lifetime, she remembered camping with Sam. She kept her head down, hoping to avoid eye contact with him.

When they had all finished eating, Sam excused himself from the table and gave Patricia a peck on the cheek. "Thank you for dinner. It was delicious." He turned to Charlie and hugged him goodbye. "I'll see you soon." With a final wave to everyone at the table, he headed toward the front door and let himself out.

Jim took Charlie's hand and led him back to the den to watch the rest of the game. Patricia helped Stevie carry the dishes to the kitchen.

"See? It wasn't so bad having Sam here for dinner." Patricia used her very best I-told-you-so voice.

"Please don't start on that again, Mom." Stevie stepped to the sink and turned on the water.

"Fine." Patricia sighed with mock exasperation. "I'll go see if Charlie wants to play."

"Before you go, I have to ask you about something." Stevie turned around, only to discover that her mother had already left the kitchen. "Well…I guess it can wait."

Stevie finished the dishes and wrapped up the leftovers to store in the refrigerator. As she wiped the countertops clean, the sound of her mother's panicked scream tore through the house.

Chapter ten

Vanessa

Vanessa ran her hand along the glossy teak railing on her new seventy-foot yacht. She'd toyed with the idea of renting one of the historic houses in town, but she settled on purchasing the yacht because it was much sexier than rocking chair porches and stuffy old rooms. The yacht's quarters were somewhat smaller than she was accustomed to, but she enjoyed it nonetheless. What it lacked in space, it made up for in luxury.

The sun was just about to set on her second day back in Beaufort. Most of the tourists had returned home for the season, and the locals were in the process of reclaiming their little town. The unmistakable scent of fried shrimp wafted from a nearby restaurant, distracting Vanessa from her focus. She could almost taste the succulent seafood she'd adored as a child and missed during her time on the run. Just another one of the many things she'd gone without because of the coven. Her focus renewed, she grabbed her car keys and left her floating palace in favor of dry land.

As she pulled out of the small parking lot near the docks in her convertible, the salty breeze danced through her hair. Reveling in the sensation, she left behind the restaurants and businesses of the waterfront and cruised west along Front Street toward the historic residential area. A few couples strolled along the sidewalk, enjoying the peaceful evening. She turned down her radio as she passed them. She didn't want to call attention to herself.

Vanessa slowed her car as she neared Stevie's house. No lights were on. It was clear that the place was empty. She cursed under her breath.

Glancing in her rearview mirror, Vanessa spotted one of the strolling couples continuing down Front Street in her direction. She groaned and tapped the accelerator before they could get a good look at her and her vehicle. By the time she finished her tasks, there would be plenty of questions, and she couldn't afford to be implicated.

As she passed in front of Dylan's house, she stomped on the brake pedal, bringing the car to a hard stop. Light emanated from the living room, and the rockers on the front porch swayed in the breeze. That bastard had returned from London. She smacked the steering wheel and released a string of curse words that would have made a sailor blush. When she last checked with her private investigator, he'd assured her Dylan was still in London. Between now and then, he must have made the trek across the ocean. She ground her teeth. He would have only come back for one reason…her.

Vanessa sensed a sudden movement just outside her car. Before she could turn around, someone jerked her head back.

"I should kill you right now." Dylan clutched a handful of her long hair.

In spite of the pain, Vanessa smirked. "Why don't you try? Or, are you afraid that Patricia won't approve?"

"The only thing saving you right now is the fact that we're in public." He clenched his jaw as he glanced toward the couple walking in their direction. "You're not worth exposing the secret for."

"That's a pity. I was looking forward to a fight." Though her heart raced, she kept her voice steady. "Another time, perhaps?"

"Count on it." Dylan released his grip.

Vanessa turned to face him, meeting his glare with unflinching calm. "It's really too bad that you have to be a slave to all of those pesky rules."

She rammed the accelerator to the floor and raced to the road's dead end. The tires squealed as she spun the car around to take another pass by Dylan. With no further need to be subtle, she cranked up the volume on the stereo and sped down Front Street, exhilaration flowing through her veins.

There was no point in hiding now; they knew she had returned.

And they know exactly what I am capable of.

chapter eleven

Stevie

At the sound of her mother's scream, Stevie raced to the den. She searched first for Charlie and found him rocking in a corner with his hands over his ears. Other than his reaction to Patricia's scream, Stevie could see nothing wrong with her son. Bewildered, she looked to her mother, who held a phone to her ear and recited her home address. Stevie turned her focus to her father, who was reclined in his favorite chair. His skin was pale, and his eyes were closed. He was very still. Too still. She clasped her hand over her mouth.

"Dad!" She rushed to his side. His breaths puffed out, shallow and weak, and a hint of blue had begun to encircle his lips. "Oh, Daddy." She buried her face beneath his neck.

"An ambulance is on the way." Patricia stroked her husband's cheek with her trembling hand.

"What happened?"

"I was with Charlie over there on the floor." Patricia pointed to the corner where the little boy continued rocking back and forth. "He had lined up all of his cars in row, the way he usually does. He was totally focused on it, but then he stopped and looked up at Jim all of a sudden. So, naturally, I looked too. Then I saw him like this. I thought he was…dead." Patricia's voice shook.

Stevie nodded, still shaken by the sight of her father. She turned to Charlie, who had lowered his hands but continued to rock back and forth.

Knowing an ambulance was on the way, she wanted to spare her son the sight of what was about to come. "Charlie, please go to the kitchen. I'll be there in a few minutes." She forced herself to sound calmer than she felt.

Charlie's rocking began to slow. Stevie waited several seconds before she spoke again. "Go on now. I'll meet you in there soon."

He rose from his spot in the corner and left the room. Stevie wanted to comfort him, but she could not bring herself to leave her father's side. She turned to Patricia, seeing her own agony echoed in her mother's eyes.

The doorbell chimed. "EMS," a stranger's voice called.

"Come in! We're back here!" Stevie yelled to guide them.

Three men entered the room, carrying a portable gurney and a large orange box. Stevie pulled herself away from her father and stepped back to stand beside her mother, allowing the technicians access to do their work. Right away, one of them opened Jim's shirt and began to place electrodes on his chest. Another secured an oxygen mask to his face. The third wrote down numbers on a clipboard as his partners called them out. Together, they lifted Jim onto the gurney and wheeled it through the house to the ambulance waiting outside.

Patricia walked behind them, wringing her hands. She turned to Stevie. "Call Randy. Tell him to meet us at the hospital."

Stevie let out the breath she had been holding as she tried to focus on what she needed to do. More than anything, she wanted to hop into that ambulance and hold her father's hand as he rode to the hospital. But deep down, she understood that her presence would be more a hindrance than a help, so she nodded to her mother and headed toward the kitchen. She would call Randy as requested, though she was not sure why her mother would want him there. The old man was a family friend and a doctor, but he had retired long ago.

Stevie went into the kitchen to check on Charlie and found him typing on his tablet. She looked at the screen. *Grandpa go.*

"Oh, Charlie." She wrapped her arms around her son. She had no idea what he must be thinking or what he understood about all that had just happened, and she wondered if he realized how much danger his grandfather was in.

"Grandpa is very sick. Those men are taking him to the hospital so a doctor can check on him." She wanted to tell him that everything was going to be fine, but the words died on her lips. Tears welled in her eyes, and she blinked them back. The truth was, she had no idea what would happen to her father, and she didn't want to lie to Charlie.

She found Patricia's address book by the telephone and dialed Randy's number, tapping her fingers on the counter as she waited for him to pick up. When he answered, she explained what happened to her father and relayed her mother's request that he meet them at the hospital.

After she completed her call to Randy, she dialed Sam's number. If he could come and get Charlie, she could wait with her mother and not have to expose Charlie to all the unfamiliar sights and sounds at the hospital. When her call went to Sam's voicemail, Stevie remembered he'd mentioned that he would be working late.

She disconnected the call without leaving a message and turned to Charlie. "Let's go to the hospital to check on Grandpa."

She spotted Patricia's car keys in a basket on the kitchen counter. She grabbed them, as well as Charlie's hand, and rushed out the front door. The ambulance had already pulled away by the time she left the house, but several neighbors had gathered on the street, wondering aloud about what might have happened to Jim Guthrie.

"Do you think he's going to make it?" One concerned neighbor glanced at another.

"I bet he had a stroke." An old lady nodded to another.

A man with a baseball cap frowned. "Could have been a heart attack."

In a small town, rumors spread like wildfire. Stevie suppressed a sigh as a few of the women hurried toward her. She knew they were dying to pump her for information about what had happened inside the Guthrie household, but she didn't have time for them or their gossipy nonsense.

Paying them no mind, she buckled Charlie into the car, hopped in the driver's seat before the old ladies reached her, and began the short trip to the county hospital in Morehead City. After a few minutes, she stole a glance in the rearview mirror to check on Charlie. He was gazing out of the window as they passed over the bridge into the neighboring town. She hoped he felt as calm as he looked.

Once at the hospital, she parked her car in the lot designated for the emergency department. As she stepped out of the car and took in the sight of the large brick building, her knees went weak with fear, apprehension, and sheer exhaustion. Somewhere inside that building, a team of nurses and doctors worked on her father. And she prayed he was still alive.

Chapter twelve

Stevie

Stevie held Charlie's hand while she checked in at the emergency department reception desk. The lump in her throat almost prevented her from giving the receptionist her father's name, but she managed to eke it out.

"I'll let your mother know that you're here." A nurse offered a smile, but it did little to alleviate Stevie's fears.

Stevie forced her voice to remain steady. "Thank you." She turned and headed toward the waiting area. She led Charlie to two empty chairs that provided a clear view of the wall-mounted television and hoped he would be satisfied with watching cartoons for a while.

Within a couple of minutes, Stevie realized that Charlie would not be able to wait in the room for long. He had closed his eyes and started tapping his hand on his leg. Her heart constricted. She recognized the problem right away, though she was at a loss to help him. The crowded waiting room provided a torrent of sensory assaults. She knew the fluorescent lights bothered him. They were not only far too bright, but their constant hum hurt his ears. Most people could not actually *hear* the lights, but Charlie could. And right now, they made him miserable.

In addition to the humming lights, she knew that he could not ignore the whooshing noise the automatic door made as it opened and closed at unpredictable intervals. Across the room, a woman coughed. Too many people spoke at once. Babies cried. Another person coughed. Charlie pressed his hands against his ears and began to rock in his chair.

Stevie squeezed her eyes shut. If she couldn't get Charlie out of here soon, she might have to leave before they got a chance to see her father. And it might be her *last* chance to see him. A fresh wave of tears welled in her eyes. To be forced to make such a choice…

Defeated, she'd just started to stand when she heard the whoosh of the automatic door and found Deborah and Lexi hurrying through the entrance toward the waiting room.

"Did my mom call you?" Stevie blinked, still trying to figure out how they'd appeared in the hospital at the exact moment she needed them.

Lexi shook her head. "Small town, word gets around fast."

"How is he?" Deborah tugged the strap of her canvas bag, pulling it higher on her shoulder.

"I don't know yet. Mom is still back there with him." Stevie bobbed her head toward the heavy door separating the emergency department from the waiting area. "I haven't heard anything new." She took a deep breath and tried her best to explain what had happened at the house.

Lexi reached for her hand and gave it a supportive squeeze. "I'm sure we'll hear something soon."

Deborah's gaze fell on Charlie. "He's having a tough time, isn't he?"

Stevie nodded. "He's not comfortable here, and I'm sure he's worried sick about his grandpa." She paused for a moment. "I think I'm going to have to take him home. I can't put him through this."

"I have an idea." Lexi squatted down to Charlie's level. "Would you like to spend the night at Auntie Lexi's house?"

He pulled his hands away from his ears and typed on his tablet. *Yes.*

Charlie had always adored Lexi, but right now, Stevie suspected that he would leave with anyone as long as it meant getting away from the emergency department waiting room. She sighed, relieved that she would be able to stay at the hospital after all.

"That would be great. Are you sure you don't mind?" Stevie pulled Lexi into a quick hug.

"No problem at all. I love hanging out with Charlie." Lexi took his hand, and he stood.

Stevie gave Lexi a grateful smile. "There's a car seat for him in my mom's car. It's unlocked."

"No worries." Lexi winked. "I'll take care of it."

Stevie hugged Charlie. "Have fun. I'll see you in the morning."

"I'll drop him off at your house after breakfast." Lexi waved and led Charlie toward the door.

"Thank you." Stevie sat back down and watched them go. A part of her missed her son already, as she did when he spent the night with Sam, but the other part of her bubbled with gratitude that she could remain here with her parents in their time of need. The farther he got from the waiting room, the more Charlie's shoulders relaxed. Some of her own tension slipped away with his.

Deborah took a seat next to Stevie and went right to work on her knitting, starting a new line of pink yarn on the blanket she carried in her canvas bag.

Stevie rubbed her forehead as she imagined every possible outcome for her father. She glanced at the clock and watched long minutes tick by as no news came. *Is he okay?*

The doors swung open again and more members of the Historic Society poured in—Alice Gillikin, followed by Ruth Turner and Dr. Randy Davis. Stevie waved them over. Alice wore a warm smile on her chubby face, a sharp contrast to Ruth's thin-lipped, permanent scowl. Randy's white eyebrows were drawn together in concern. If nothing else, these friends would help support her mother, and for that, Stevie could have hugged them all. The deepest part of her heart warmed with the flame of lifelong friendship, like the one she shared with Lexi. These people, though not bound to her by blood, constituted her family, and their very presence here now proved it.

Ruth crossed her arms and lorded over Stevie and Deborah. "Any news?"

"No, not yet." Stevie stood to make her chair available in case one of the elderly members of the trio wanted to rest. "Thank you all for coming."

"If any one of us were in the same situation, Patricia would be here too." Alice patted Stevie's cheek. Deep lines, marking a lifetime of smiles, adorned her brown eyes.

"Come here, sweetie." Alice stretched out her hefty arms for a hug and buried Stevie's face in her ample bosom. Stevie gasped for air to prevent herself from suffocating right there in the swell of the old woman's enormous breast. At last, Alice freed her from the well-meaning, yet terrifying, embrace. Stevie offered a polite smile as she took in a grateful breath and backed away, putting a little distance between herself and any additional hugs from Alice.

Ruth glowered as she glanced around the waiting room. Of all the members of the Historic Society, she made Stevie the most uncomfortable. Prone to pontificating diatribes, Ruth never missed the opportunity to complain or point out flaws. Given the events of the day, Stevie didn't relish the idea of smoothing over any hospital staff's feathers that Ruth might see fit to ruffle. A nurse, who'd been headed their way, caught sight of the scowling gray-haired woman and reversed course. Ruth's reputation preceded her. Though she'd long since retired from her job as a teacher, rumors of her "charm" still circulated through town like the weekly news. Stevie shook her head. Those poor students who'd had the misfortune of studying under Ruth's tutelage...

For now, at least, the old woman remained silent.

Randy rested his hand on Stevie's shoulder, his blue eyes twinkling under a crown of white hair.

"Can you get us in to see my dad?" Stevie gestured toward the emergency room door.

Randy nodded. He rarely said much. But then again, he was usually napping. He had the uncanny ability to fall asleep just about anytime and anywhere.

They left the impromptu gathering of the Historic Society and crossed the waiting room to the reception desk. Though Randy hadn't practiced medicine for several years, the nurse at the desk recognized him. When he asked her to buzz him through the secured door to the emergency department, she did not hesitate to comply.

Stevie followed Randy through the door. She scanned the wide space in search of her parents and spotted them in a room to the right.

She gasped at the sight of her father. Buried under a net of electrodes, wires, and tubes, he lay unconscious in the narrow hospital bed. Her mother sat next to his bedside, resting her tearstained cheek on his hand.

"Mom?" Stevie entered the small room, attempting to decipher her father's prognosis by the expression on her mother's weary face.

Patricia sat upright, but her gaze traveled past Stevie and fell on Randy. "I'm so glad to see you." She exhaled what appeared to be a long-held breath.

Randy approached Jim. Ignoring the digital displays and the monitor's beeps, he rested his hand on her father's chest. Stevie furrowed her brow. Everyone in Beaufort marveled at Randy's medical skill, but even he couldn't diagnose her father's condition with just a touch.

Patricia looked at Stevie. "I'm sorry. I should have come out there and told you what was happening, but I was afraid to leave him."

"That's okay." Stevie stepped closer to her mother. But she kept an eye on Randy, craving any information the retired doctor might be able to share. "Do we know what happened to him?"

"They think it was a heart attack, but we're waiting on some test results." Tears welled in Patricia's eyes. "I really thought I was going to lose him." She blinked, dried her watery gaze, and turned her attention to Randy.

"Jim's in good hands here." Randy moved away from the bed. "I'm going to go back to the waiting room now. If you need anything, just let me know."

"Of course." Patricia smiled. "Thank you, Randy."

She eased back in her chair. The deep creases across her forehead had smoothed out, revealing a more relaxed expression. Stevie tilted her head, baffled that Randy's quick, low-tech assessment had had such an impact on her mother. He hadn't actually *done* anything.

"Is Dad going to be all right?" Stevie grasped for any scrap of optimism to hold on to.

"The doctor didn't say, but yes, I think so. We'll have more information soon." Patricia rested her head on the back of her chair and closed her eyes.

Stevie crossed the small room to the other side of her father's bed and wrapped her hand around his. "Has he been unconscious the whole time?"

"He woke up but fell asleep again after only a few minutes. The doctor said that was normal." Drowsiness tinged her mother's words.

It was hard to imagine that there was anything normal about this, but Stevie did not argue. They waited together, listening to the steady beeps provided by the electronic heart monitor, until the emergency room physician returned, carrying Jim's chart. Stevie braced herself for news.

He looked up from the clipboard and greeted her with a firm handshake and an emotionless expression. "I'm Dr. Farr. As expected, the bloodwork confirmed that he did indeed have a heart attack. We'll need to run some more tests to determine the extent of the damage."

Damage. Stevie bit down on her lip and cast a worried glance at her mother. But Patricia appeared unfazed by the idea of permanent injury from the heart attack.

A calm façade. She's stronger than I am.

Patricia nodded. "What happens next?"

"I'm going to admit him now." Dr. Farr checked the monitors as he spoke. "We'll have a clearer picture of what we're dealing with after we complete those additional tests. But I can tell you that he will almost certainly need to make significant lifestyle modifications."

"What kind of modifications?" Stevie's stomach tightened.

"Less red meat and beer. More vegetables. He'll also need regular exercise." The doctor scribbled a note in the chart. "I'll have the nutritionist meet with you to go over the specifics."

Patricia glanced at her husband, who still slept in the bed. "That's a tall order. He's pretty set in his ways."

Dr. Farr, who'd started to walk out the door, paused. "Heart attacks can be very motivating for some patients. He may surprise you."

When the doctor left, Stevie stepped away from the bedside. "I guess I'll go share the news with the Historic Society."

"They're all here?" Patricia chuckled as she shook her head. "Of course they are." She rose from her chair. "I'll go with you."

They entered the waiting room to find Deborah knitting and Randy dozing in the chair next to her. Alice sat nearby, shaking her head in disapproval as she watched Ruth on the other side of the room.

"What did you do to this coffee?" Ruth smacked a cup down on the counter in front of the receptionist. She pinched her face in disgust as a few stray drops hit her hand. "I bet you emptied the bedpans into the coffeemaker. This stuff tastes like sh——"

"Ruth!" Patricia commanded the older woman's attention before she could finish her tirade—but not before some of the other patrons took a second look at their own cups of coffee and opted to throw them away.

Ruth shot the receptionist one more scathing glare before abandoning her outrage to hear the news regarding Jim's condition. She rejoined the Historic Society members on the other side of the waiting room.

"How is he?" Deborah reached for her best friend's hand.

Patricia began to relay the most recent information regarding Jim's condition, but Stevie stopped her. "Should we wake up Randy?"

"Oh." Patricia glanced over to the snoozing doctor and gave a slight shake of her head. "No. Let him rest."

The members of the Historic Society listened to her mother finish her update, which included no information about possible heart damage. Stevie watched their worried expressions soften. By the time Patricia reached the end of her story, their frowns had evaporated. Except for Ruth. She still looked miserable. But then again, she always looked miserable.

Stevie fiddled with the hem of her shirt. She admired her mother's optimism, but the doctor hadn't said anything that would warrant the relief she saw on Patricia's face.

"Thank you all for coming." Patricia met the gaze of each person. "But there's really no need for you to stay here."

"Okay, let's get out of here then. Wake up, Randy!" Ruth snapped her fingers. "Let's go find some decent coffee." She glared at the nurse behind the reception desk…again.

"Are you sure? I don't mind staying." Alice offered a sweet smile.

"Mom, I can stay with you. Charlie is with Lexi." Stevie started to head back toward her father's room.

"No. I won't have it." Patricia grabbed Stevie's arm and spun her around in the direction of the exit.

"But Mom, I *want* to stay." Stevie couldn't fathom the thought of leaving her father now.

Patricia drew in a deep breath. "Honey, I think it's best if he doesn't have more than one visitor tonight. Let him get some rest, okay?" She hugged Stevie. "You can come back tomorrow."

Stevie couldn't argue with that logic. "Will you call if anything changes?"

"Of course." Patricia patted her arm. "Now, I just need to find a book to read, and I'll be all set for the night."

Deborah reached into her overstuffed canvas bag and pulled out a paperback novel, which she held up for Patricia to see. "How about this one?"

"Perfect. Thank you." Patricia smiled as she accepted the book. "Now get going. I mean it." She shooed them all out through the door.

Stevie returned to her empty house. With Charlie at Lexi's and her parents at the hospital, a new level of loneliness enshrouded her. Intending to relax, she took a hot bath, soaking until the water became too cool. She tried to forget the haunting image of her father as he'd suffered his heart attack. But the events of the day refused to be washed away. After her bath, she slipped into her favorite yoga pants and a tank top.

She glanced at her bed, wishing she could climb in and go to sleep. However, the knots in her stomach threatened a far less peaceful night than she craved. With a sigh, she turned away. But something, an unexpected difference, caught her attention, and she spun around once more.

The coverlet gleamed, stark white against the sheets. She hadn't washed the bedspread in weeks, so its renewed vigor made no sense. After rubbing her eyes, she glanced around the room. Everything sat where it always had, yet it all shined with a newness. She'd practically grown up in this house. She knew every nook and cranny. But today, the colors and lines jumped out in ways they never had before. Almost as if she could see clearer.

I'm losing my mind. My father's sick, and I'm a nutcase. Super.

She ran her hand along the bright white coverlet and stared at her empty bed. More than just her eyesight had changed. She'd been alone since the divorce and it hadn't bothered her. Until now.

Maybe Lexi has it right. Maybe I should just go into a bar and leave with someone. No strings. No commitments. Stevie shook her head. She wasn't ready to go that far, but she knew she didn't want to be alone on this night.

Not much I can do about that now.

She sighed. Deciding that a glass of wine would help her relax, she padded back down the stairs. Stepping into the foyer, an odd sensation struck her, compelling her to stop in her tracks. She had a strong, inexplicable instinct to simply pay attention. To what, she did not know.

She remained in place but began to scan her surroundings. The front door was locked. The rug was undisturbed. She noticed a dust bunny in the corner, but that was no cause for alarm. Everything was just as it should be; nothing was out of place. She let her gaze wander up the wall until it settled on the old portrait, and she gasped in surprise.

As she looked upon the image, she recalled the strange vision from earlier. She'd seen these women from the painting—Hannah, Catherine, and Charlotte—on the island in her daydream. Her pulse quickened, just as it had when she held the amethyst. She sunk down, taking a seat on the staircase.

What the hell is wrong with me?

That portrait had hung in the same spot for her entire life. She hardly noticed it anymore. And yet, twice in the last few days, it had commanded her attention. First with Charlie's sudden interest in it, and now *this*…whatever *this* was.

Stevie lowered her head, studying the worn grain on the hardwood floor, as her mind raced to find an explanation for the strangeness of the day. *I'm either going crazy or suffering from an overactive imagination.* She ran her hand through her damp hair. Neither theory quite fit, but she'd rather blame imagination than swallow the tougher pill of a descent into insanity.

As her pulse returned to normal, she stood up, more than ready for the glass of wine that had brought her downstairs in the first place. On her way to the kitchen, the doorbell rang. She jumped at the unexpected sound and wondered who could be at her door at this hour. She wasn't expecting anyone.

Stevie opened the door, relieved to see a familiar face. "Hi."

"I just heard about your dad. Are you okay?" He reached out and touched her cheek.

I am not anywhere close to okay.

A new boldness took hold of her. She bit her lip in a half-hearted attempt to restrain herself. "Stay with me tonight."

He stepped inside and closed the door behind him. Without hesitation, he lifted Stevie in his strong arms and carried her up the stairs.

Chapter thirteen

Stevie

The birds in the magnolia tree outside Stevie's bedroom window chirped their morning alarm. She feigned sleep for a few extra moments, hoping her overnight guest would get up and leave before she had to abandon the refuge of the sheets to go search for her clothes.

What was I thinking?

There was an abrupt change in the rhythm of his deep, even breaths. He stirred, moving closer to Stevie, and wrapped his arm around her. She eased away from him and slipped on the yoga pants she had tossed on the floor the night before. Scanning the room, she saw no sign of the top she'd worn, though his clothes were scattered everywhere. When he stirred again, she hurried to her dresser to find another shirt.

Stevie felt his eyes on her bare back and winced. She must have woken him when she got out of bed. She threw on an old t-shirt and took a deep breath before turning to face her ex-husband.

"I should have fought for you." Sam's eyes gleamed with fierce earnestness.

"There was nothing left to fight for." Stevie averted her gaze. She'd give just about anything to *not* have this conversation.

He shook his head. "How can you say that after last night?"

She swallowed the bitter tang of regret. "Last night was a mistake. I'm sorry."

"No, Stevie. We're still good together." He sat up in the bed, his blond hair disheveled. "We never should have gone through with that divorce."

She sighed. Sometimes, she also doubted whether they should have gotten divorced. She couldn't deny that she still loved him, nor could she deny the misery she had suffered when they fought all the time.

"Sam, we don't have time to discuss this right now. Charlie stayed at Lexi's last night, and he'll be home any minute. If he sees you here, it will be confusing for him." She collected his shirt from the floor and tossed it to him.

"That's just perfect. You're saying that I can't be in *my* house, with *my* wife, when *my* son gets home?" His voice rose in anger.

"This was never *your* house, and I am not *your* wife. Not anymore." Her hands trembled, as they always did when arguments ramped up.

"So, what exactly was last night about?" Sam yanked the shirt over his head.

I have no idea. I don't know what came over me.

Stevie looked through the window at the magnolia tree, as if the answer to Sam's question hid among its glossy leaves. She turned to meet his scorching gaze. "I was upset. And weak." She softened her tone. "I already said I'm sorry." She shrugged. She knew it wasn't enough, but it was all she had to offer.

"So, it was just a one-night stand?" His cheeks flushed.

"I guess so." Stevie cringed at the thought and dropped her gaze to the floor. She vowed never to judge Lexi's promiscuous behavior again.

"This isn't like you." Sam clenched his jaw. "I'm not buying it."

"Suit yourself." She faced him once more. "But you still have to leave now."

She bit her lip. She hated herself for being so cold to Sam, but there was simply no time to discuss what had happened between them. Even if they'd had the time, she had no way of explaining her behavior.

He threw the covers back, unashamed to be half naked in front of her, and snatched the rest of his clothes from the floor. He dressed and then stormed out of the bedroom. Stevie listened to his footsteps retreat as he stomped down the staircase. The front door slammed behind him.

Stevie stepped out of her bedroom and walked down the hallway toward the stairs. Near the landing, she found the tank top she'd worn the night before. She picked it up and closed her eyes, reveling in the memory of their passionate encounter.

Yes, it was a mistake, but it was an exceptionally enjoyable one.

Stevie heard Lexi let herself in through the front door and let out a relieved sigh. They had missed Sam by only a few minutes. It had been close, but she was grateful that she would not have to answer any uncomfortable questions about her ex-husband's presence in her house so early in the morning.

"I'm in the kitchen," Stevie called out to them.

"He was an absolute angel." Lexi beamed as she entered the room with Charlie at her side. "He should hang out with me more often." She looked down at him. "Right, little dude?"

Stevie chuckled as Charlie held his tablet up so Lexi could see the text he'd already typed on the screen. *Name Charlie.* By the expression on Lexi's face, Stevie knew this wasn't the first time Charlie had reminded her to call him by his real name.

"Oh, right. I'm sorry, Charlie." Lexi winked.

Stevie hugged her son before he ran off to watch cartoons in the den. She turned her attention to Lexi. "Have you guys had breakfast yet?"

"Yep. I fixed him bacon and eggs at my apartment." Lexi puffed her chest out with pride. "Totally gluten and casein free, by the way. Charlie gobbled them all up."

"Thanks for keeping him last night. It was a big help." Stevie hugged her.

"No problem. How's your dad doing?" Lexi took a seat in a nearby chair.

Stevie updated Lexi on everything she had learned before she left the hospital the night before. "There are more tests scheduled for today, so I'll go check on him this afternoon."

"Uh-huh." Lexi eyed Stevie with suspicion. "Are you all right? You seem a little…different this morning."

"Yeah, I'm fine." Stevie avoided Lexi's narrowed gaze. She would never hear the end of it if Lexi found out about her night with Sam.

"Fine, huh? Then can you tell me why your underwear is falling out of your pants?" Lexi pointed to the lacy fabric peeking out from the bottom of Stevie's pant leg.

"Must've gotten m…mixed up in the laundry." Heat rose in Stevie's cheeks. She snatched the telltale garment from its perch on her ankle and rushed past Lexi to toss it in the laundry room.

"Don't you try to lie to me!" Lexi stayed on her heels. "You had sex, didn't you? Finally!"

Stevie spun around to face Lexi. "Shhh!" She jerked her head toward the living room where Charlie sat watching his cartoons. "We're not going to discuss this."

"Just tell me who it was? It was Dylan, wasn't it?" Lexi clapped her hands together.

97

"You have an unnatural obsession with my love life." Stevie pointed an accusatory finger at her best friend.

Lexi clapped again. "I just want you to be happy. That's all. Now, you've got to tell me." She grabbed Stevie's arm. "Was it Dylan?"

"No." Stevie wiggled away.

"Oh come on, Stevie! You have to tell me who it was." Lexi grinned. "You know I'll get it out of you eventually. So there's really no point in fighting it."

"I'm not talking," Stevie crossed her arms in defiance.

"Did you meet a cute doctor at the hospital last night?" Lexi waggled her eyebrows.

Stevie threw her head back and stared at the ceiling for an exasperated moment before responding. "You think I left my dad in the emergency room and picked up a doctor on my way out? Seriously, Lexi, who does that?"

"It happens." Lexi shrugged.

Stevie snorted. "Maybe in *your* world it does…"

"I'm not giving up." Lexi placed her hands on her hips as if to punctuate her intention to torment Stevie until she extracted a full confession.

Stevie hesitated for a heartbeat before she realized she would not be able to keep her encounter a secret from her best friend. "It was Sam." She hung her head in defeat.

"Whoa! Does this mean…?" Lexi's eyes grew wide.

"It means nothing." Stevie waved the question away. Of all people, Lexi would understand how that worked. "He stopped by last night and it just happened."

The doorbell rang, sparing Stevie from Lexi's relentless inquest.

"Expecting someone?" Lexi raised her eyebrows in curiosity.

Stevie shook her head. "No."

Lexi joined her as she made her way to the front door. "Well, try to control yourself. You don't have to sleep with everyone who stops by." She chuckled at her own joke.

"Look who's talking." Stevie rolled her eyes, and Lexi landed a playful punch on her arm.

Stevie opened the door and rocked back in surprise. "Hey, Dylan."

He wore a red polo shirt and khaki shorts, already looking more like a local than the international businessman he was. Her gaze shifted to the now empty spot on the street in front of her house. She hoped he'd not seen Sam's truck parked there overnight. She looked back at Dylan and mirrored his cheerful smile, only to catch his waver. The corners of his eyes wrinkled as the slightest grimace flashed across his face. It was gone in an instant, and his full smile returned. Stevie tilted her head, wondering what had bothered him, but she didn't ask.

"I heard about Jim's heart attack, so I just wanted to check on you. Do you need anything?" He leveled his gaze to hers. "Is there something I can do to help?"

"That's so thoughtful." Stevie raised her hand to her chest. "My mom is with him now, and we're all just waiting for more information. So, there's really nothing to be done until we know more."

"Whoa!" Lexi pointed past Dylan. "Is that a new boat?"

He glanced back to the long red speedboat tied to his private dock across the street. "Yeah, it is." He rubbed the back of his neck as the color rose in his cheeks. "An indulgence."

"She looks fast." Lexi let out a low whistle.

"That's why I got her."

"Very cool." Lexi glanced between Dylan and Stevie. "Well, I have a painting to finish." She scooted past him as she walked out the door. "I'll see y'all later."

99

"Bye, Lex." Stevie waved to her before turning back to Dylan. "Would you like to come in for coffee?"

"Sure." He hesitated. "If I'm not catching you at a bad time."

Stevie winced and remembered how Sam had been in her home, in her bed, less than an hour before. "No, not at all." She gestured for him to follow her.

In the kitchen, Stevie poured two cups of coffee while Dylan sat at her tile-topped table. He traced the outline of the floral pattern on one of the squares.

"Do you remember when we were kids and your grandmother would make us those chocolate chip cookies?" A wistful grin graced his lips. "We'd sit right here at this table and eat them."

Buoyed by the sweet memory, she smiled back at him. She'd spent a lot of time in this house as a child, and with Dylan right next door, she'd always had a playmate available. "Do you remember the hideout?"

"How could I forget?" He chuckled.

"Charlie has inherited it now. He loves it in there." Stevie passed a mug to him.

"Can't say that I blame him." He took a sip. "It's a pretty cool place to hang out."

Charlie ambled into the kitchen, carrying his tablet. He walked over to Stevie, took her hand, led her to the pantry, and placed her hand on the doorknob. She opened the door and lifted a bag of gluten-free cookies from the middle shelf.

"Snack time." She placed a few of the cookies on a plate and delivered them to the kitchen table.

Charlie sat down while Stevie poured a cup of almond milk for him. She'd planned to explain her son's behavior to Dylan before they met, but now he'd just have to experience it firsthand.

"It's nice to meet you, Charlie." Dylan cocked his head as he gazed at the boy.

Charlie concentrated on eating the cookies without looking up. His tablet sat unused on the table.

"Charlie, please say hello to Dylan." Stevie nudged the tablet toward him.

He poked his finger against the screen and typed. *Hello.*

Charlie held it up for Dylan to see before placing it back on the table.

Stevie didn't know if Dylan had ever met someone with autism. But given the way he accepted Charlie's use of the tablet and lack of eye contact, she suspected that he had.

"Would you two like to join me for a boat ride?" Dylan directed the question at Charlie first and then Stevie.

"That sounds like fun." Stevie nodded. "Charlie, what do you think?"

He tapped on the screen again. *Yes.*

"I just need to get cleaned up." Stevie stood, remembering that she was still in yoga pants and an old t-shirt. "I'll be right back."

She took a quick shower and changed into a fresh tank top and shorts. After pulling her hair back into a loose ponytail, she applied some pink-tinted lip balm. In only a few minutes, she descended the stairs, ready to go. She glanced down at her no-frills outfit. Lexi would chide her for being low maintenance, like it was a bad thing, but Stevie considered it an asset. She raised her chin and headed toward the kitchen.

Stevie strode down the hall, planning to alleviate the awkward silence that was surely happening in the kitchen. However, as she neared the doorway, she stopped short.

"So, what's your favorite color?" She heard Dylan ask Charlie.

"That's my favorite too," Dylan said. "What do you like to do for fun?"

There was a short pause before Dylan spoke again. "I'd love to see them sometime."

Stevie drew her hand up to her mouth, astonished. Charlie had never demonstrated enough of an expressive vocabulary to be typing the words he must have used to answer Dylan's questions. More importantly, Charlie was involved in a *conversation*. That had never happened before. Dylan continued talking, and Stevie was unable to stop herself from eavesdropping.

"Your mom and I have been friends since we were your age."

There was another pause. Then Dylan said, "I think she's special too."

Stevie heard the smile in his voice.

Unable to wait any longer, she rounded the corner into the kitchen, announcing her presence with a conspicuous cough. Dylan sipped from his coffee mug, and Charlie stood next to him, flapping his hands. His tablet sat on the other side of the table, powered down.

The crushing weight of disappointment hit her. She pressed her lips tight as she realized that Charlie had not been having a conversation at all. Dylan had only been playing with him, indulging in an imaginary discussion with her son. Though Stevie could tell by Charlie's flapping hands that he had enjoyed it, the whole charade turned her stomach. She made a mental note to talk to Dylan about it later.

"Okay, guys. Let's go." She forced enthusiasm to mask her dismay.

They walked through the front door and down to the street. Stevie stopped at the curb and made a point of looking both ways to make sure that there were no cars coming, a habit she was working to instill in Charlie.

"See? We always stop and check." She turned her head to the left and then to the right once more for good measure." There wasn't a car in sight. "Okay. All clear." They stepped off the curb and crossed the street together.

"I just need to grab Charlie's vest and headphones from my skiff. I'll be right back." She scurried off while they continued walking toward the end of Dylan's dock. When she rejoined them, Dylan stepped onto the deck of his sleek red speedboat first and turned to lift Charlie aboard. Her son settled in on one of the white, padded benches and put on his life vest. Dylan turned back to Stevie, offering his hand to support her. Having spent her entire life on the water, she didn't need help boarding the vessel. But she accepted his help anyway, biting back a smile as their hands touched.

Dylan waited until Charlie put on his headphones before he coaxed the powerful engine to life. They cruised through the calm, deep waters of Taylor's Creek, passing by Carrot Island on their right and the waterfront businesses on their left. As soon as they emerged from the confines of the no-wake zone, he dropped the boat into gear and revved the engine.

They were traveling fast now, though Stevie had no doubt the boat could go much faster. She glanced back at her son, who smiled as the wind ruffled his blond curls. Her heart swelled at the sight. A smile from Charlie was brighter than the sun, a rare gift that she would never take for granted.

She inhaled, allowing the pure air to fill her lungs. She had always enjoyed the salty breeze, but today, as the wind whipped through her hair, a new energy coursed through her veins. For the first time in a very long while, she was happy.

She continued to breathe it all in, filling herself with new life, born of the water and carried by the wind. She glanced at Dylan, overcome with the same desire that had resulted in her dalliance with Sam. Their eyes met, and she looked away after only a second, fearing the intensity of her thoughts would somehow be visible on her face.

Since it was early on a Monday morning, there was little traffic. They continued all the way to the lighthouse at Cape Lookout. Dylan slowed the boat until it was just drifting on the water, allowing them time to enjoy the view.

Stevie took in the familiar sight of the lighthouse. Its unique black-and-white diamond pattern stood stark against the pale blue sky.

"Sometimes I wish I had never left this place." Dylan cast a meaningful glance at Stevie.

"I'm glad you came back." *You have no idea how glad I am.* She frowned at her wantonness. Her behavior of late would shame even Lexi. *What is wrong with me?*

"I should have done a better job of keeping in touch." Dylan glanced back toward the lighthouse. "I'm sorry."

Stevie grimaced, feeling guilty for not contacting him since he'd left. "Phones work both ways, you know. I could have done better too."

Dylan nodded. "We'll just have to agree not to let the years get away from us again."

"Sounds like a deal to me." Stevie extended her hand.

"Deal." Dylan clasped his large hand around hers, sealing the agreement with a firm shake. He held on to her longer than was necessary, and she wondered if he wanted to say more. But, with a glance back at Charlie, Dylan let go.

Stevie's heart fluttered. "Thanks for taking us out here today. Charlie's having a great time. And so am I."

"It's my pleasure. We were lucky the rain held off for as long as it did." He nodded toward the dark gray clouds moving in from the south. "Guess we should start heading back." He turned the boat around for the trip home.

When they reached Dylan's private dock, Stevie returned Charlie's headphones and life vest to her small skiff. Dylan took Charlie's hand

and walked with him across the street, where they waited for her on the porch.

Those two have really hit it off.

With a pang of sadness, she remembered the pretend conversation Dylan had orchestrated earlier.

Stevie approached the house. "Charlie, go on inside. I'll be there in a minute."

She watched as her son walked inside, and once he closed the door, she turned to Dylan. "I heard you talking to Charlie in the kitchen earlier. That was sweet, but I'm not sure that it was a good idea. You don't know what he's thinking, so it's best not to make assumptions. I think it might be confusing for him."

Dylan nodded, but a knowing grin flitted across his face. "I'm sorry. I won't do it again."

Chapter fourteen

Stevie

The next morning, Stevie stood beside her father's hospital bed while her mother rested in a chair nearby. "How are you feeling today, Dad?"

"I'm feeling fine, honey. Just ready to go home." He ran his hand through his thinning hair. "I'm tired of getting poked and prodded. By now, they've got to be out of tests to run."

Patricia leaned forward and patted his leg. "They're just being thorough, Jim. You made an unusually fast recovery. I'm sure they want to make sure that they haven't missed anything."

Stevie smiled as she took in the sight of her father. The color had returned to his cheeks, and his eyes were bright once again. The nurses had removed all of the wires and tubes, except for the IV in the top of his left hand. Even that was capped and no longer connected to anything. The monitor that had once displayed his vital signs stood, unplugged, in the corner of the small hospital room.

Patricia settled back in her chair. "He'll probably be allowed to come home today. We're just waiting for the doctor to stop by and give the okay."

Stevie found it hard to believe that only two days earlier he'd been so close to death. The image of him lying in his recliner, his lips blue from lack of oxygen, jarred her out of sleep at night and haunted her during the day. She stared at him, memorizing his every feature, in hopes that seeing him healthy again would replace that unwanted memory.

"They say I was really lucky. The attack didn't do any damage." Jim tapped his chest and beamed with pride.

"Really?" Stevie's eye widened in surprise, and she looked to her mother for confirmation.

"That's the same look the doctor had on his face when he gave me the news." Jim chuckled. "Guess it's going to take more than a massive heart attack to bring me down."

Patricia shook her head. "You still have to be careful. You were lucky this time. If you have another heart attack..." She swallowed hard. "Who knows what will happen?"

Jim gave a slight nod as he cast a sidelong glance at his wife, offering an unspoken assurance that he understood the seriousness of the situation.

Patricia cleared her throat. "Where's Charlie?"

"He's fishing with Sam. He starts school tomorrow, so they're enjoying the last day of summer break together."

"Hard to believe he's starting school already." Jim scratched his head.

Stevie gulped. *My thoughts exactly.*

A knowing grin stretched across Patricia's face. "They grow up fast, don't they?"

"Too fast. I'm not sure I'm ready for this." Stevie fiddled with the hem of her shirt. In fact, she was quite sure she *wasn't* ready at all. Her life had taken one weird turn after another in the last few days. And the stress of sending her son to school for the first time was the last thing she needed.

"I had the same worries when you started kindergarten. I think all moms do." Patricia rose from her chair and walked around to the other side of the bed. "You'll get through it just fine, honey." She wrapped her arms around Stevie and gave her a tight squeeze. "I promise."

Stevie pulled away and mustered a half grin for her mother. She appreciated the vote of confidence, but sending Charlie to school wasn't the same as sending any other kid. Everything was more complicated for him. And when things were tough for him, they were tough for her.

A tall, trim woman bustled into the room. She greeted them and introduced herself as the hospital's nutritionist. "We need to discuss your new dietary restrictions before we discharge you."

Jim groaned and clutched his chest. "I think I feel another one coming on."

"Stop that!" Patricia swatted his hand. "This is important."

"Guess that's my cue to leave." Stevie didn't want to witness her father's reaction to learning about his limitations regarding butter, salt, and fried food. She bent over the bed and hugged him. "I'm glad you're better, Dad."

"I'll call you when we get back home." Patricia sent an air kiss as Stevie walked out the door.

Stevie leaned in to whisper to the nutritionist on her way out. "Good luck with that one."

Chapter Fifteen

Stevie

That afternoon, Stevie waited for Charlie to return from fishing with his dad. To pass the time, she sat at her kitchen table and busied herself by cutting the tags from his new school clothes. She removed not only the price tags but the inner labels as well. Something as insignificant as a size label on one of his cotton t-shirts could cause Charlie great distress. Though she knew most mothers never had to bother with this chore, Stevie didn't mind doing it. In fact, there were so many issues that she was helpless to fix for her son, she was happy to do this one small task to make his life a little easier.

In the quiet of the empty house, Stevie let her mind wander. Her thoughts drifted to her boat outing with Dylan, and she wondered if he'd enjoyed their time together as much as she had. She snipped another tag from one of Charlie's new shirts, smiling for no reason in particular.

Recalling the look in his eyes when he'd touched her hand, a quiver raced throughout her body. She lowered her scissors to the table and rested her hand against her thudding her heart. *If he'd been the one who showed up at my door on Sunday night instead of Sam...* She shook her head.

Though she was alone, her cheeks grew hot with embarrassment.

Her recent lack of inhibition still surprised her. Lexi had often teased her, claiming she was "repressed," but now her best friend would have to find something else to tease her about. She was changing, but she didn't know why.

The resurgence of her infatuation with Dylan explained her racing heart and fluttering stomach. She could even credit him with the newfound exhilaration that coursed through her veins. Those things were explainable, but the other changes weren't.

Her heightened senses and that strange vision still baffled her. Then there was the constant sense of anticipation, as if something amazing waited just around the corner for her. It was the same sort of excitement she'd always experienced at the start of spring, when the chill of winter surrendered to bright sunshiny days and the promise of new life. But *this*, she knew, was not the expectation of changing seasons. It was something much stronger.

The sound of a breaking twig just outside the open kitchen window interrupted her thoughts. With a start, she looked up and saw a blur of black sprint out of view. Certain that someone had been peering in at her, she raced to the back door and threw it open.

"Who's there?" She stepped out onto her back porch. "Hello?" She looked in every direction but saw no one.

Suddenly, Dylan's back door flew open, and he dashed outside. "Everything okay, Stevie?"

"I—I saw someone looking in my window." She groaned inside, fearing she sounded like a damsel in distress.

He scanned the area, his shoulders drawn up and his eyes alert.

"I think it was a woman." Stevie frowned and tried to recall more details. "I didn't get a good look at her face, but I'm pretty sure I saw long black hair."

Dylan clenched his jaw. "Go back inside, and lock your doors. I'll

110

take a look around."

Stevie did as he asked. She watched through the window as he leaped over the railing of his porch and jumped the picket fence that separated his property from hers. He landed in her yard and rushed around the exterior of her house, searching for any sign of the trespasser. When he returned to her back door after patrolling the perimeter, she let him inside. His eyes had grown darker, and he furrowed his brow with worry.

"I'm sure it's no big deal. Probably just a kid goofing around." Stevie shrugged, finding it odd that she was the one doing the consoling.

"I'd like to look around inside, if you don't mind." Without waiting for a reply, he walked over to the kitchen window, pulled it closed, and engaged the lock. He slipped past her to check the other windows, giving each room a visual sweep as he entered it. When he finished, he climbed the stairs to the second floor.

"She'd have to be awfully tall to peek in through those windows." Stevie laughed at her awkward joke as she trailed behind him on the stairs.

"Just being thorough." He glanced over his shoulder before heading for her bedroom.

Since she didn't trust herself to go in there with him, she waited in the hallway when he entered her bedroom. But Dylan remained businesslike, tugging on the windows and looking under the bed, before he moved on to the other rooms. When he finished his security check, they walked back down the stairs.

Dylan touched her arm. "Call me right away if you see her again." The hard edge in his voice and the concern in his eyes jolted Stevie.

She rubbed the goosebumps on her forearm. "Sure, but I—"

The chime of the doorbell interrupted her.

"Charlie?" Dylan nodded toward the door.

"Yes. And Sam too." Stevie glanced in the same direction. If Sam saw Dylan in her house… She frowned.

"Don't worry." Dylan winked. "I'll just go out through the back. See you later."

"Thanks." She flashed him a grateful smile. The tension in her shoulders loosened as she watched his retreating frame head toward the back door. He'd left without her even having to ask. Like he'd known she wanted him to. She couldn't remember the last time anyone had paid that much attention to her. It was almost unnerving how well he knew her.

By the time the doorbell rang a second time, Dylan was already gone.

"Hey, Charlie!" She opened the door, a big smile on her face. "Did you have fun?"

"I think he did." Sam lifted the small cooler he held in his right hand. "He caught a couple of fish all by himself." Beaming with fatherly pride, he passed the cooler to Stevie.

"Great job!" Stevie knelt down and gave Charlie a quick hug. As soon as she let him go, he began to walk down the hall.

"I'd better get a snack ready for him." She gestured toward the kitchen. "Would you like to come in for a while?"

Sam shook his head. "No, thanks. I have to get back to the boat. I'm taking some folks out to Cape Lookout this afternoon." He turned to walk back to his truck.

"Okay. See you later then." She waved and tried to look casual, but inside, she breathed a sigh of relief that he'd declined the invitation. They'd done a good job of pretending nothing had happened, but the fact remained. Something *had* happened. Stevie had a strong suspicion it would not be long before Sam insisted on bringing it up again.

As Sam drove away in his pickup truck, a champagne-colored Buick pulled up and parked on the street in front of Dylan's house. Randy climbed out of the driver's side. Then he walked around the car to open the doors for his elderly companions, Alice and Ruth. Alice carried an overstuffed basket of homemade baked goods, and they proceeded up the walkway to Dylan's front porch. Stevie stepped out onto her own porch and waved to her mother's friends.

Dylan opened the door before they even had a chance to knock. "I've been expecting you," Stevie heard him say. "It seems we have quite a bit of work to do." He looked in Stevie's direction, as if aware that she was listening. "Please come inside." He ushered the three senior members of the Historic Society into his home.

chapter sixteen

Stevie

Stevie sliced a red apple and set it on the table for Charlie, who stared off into space as he waited for his snack. While he ate, she assembled the ingredients she needed to bake a loaf of gluten-free bread. She wanted to have plenty on hand to use for Charlie's school lunches. Humming, she reached into the cupboard and selected a bag of organic brown rice flour.

A sudden movement outside the window caused her to jump, and she dropped the bag onto the area rug. It exploded, sending send white dust all over the kitchen floor.

Stevie squinted, ready to note every detail about her intruder. But it was nothing more than a lone tree branch swaying in the breeze. She let out an exasperated sigh, frustrated with herself for being so jumpy. She swept up as much of the flour as she could, but she knew she would have to vacuum the rug after Charlie finished his snack.

When the last apple slice disappeared from his plate, Stevie warned him. "Charlie, vacuum."

The boy hurried out of the kitchen and ran upstairs. As Stevie pulled the vacuum cleaner from the hall closet, she counted to twenty. By then, she knew Charlie would have had time to secure himself within the hideout, safe from the terrible sound she was about to make. She cleaned up what was left of the mess on the kitchen rug and stowed the vacuum away.

She went upstairs to her son's room and knocked on the door to his hideout. "All done, Charlie."

He pushed open the hidden door and drifted to his Lincoln Log collection. Stevie watched him cross the room without even the briefest glance in her direction. She sighed, longing for him to connect with her with a word or a smile. She had grown stronger in the years since his autism diagnosis. But there were still moments, like this one, when grief rose to the surface. Powerless to stop its gnawing ache, she pressed her hand against her chest as if to hold the pieces of her broken heart in place. Saying nothing more, she turned and left the room.

Back in the kitchen, Stevie found another bag of flour and busied herself with the work of making bread. She mixed the ingredients, remembering how she'd never been much of a cook before Charlie's special diet. In her life before autism, take-out menus had reigned supreme and even Pop-Tarts went untoasted. Now, she could bake a loaf of gluten-free bread from scratch without even glancing at a recipe.

Once she'd prepared the dough to rise, Stevie went back upstairs to find Charlie. He still stood at the long table on the far side of his bedroom, building a small house with his newest set of Lincoln Logs.

"It's so pretty outside. How about we go play some ball?"

Charlie added a green plastic roof to the top of his latest log cabin creation, adjusting it until it fit just right. Then he walked to his toy bin and selected a red ball. Stevie watched his expressionless face and wondered, once again, what her son was thinking.

"Okay. Let's go." She tried to summon enough enthusiasm for both of them.

They went to play in the freshly cut grass of the front yard. Curious about Dylan's business with the Historic Society, Stevie angled herself so she could see when his guests left. Charlie threw the ball to her, and she caught it. With a gentle toss, she sent it back to him.

After several minutes, Dylan's front door opened, and the three guests stepped out onto his porch. Stevie caught the ball again and held it for a moment while she listened in on the conversation next door.

"Of course, Patricia wanted to come in person, but she's taking care of her husband today. She'll be in touch soon." Randy shook Dylan's hand.

"It's good to have you back home, Dylan." Alice patted his cheek in her grandmotherly way.

"It's good to be back, though I wish the circumstances were better." Dylan made eye contact with each of them before stepping back inside his house. "Thanks for stopping by. I'll see you all again soon." He closed the door.

What circumstances?

Stevie tossed the ball back to her son. The movement must have caught Alice's attention because she waved and began walking in their direction. Ruth and Randy joined her.

"We heard you had a bit of a scare today, sweetie. Are you okay?" Alice wrapped her beefy arm around Stevie and squeezed.

"I'm sure it was no big deal. Probably just a curious kid or a tourist wanting to take a peek inside my old house." She slipped out of Alice's grip before she ended up drowning in the woman's bosom again. But her heart skipped a beat as she realized Dylan must have told them about the encounter. So, he'd been talking to them about her. But why?

"Yeah, right." Ruth snorted. Alice elbowed her in the ribs.

As they talked, Charlie amused himself by bouncing the red ball on the walkway. On the third bounce, it hit his foot instead of the sidewalk and rolled into the street. In spite of Stevie's countless attempts to teach him, Charlie never checked for cars before crossing the road. This time was no different. Out of habit, Stevie checked for oncoming traffic as she neared the curb. Seeing that the coast was clear, she did not stop him from chasing after his ball. He scampered out into the middle of Front Street.

A car engine roared to life just two houses away. Stevie whirled toward the source of the sound to see a silver sedan whip away from the curb and tear down the street, accelerating at an impossible rate. She jerked her head back toward Charlie.

It's heading straight for him! Her heart thundered within her chest.

Held hostage by the noise of the revving engine, Charlie stood frozen in the middle of the street with his hands clamped over his ears. The speeding car raced toward him, getting louder and louder as it approached. Charlie squeezed his eyes shut.

Stevie sprinted forward in a futile attempt to save her son, her feet pounding against the ground as she tried to outrun the speeding vehicle.

A new heat pooled in her blood as the icy chill of fear gave way to sheer determination. An electric sensation zipped through her body. She thought of nothing else but rescuing Charlie from the unimaginable fate that bore down on him.

"Charlie!" Her soul-wrenching scream echoed across Taylor's Creek. She stretched out her hands as if she could stop the car by the force of her will alone.

And the car...stopped. Mere inches away from Charlie. With no skid marks and no indication the brakes had been used at all. A fraction of a second earlier, the vehicle had been barreling down the street at incredible speed. Now, it sat motionless except for the idling engine, proof Stevie had not imagined the whole, horrific incident.

She pulled Charlie into her arms and pressed him against her like she never intended to let him go. With trembling hands, she rubbed his hair and thanked the heavens he had survived. All of a sudden, Dylan appeared beside the car and flung open the door. Stevie strained to see the person who'd almost killed her son, but no one occupied the driver's seat. Dylan rounded the car and slammed his fist on its roof.

He took a deep breath and walked over to Stevie and Charlie. "Are you okay?"

Stevie, unable to speak, nodded. Pale and shaking, she picked Charlie up and carried him to the safety of their yard. Without a word, she fell to her knees and rocked her precious son as tears rolled down her cheeks.

Snippets of conversation Stevie didn't understand floated around her. She glanced up at the members of the Historic Society.

"Look, I'd do anything to save the kid too, but don't you think you could have been a little more subtle?" Ruth asked.

"It wasn't me." Alice shook her head. "I don't think any one of us could have stopped that car on our own." Both women turned to look at Randy.

"Wasn't me either." Randy glanced toward the car. "It all happened so fast, we didn't even have a chance to try to help." He paused for a moment. "Dylan was inside when it happened, so it couldn't have been him."

In unison, they turned to Stevie.

Ruth's gray eyes lit up. "Well it's about damn time!"

"I'll call Patricia." Randy pulled his cellphone out of his pocket and stepped away.

"I'll make the tea." A broad grin stretched across Alice's face.

chapter seventeen

Stevie

E verything's all right. You're safe now." Stevie ignored the bizarre chatter around her and attempted to soothe herself as
much as her son.

"Let's get you inside." Dylan bent down to help her up, still scanning the street for any sign of further trouble. When Stevie glanced
up at him, the rage that burned in his eyes melted into compassion.
He held out his arms, offering to carry Charlie for her.

"No, I've got him." She tightened her hold on her boy. He'd
calmed down, and she didn't want to upset him. But in truth, she
couldn't bear to let him go.

"Okay." Dylan helped ease her onto her feet. With a protective
arm around her trembling shoulders, he escorted them toward their
home.

When Stevie reached her porch, she turned around to take another look at the silver car that had nearly slammed into Charlie. None
of it made any sense. She stared at the vehicle, seeking answers that
were not there.

Randy stood in her yard, holding his phone to his ear. She detected
his hushed, urgent tone but couldn't make out his words. He hung up,

119

returned his phone to his pocket, and faced Alice and Ruth. "Patricia will be here soon. She just brought Jim home from the hospital, but she's going to get a neighbor to come sit with him so she can leave."

"Better get that car out of the road before someone starts asking questions." Ruth pointed a bony finger at the silver vehicle.

"We should be with Stevie." Alice escorted Ruth toward the house.

The two women climbed the steps to join Stevie and Charlie on the porch. Together, they watched Randy drive the silver car back to its original location farther up the street.

"At least there were no witnesses." Though Ruth whispered to Alice, Stevie still heard.

"Amen to that." Alice pressed her hands together as if in prayer. "Can you imagine trying to explain this?"

Puzzled by their comments, Stevie pulled Charlie closer. "Explain what?"

"Nothing, dear." Alice waved her hand to dismiss the question. "Let's get you settled inside."

Lacking the energy to form an argument to the contrary, Stevie complied. Alice placed her hand on the small of Stevie's back and nudged her toward the living room.

Stevie perched on the dark green sofa, still cradling Charlie in her arms. Dylan sat down beside her and began smoothing her hair with his hand. At his touch, the tension in her shoulders eased a bit. She took several deep breaths. Though the shock had begun to wear off, she still found herself at a loss for words. Questions formed in her racing mind but never quite made it to her lips.

Ruth entered the room and slumped down into a hand-carved walnut side chair. Alice stood next to her, with bright eyes and clasped hands.

"Can I get you anything?" Alice smiled at Stevie.

"No, thank you." Stevie focused on snuggling Charlie and taking in the fresh scent of his shampoo.

"You can get me a beer." Ruth scowled up at Alice.

"I don't believe I asked you." Alice rolled her eyes at Ruth and then turned toward Randy as he joined them in the living room. "Can you drive me home? I need to pick up a few things."

"Sure." He shuffled toward the door, and the two left.

When her heart returned to its normal beat, Stevie loosened her hold on Charlie. She hesitated to let him go and paused to take a good, long look at his face. From his blond hair to his blue eyes to his expressionless face, he was everything to her.

He's not hurt. That's all that matters.

"You must be getting hungry for dinner." Stevie mustered up a smile for him.

He climbed down from her lap but remained close as she stood and crossed the room to the hallway. When she reached the threshold, she overheard an odd exchange between Ruth and Dylan.

"Been a while since we've had to do one of these," Ruth whispered.

"I was the last one, and that was twelve years ago," Dylan replied.

Stevie stared at them, seeking some explanation, but their smiles—bizarre mixtures of sympathy and excitement—only confused her more. Charlie tugged at her hand, so she continued down the hallway.

In the kitchen, Stevie noticed the dough had plumped up over the sides of the loaf pan. She placed it in the hot oven and set the time for one hour. Though she had no appetite, she wanted to be sure that Charlie ate a good dinner. She found leftover chicken in the refrigerator and reheated it along with some peas.

It felt strange, being in the kitchen, performing such mundane chores after what had happened. The out-of-control car and its missing driver continued to occupy her thoughts. The shocking scene replayed in her mind over and over in an endless loop. With each intrusive flashback, new questions cropped up. Nothing made sense.

She sat down at the table with Charlie while he ate his dinner. After a few moments, Ruth and Dylan joined them in the kitchen.

"That girl needs some booze." Ruth pointed to Stevie.

"I wouldn't mind a glass of wine." Her voice sounded odd and stilted to her ears.

Dylan opened the cupboard to retrieve a wineglass. Then he filled it with chardonnay and handed it to Stevie.

"Thank you." She accepted the glass with a wobbly grin. "There's beer in the fridge too. Please help yourself."

"You don't have to tell me twice." Ruth flung open the refrigerator door and grabbed herself a bottle of beer.

"There was no one behind the wheel." Stevie brought the wineglass to her trembling lips. "They must have run while I was busy with Charlie."

Ruth and Dylan exchanged a glance.

"I think it's best if you don't worry about that right now." Dylan slipped his warm hand over her freezing one.

Stevie tensed. "You've got to be kidding me! How can I not worry about it? Charlie could have been…" She stopped. She didn't want to finish that sentence in front of her son.

"You just need to relax for a bit." Ruth tipped her beer bottle in the air in mock cheers. "We'll talk more about this later."

"Relax. Yeah, right." Stevie rolled her eyes as she guzzled down the remaining wine.

When Randy and Alice returned, they let themselves in through the front door. Randy carried Alice's floral tote bag into the kitchen and set it in a corner.

"Thanks, Randy. We'll get everything set up shortly." Alice trailed behind him carrying a small, mesh bag filled with loose tea leaves.

Stevie filled her glass with more wine and didn't even bother to ask what Alice meant. They wouldn't tell her anyway. She scowled at Dylan and Ruth. This secrecy drove her mad. They should be out there tracking down the absentee driver and hauling him into the police station, not sitting here drinking and making tea like nothing had happened.

Charlie finished his dinner and carried his plate to the sink. Stevie's heart twinged. He'd been through a lot, and it was getting too crowded in the kitchen for him. She knew he wanted to escape to his bedroom, either to the quiet solitude of the hideout or to the safe predictability of another Lincoln Log project.

She reached out for him as he walked past and held him once again. "I love you, Charlie." Tears swam in her eyes as gratitude that he'd somehow managed to remain unharmed flooded through her once more. She released him and watched as he walked out of the room. When she could no longer see him, she turned back around, lifted her wineglass from the table, and emptied it in one long sip.

Alice stepped forward and took away the empty glass before Stevie had a chance to return it to the table. "I'm going to make you some tea now, dear. It will help you feel better." She filled a stainless steel kettle with water and placed it on the stovetop.

"Thanks, Alice. But really, it's not necessary."

Alice chuckled. "Oh, but it *is*."

Stevie heard the front door open again. She listened to Patricia, Deborah, and Lexi's excited chatter as they walked toward the kitchen. They fell silent when they entered the room. Lexi bounced to Stevie's side and hugged her. Deborah's wide grin seemed out of place given the terrifying events of the day.

Patricia passed through the knot of visitors and took her daughter's hands. Stevie met her intense gaze and frowned in confusion at the joy dancing in her mother's eyes.

"Mom." Stevie's voice shook. "What's going on?"

"We have so much to tell you, honey." Patricia kissed her cheek.

"Give us a few moments. It will all become clear soon enough."

Twilight settled on the world outside while Stevie sat at the table. Exhausted and confused, she watched Alice prepare a rather complicated cup of tea. Alice took several pinches of dried leaves from the mesh bag she'd brought with her and placed them in the bottom of a mug. Then, she drew a small vial filled with an amber liquid from her pocket.

"One, two, three." She counted aloud as the drops fell from the vial.

Pausing, she stole a glance at Stevie, tilted her head, and then proceeded to add a couple more drops to the mixture. When the kettle whistled, she poured the boiling water into the mug. Alice stirred the tea and placed it on the table in front of Stevie.

"Thanks." Stevie watched the steam rise from the mug with a twinge of disappointment. After the day she'd had, she would have preferred another glass of wine.

"Drink it, Stevie." Patricia lifted the mug and handed it to her.

"I need to go get Charlie ready for bed." She started to stand.

Patricia placed a hand on Stevie's shoulder. "Stay here."

"I can take care of him." Ruth stood with a grunt and headed toward the stairs. "I'll make up a real nice bedtime story for him too!"

Stevie shuddered as she tried to imagine what kind of story Ruth might conjure up. Since her son had been traumatized enough for one day, she called, "Maybe you should just let him choose one that he already has."

"If you say so…" By the sarcastic tone of Ruth's voice, Stevie knew the old woman would do whatever she pleased.

Lexi leaned toward Patricia. "Should I go ahead and get everything ready?"

"Yes, please." Patricia nodded. "It won't be long now."

"I'll help her." Randy followed Lexi out of the kitchen.

Stevie glanced over at Dylan, hoping for answers. When his eyes met hers, he smiled but said nothing.

The people she'd known and trusted for her entire life now filled her kitchen, bustling about with busy, purposeful energy. Like they'd all been planning some party she had no idea about. With her addled mind, she tried to puzzle out what they could be doing, but nothing came to her. Tea, setting up, all of their weird smiles—none of it pointed to anything other than a boring meeting.

She froze. *Are they initiating me into the Historic Society? Today of all days?*

"Drink the tea, Stevie," Dylan coaxed her.

She took a sip, finding its sweetness surprising. "What kind of tea is this?"

"It's my very own special blend, dear. The recipe is a secret." Alice winked.

Stevie nodded and sipped again. The tightness in her body began to roll away, a welcome sensation after such a trying afternoon. The thick, homey scent of the bread baking in the oven permeated the air, wrapping around her like a warm blanket.

After a while, Ruth returned from upstairs. "He's asleep now."

"Thank you." Stevie took another sip of the tea and refrained from asking about the bedtime story.

"Just so you know, *he* chose his story tonight." Ruth crossed her arms and jutted out her hip. "It was some trash about a pasty hussy shacked up in a house in the woods with a bunch of midgets."

"I think you mean *dwarves.*" Alice shook her head and tsked.

All of a sudden, Stevie's limbs drooped like they were made of lead, and it became difficult to hold the ceramic mug. She placed it on the table, allowing her arms to fall by her sides.

125

The timer dinged, but Stevie paid it no mind. Alice turned off the oven and removed the freshly baked bread.

Lexi flitted into the kitchen. "We arranged the chairs and set out the candles. I smudged the room with sage, so it's ready." She nodded in Stevie's direction. "From the looks of it, I'd say she's ready too."

Stevie giggled for no particular reason. Her eyelids had grown heavy, so she let them close.

Dylan slid his arms underneath her and carried her down the hall. She fluttered her eyes open as he laid her on the sofa in the dark living room.

He leaned in and stroked her cheek. "Tonight, Stevie, everything is going to change."

Patricia waited as the others filed in. She waved her hands, and all of the candles in the room lit at once. "Let us begin."

Chapter eighteen

Stevie

Stevie fell deeper and deeper into the black abyss. She tried to raise her arms, reaching for something to stop the fall, but her limbs were as cumbersome as tree trunks. She couldn't get them to budge.

"Don't fight it, dear." Her mother's voice drifted down from a distance.

The free fall slowed, and Stevie landed on a sandy island beach. She scanned the area, searching for a landmark to help identify her location. Assuming she was on one of the islands near her home, she looked to the horizon but could not see the lighthouse.

Her mother's voice carried above the crash of the waves. "Our people have existed throughout the ages. But the history of *our* coven begins in the summer of 1718, on a small island off the coast of North Carolina."

Stevie began to walk along the pristine shoreline. As she came around a bend, she spotted a small village in a grassy area just beyond the beach. Near the water, she saw the same four women she had seen when she held the amethyst pendant at her mother's house.

Patricia called out to her again. "They can't see you, Stevie. Get closer."

Stevie approached the women, consumed with the same overwhelming sadness that had accompanied her earlier vision.

"Charlotte, Hannah, and Catherine." Stevie's words slurred.

"That's right." Patricia's voice helped soothe some of her sadness. "They are with Lucia, Charlotte's mother and our ancestor."

"Why are they so sad?" Stevie furrowed her brow, trying to understand.

Her mother's voice pierced the vision again. "Keep watching. You will see."

As Stevie looked on, a tall man stepped onto the beach, accompanied by twenty-five men from his crew. Most of them were dressed in rags. What they lacked in teeth, they made up for in filth and unhealthy levels of testosterone. Her gaze shifted to the three crowded sloops and the much larger flagship anchored offshore. She suspected those vessels contained hundreds more vile crew members.

Their leader stood out from the group, not only in height but in appearance as well. Dressed in a velvet jacket and polished knee-high boots, he wore his long black beard in braids tied with ebony ribbons. He had tucked slow-burning matches under his hat, leaving tendrils of smoke to curl menacingly around his face. He was a living demon, no doubt ready and able to exact unimaginable destruction upon those who dared to challenge him.

Stevie recognized him right away. *Blackbeard*. Her pulse quickened.

Lucia, Charlotte, Hannah, and Catherine stood shoulder to shoulder, their gazes locked on the unwelcome visitors.

"I see the witches wait for me." The pirate captain grinned with lecherous exuberance as he approached. "So, you knew I was coming."

"There are no witches here. We are a small village, settled here decades ago." Lucia's face remained impassive. She held her chin high.

"Where are your men?" Blackbeard glanced around at the few modest structures that made up the village.

"Fishing." Charlotte offered no more information than the question required. She mirrored Lucia's example, keeping her voice steady and her expression inscrutable.

The pirate turned to his men. "Surely if they possessed magic abilities, they would have stopped us by now." His crew answered him with a low murmur of agreement. "But I am not yet convinced." He moved closer to the four women and narrowed his black eyes. "Witches are well known for their cunning."

He stopped in front of Lucia, studying her. "Do you know the true test of a witch?"

"I am familiar with the stories." Lucia's reply held no emotion.

Blackbeard hunched toward her but spoke for all to hear. "If I bound you to a chair and threw you into the ocean, would you sink to the bottom or float to the surface?"

"I would sink, just as surely as you would."

The pirate removed one of the sharp daggers from his belt and, with a swift lunge, held it tight against Lucia's neck. She stood firm, though the younger women gasped in horror. "If I cut you, will you bleed?"

"Of course." Lucia still showed no signs of alarm.

"I'll see about that." He raised the dagger above his head and drove the knife down toward her heart, stopping a mere hairsbreadth from her skin.

129

Catherine's terrified wail sliced through the wind and rose above the crash of the waves, but Lucia did not flinch.

"Claims of magic and witches..." The pirate captain scoffed. "There are no witches here." His men grumbled in disappointment at the lack of bloodshed.

Blackbeard dragged the tip of his dagger along the exposed skin of Lucia's chest, grinning with delight at the sight of her blood as it trickled down to stain her white dress. "You are fortunate I chose not to pierce that heart of yours. You possess no power to stop me. No power at all."

He left Lucia and stood before Catherine, studying her petite frame and youthful features. He said nothing, nor did he have to. His presence alone caused her to shiver.

He moved on to Charlotte, hungrily eyeing her auburn mane. "Red hair." He twirled a tendril around his filthy finger. "I bet this one has a temper."

"But you." He moved to Hannah, glaring into her deep, green eyes. "You're the feistiest of them all, aren't you?" He clutched her throat in his hand. "I shall take you first."

Lucia's face pinched in agony, and she hung her head.

Blackbeard released his grip on Hannah and turned to address Lucia. "Are they all your daughters?"

She raised her chin once more. "I love them all." She scowled at him, revealing her growing anger.

"Then this will be a very sad day for you." The pirate returned his dagger to his belt.

"We have surrendered peacefully to you." Lucia's intense gaze bore into him.

"Indeed you have, and that is the only reason you are still alive." He sighed and called to his men. "There is no magic here, but I do believe I have found three new wives." A rumble of laughter coursed through the crew.

He leered at the young women. "Will you walk with us? Or must my men drag you to the ship?"

Charlotte pursed her lips. "We will walk on our own."

"Very well then. Let's go. Leave the old one. I have no use for her." He sauntered away without sparing another glance in Lucia's direction.

The crew encircled the young women as they followed the pirate captain. Charlotte stole a final look back at her mother. Lucia blew her a kiss as the first tears streamed down her cheeks. She remained on the shore, watching as Charlotte, Hannah, and Catherine drifted away on a boat headed toward the pirate's flagship.

Stevie shuddered. Though she'd merely witnessed these events from long ago, her throat tightened as if Blackbeard's evil had reached through the centuries and squeezed her neck. She struggled to pull herself through the abyss, desperate to return to her own time and leave Blackbeard and his crew far behind.

"Stay still, Stevie." Her mother's voice resonated from far away. "There's more. Watch."

In an instant, Stevie found herself in a grimy hold below the ship's deck, along with Charlotte and Catherine. Thin shafts of sunlight beamed through the lattice of the overhead hatch, revealing dusty crates, cannonballs, and ballast stones cluttering the cramped space. Skittering sounds came from the spaces between the crates, and Stevie caught sight of a long, hairless tail just before it disappeared into a dark corner. The squalid surroundings were a far cry from the island paradise she had just visited.

Charlotte paced back and forth in the small hold as Catherine huddled in a corner, swatting at the hungry rats with an ax handle she'd found on the wooden floor. Though neither spoke of Hannah, Stevie had no doubt Blackbeard held the missing witch.

"How are we going to get out of here?" Catherine rose to her feet, the ax handle still in her hand. "I don't see how we can do it without using our magic."

"We have to keep our magic a secret. Even now." She continued to pace, deep in thought, as Catherine struggled to keep the hungry rats at bay.

Time passed, and the *Queen Anne's Revenge* sailed on. Stevie listened to the activity of the men on deck. Their heavy footsteps and occasional yells offered no clues to their destination.

Charlotte paused her pacing to look through the lattice in the overhead access. "There's a seagull!"

"Seagulls always fly over the ocean." Catherine sighed.

"Yes, but only close to land." Charlotte raised a finger. "I have an idea, but we should wait until Hannah is with us."

Catherine was a quiet for a moment, appearing to listen to something only she could hear. She nodded. "Yes, I think that will work."

Before long, they heard Blackbeard's voice overhead. "Put this one in the hold with the others."

Stevie's breath caught as she awaited Hannah's return. The hatch flew open, and she shielded her eyes from the glare of the bright sunlight until the silhouette of a pirate blocked it, casting a long shadow onto the hold below. He moved away from the opening, and a smaller silhouette took his place.

Hannah.

She climbed down the ladder as the pirate slammed the hatch shut. When she reached the floor, she turned to Charlotte. Her eyes were black with rage. "I have obeyed our rules this time, but I cannot promise that I won't seek revenge against him." A snarl flitted across her lips.

132

"You may get your chance." Catherine pointed to Charlotte. "She has a plan."

"Oh?" Hannah raising a dark eyebrow. "Does it involve me killing him?"

"No. I'm sorry." Charlotte shook her head. "But there is a way we can escape with our secret still intact." She described her plan to Hannah. "Join me." She extended her arms and took their hands in hers.

Stevie watched, almost expecting Charlotte to lead a fervent prayer for their salvation. But she knew, in her heart, something else loomed on the horizon.

The three women formed a circle and closed their eyes.

"One mind, one spirit, one focus." Charlotte swayed a little as she whispered.

A gold chain holding an amethyst pendant materialized around Charlotte's neck. The purple stone began to glow.

Magic. Stevie gasped.

From several feet away and three hundred years apart, Stevie sensed the power of the amulet intermingling with that of the women. She watched them concentrate as their magic began to swirl within the open bowl of their outstretched arms. She closed her eyes, reveling in the electric sensation that now coursed through her own body.

In her mind's eye, she saw tiny, vaporous drops of force drip from their swirling pool of energy and plummet down through the thick hull of the ship into the water below. She visualized the magical droplets falling to the sandy bottom, each engulfing and combining with a grain of sand.

At first, only a few grains responded to the combined power of the witches, but soon, billions of particles ascended from the bottom of the ocean. They rose through the water, piling up in a great swell, remaining just beneath the surface.

Stevie opened her eyes and stared at Charlotte, Hannah, and Catherine, awestruck.

The young witches had willed a massive sandbar into existence directly in the path of Blackbeard's ship. Each woman exhaled an enormous breath, sending her energy swirling upward through the hatch. The wind they'd created gathered behind the ship's sails, propelling the vessel faster. When the ship lurched forward, Catherine stumbled.

Stevie heard the chatter of the crewmen go from relaxed banter to confused alarm.

With their spell complete, the women dashed to a corner of the hold where they huddled together, bracing themselves for impact. They listened to the panicked calls of the men on the deck as the sandbar came into view, far too late for them to avoid it. The strange wind continued to fill the ship's sails, thrusting the *Queen Anne's Revenge* toward the sandbar.

With a long scrape, followed by crackling sounds of splintering wood, the pirate flagship smashed onto the bar. The women, already braced against the forward bulkhead, barely managed to keep their footing as the ship listed sideways.

"It worked." Catherine clapped.

"Hush." Charlotte put her finger to her lips. "They can't suspect that we caused this."

The deck heaved as the ship lost its seaworthiness. The witches grasped onto each other to keep from falling. They heard a second deafening crunch as one of the accompanying sloops also ran aground. Mayhem broke out on the deck as the men scrambled to secure their escape.

"Grab the gold! Get the loot into the longboat!" The voice of the pirate captain blared loudest.

Catherine's eyes grew wide with fear as seawater began to seep into the hold, but she remained silent. They listened as the pirates continued their frantic evacuation. Though heavy footsteps thundered all around the hatch, no one bothered to free the captive women.

Catherine whimpered as the water rose above her knees. All three stared at the hatch, waiting for silence on the deck above.

At long last, the ship grew quiet.

"I think they're all gone now." Hannah broke away from the huddle.

"Let's take a peek." Charlotte pushed through the deepening water to reach the ladder. Her wet linen shift clung to her legs as she climbed. She lifted the hatch and, with a quick glance, confirmed that the deck was empty.

"All clear!" She motioned for Catherine and Hannah to follow her.

Stevie accompanied the women as they eased out of the hold. Once up top, they struggled to maintain their balance on the angled deck. Stevie searched for Blackbeard and spotted him on one of the remaining sloops. He had abandoned the two disabled ships, leaving much of his original crew stranded. Dozens of men floated in the ocean water. Some attempted to swim toward a nearby barrier island; others sank below the surface. No one noticed the women amid the chaos.

They moved to the opposite side of the ship, out of view of the crew. Charlotte pointed to a nearby island. "None of the pirates are swimming in that direction. We'll be safe there."

"Stevie," Patricia called. "They made it to the island where they were rescued by a merchant captain. He brought them to Beaufort."

The image of the witches disappeared as darkness surrounded Stevie once more. She listened to her mother's disembodied voice, her only anchor in the void.

"Hannah would soon realize that she was pregnant with Blackbeard's son. Catherine married a local fisherman, and Charlotte married the merchant captain who had rescued them from the island." Her mother's dreamlike voice drifted through the blackness. "They started families of their own and only spoke of magic with those who also possessed the gift, a rule we still follow today."

Patricia voice grew closer. "The magic Charlotte, Hannah, and Catherine brought to Beaufort spread among the growing population as family trees sprouted new branches. The pure blood of those original witches eventually became diluted within the family lines, and the gift became unpredictable. Mothers throughout the centuries watched their children grow, wondering if they too would share the gift. There was no way to predict who would have it, how much they would have, or when it would make itself known."

Stevie struggled to make sense of her mother's words. Nothing was what it seemed. The past held more secrets than she could ever have imagined…and those secrets were woven into the tapestry of her own life.

"Stevie," Patricia said. "It's time to come back."

Chapter nineteen

Stevie

Stevie floated up through the abyss, rising higher and higher, until she returned to her own place in time.

"Welcome back." Her mother rubbed her arm.

Wrestling with an undeniable sense of loss as she left the world of Charlotte, Catherine, and Hannah, she could not bring herself to look at those who waited for her now.

"Open your eyes, dear." Alice's cheery voice broke the spell.

Stevie blinked. "How long was I asleep?"

"Not long." Alice leaned forward, meeting Stevie's gaze. "And you weren't exactly sleeping."

Stevie's eyes took a moment to adjust to the soft candlelight in her living room. She tried to sit up, but that proved more difficult than she expected. Her head lolled, too heavy with the memories of Beaufort's first witches.

Dylan stood and walked to her side. He slid his hand underneath her back, supporting her while she lifted her head from the cushioned arm of the sofa. She opened her mouth to speak but stopped. She didn't know where to begin.

"Wake up, Randy!" Ruth nudged the old doctor. "She's back."

Randy shook off his sleepiness and straightened in his chair.

Stevie ran her hand through her hair as she recalled the events of her strange dream. It had seemed so real, and yet here she was in her own living room, surrounded by her family and friends. Under the weight of her mother's intense gaze, Stevie felt obligated to speak, but she remained at a loss for words.

The history of our coven begins in the summer of 1718. Remembering Patricia's words, Stevie shook her head in disbelief.

"Are you okay?" Dylan cupped her cheek.

"What just happened to me?"

"That was part of our initiation process. You need to know the history of our people, and that's the fastest way to deliver the information." Patricia squeezed Stevie's hand. "I'm sure you have some questions for us."

"Does this mean…" Stevie struggled to form a coherent sentence. "Are you saying that…" She drew in a deep breath and pulled together the words that she never would have imagined she'd utter. "Am I a witch?"

"Yes." Patricia beamed.

A wave of dizziness hit Stevie. She sunk back against the couch cushion and closed her eyes. *How is this possible?*

She peered at her mother again. "And you're a witch? And Grandma was too?"

Patricia nodded. "That's right. And her mother and grandmother were as well."

"And we're your coven, dear." Alice spread her arms, wide and welcoming.

"Also known as the Beaufort Historic Society." Randy yawned.

Deborah pointed at Patricia with a knitting needle. "And your mother is our queen."

Stevie hunched toward her mother, inspecting her like she'd never seen her before. "Is this really happening?"

"It is, honey." Patricia nodded. "Everyone in this room has experienced this initiation as well, so we all know how difficult it is to comprehend." She patted Stevie's hand and then sat back in her chair.

Alice inched closer. "That's why I gave you the tea, dear. It helps you relax so you can more easily accept all of this."

Stevie knew nothing about witches other than what she'd heard in fairy tales. None of the people sitting in her living room wore pointed hats, and not a single one of them possessed an unsightly facial mole.

Still dulled by the effects of Alice's tea, Stevie struggled to grab hold of her fleeting thoughts. Everyone was quiet as if they were waiting for her to speak, so she voiced the next question that popped into her mind.

"So, does this mean I have to start wearing long skirts and dancing under the full moon?" She eyed her mother's ankle-length dress with disdain.

"Dancing in the moonlight is optional." Patricia laughed.

Deborah looked up from her knitting and grinned. "It is a lot of fun though. You really should give it a try."

"The long skirts are really just a matter of personal comfort. You can focus better if you are at ease." Patricia patted her dress. "You can wear whatever you like."

"I wouldn't be caught dead in a dress myself." Ruth shifted in her chair. "If you ask me, underpants are the real problem. I haven't worn them in decades." She snapped the elastic waistband of her gray polyester slacks for emphasis.

"Now that's an image none of us will soon forget." Randy chuckled.

Alice grimaced and buried her face in her hands. "I did not need to know that, Ruth."

Lexi eased next to Stevie on the sofa and looked into her eyes. "I'm sorry I didn't tell you about this. Believe me, I wanted to."

"She couldn't tell you, honey." Patricia glanced from Lexi to Stevie. "Neither could I."

Dylan cleared his throat. "None of us could."

Stevie perched on the edge of the seat and glanced down, studying the worn grain of the wood floor. She had known these people all her life, and yet, she hadn't known them at all. At this point, she wasn't entirely sure that she knew herself anymore.

"We've waited a very long time for you." Deborah grinned as Stevie looked up to meet her gaze.

"I gave up on her ten years ago." Ruth shook her head. "Never seen anyone develop powers this late in life."

Patricia patted Stevie's knee. "I never gave up on you, honey. I knew you were just a late bloomer."

"I think the intense stress of that car barreling toward Charlie might have helped bring her magic out." Randy rubbed his chin and nodded.

Stevie gasped. She had almost forgotten about the car, it seemed so long ago. "Can someone explain what happened today?"

The room fell silent. Everyone glanced away, refusing to make eye contact.

Dylan turned to Patricia. "We have to tell her. She needs to know."

"Who was driving that car?" Stevie sat up taller, more alert than she had been all day. "It looked like it was aiming for Charlie."

Dylan stepped away from Stevie and began to pace behind the row of chairs. Alice frowned as she wrung her hands. Deborah returned her attention to her knitting, adding another row of white yarn to the seemingly endless blanket that she worked on.

Patricia drew in a deep breath. "Honey, no one was driving that car today."

Stevie's eyes grew wide. "How can that be?"

Patricia paused for moment before she spoke. "There is another one of us who lost her way."

"You are being too generous, Patricia." Dylan clenched his fist. "She is evil—pure evil."

Stevie slammed her hand down the sofa. "Just tell me what happened!"

Lexi leaned in. "Do you remember Vanessa Moore?"

"Yes. She moved away after high school, right?" Stevie frowned and shook her head. "What does she have to do with any of this?"

"We believe Vanessa tried to kill Charlie today." Patricia grimaced.

"That can't be. Why would anyone want to hurt him?" Stevie's voice quaked. The agonizing memory of her little boy standing in the street, helpless, rose to the forefront of her mind. She shivered.

"Vanessa was involved in my mother's murder twelve years ago." A tempest of anger and sadness brewed in Dylan's eyes.

"Murder? I thought that was an accident." Stevie remembered the night Rebecca had died. There had been no suggestion of foul play when her car went over the guardrail of the old drawbridge.

"It was Vanessa's mother, Susan, who caused Rebecca's accident. We believe Vanessa assisted her." Alice sighed. Sadness replaced her normal, cheery expression. "At the very least, we know she was with Susan when it happened."

"What?" Stevie turned to Dylan. "You just let her get away with it?"

"It wasn't my choice." He glanced at Patricia.

Patricia nodded. "It's complicated, Stevie. Vanessa and Susan are witches too, but they aren't like us. There's darkness in their hearts." She took another deep breath. "They both resented being bound by the rules of our coven."

"After they attacked Rebecca that night, we attempted to strip their powers from them." Randy rubbed his neck. "We were successful with Susan. But Vanessa…" He swallowed. "She proved to be more difficult to bind."

"Please, let's discuss the events of that night another time." Patricia pursed her lips.

Stevie started to press on, to seek answers about Rebecca's death, but Dylan's slumped shoulders and her mother's drawn expression stopped her.

"I still don't understand what this has to do with Charlie. Why hurt him?" Stevie glanced around the room. "He has nothing to do with this. She doesn't even know him."

"It's too soon to know if he will develop powers, but he *is* a member of the family. She may be trying to get rid of all of us to ensure that no one will ever stand in her way." Patricia pondered aloud but didn't sound confident in her assertion.

Get rid of all of us? Stevie sank back against the sofa cushion once more. It was all too much to take in. How could she possibly keep Charlie safe from a danger she didn't even understand? "Why now? Why did Vanessa come back now?"

"She returned because of the discovery of Blackbeard's treasure," Randy answered.

Stevie tilted her head, still perplexed. "If she's so powerful, why does she care about the treasure?"

"She's looking for this." Patricia pulled the amethyst pendant through the collar of her dress.

"Lucia's necklace." Stevie reached up to touch the stone but stopped when she remembered what happened last time.

"Only the members of our trusted coven know we have this necklace in our possession." Patricia wrapped her hand around it.

"Why?"

Patricia let her hands fall to her lap. "You and I are direct descendants of Lucia, and because of that, our family line has the strongest magic. We are obligated to protect the secret of our people as well as the necklace." She patted the pendant. "This amulet amplifies the power of the witch wearing it. As you might imagine, if it were to fall into the hands of someone with evil intentions, the results would be catastrophic.

"To the witches outside of this room—outside of our coven—this necklace is little more than folklore passed down from generation to generation. Not everyone witnessed the history of our ancestors the way you did. Most only heard stories shared by their parents and grandparents. Many believe that if the amulet really existed, Blackbeard must have stolen it. Since it hasn't been seen in centuries, the logical conclusion is that it sunk with the *Queen Anne's Revenge*."

"But I found it in your dining room." Stevie frowned. "Maybe you should keep it in a safe deposit box or something."

Patricia laughed. "Give me a little credit, honey. I left it there for you to find. I thought it might give you a little nudge and help your powers develop. Based on what happened today, I'd say it did the trick."

"Why didn't you try that sooner?" Stevie asked. "It sounds like I'm the oldest witch to ever develop powers."

"We've never done that before because magic in our family tends to develop during childhood. If it hadn't worked, I would've had to lie to you about the necklace, and I didn't want to do that. But with the threat of Vanessa's return, your powers became a more urgent need, and it was worth the risk to try exposing you to the amulet."

"What do we do now?" She glanced at her mother, hoping to find magical solutions to keep Charlie safe.

"You will continue with your life, starting with taking Charlie to school in the morning."

Stevie shook her head. "No way! He needs to be with me so I can protect him."

"You can't protect him yet. He'll be safer at school than at home. We have some friends there who will look out for him. After Vanessa's attack today, she'll likely lay low for a while. I'm sure she wouldn't risk being seen at Charlie's school anyway." Patricia reached forward and grabbed Stevie's hand. "And, under no circumstance, are you to attempt to practice magic until you see me tomorrow. We'll begin your training right after you drop Charlie off."

"Let us worry about Charlie." Deborah clicked her knitting needles as she spoke. "We'll keep him safe."

Lexi put her arm around Stevie. "I promise I won't let anything happen to him."

Stevie pulled away, her shoulders slumped. All she wanted was to protect Charlie. But she couldn't. Not from a *witch*. She needed help. A lot of help. She gave a reluctant nod.

"I'll stay here tonight so I can keep a closer watch on you and Charlie." Dylan eyed the front window before drawing the curtains.

"Good idea." Patricia stood and gestured for the others to follow. "I think we've covered everything we need to tonight."

Deborah packed away her knitting. Alice nudged Randy, who stood and helped her out of her chair. With a series of grunts, cracks, and pops, Ruth rose from her seat.

Lexi squeezed Stevie's hand. "Call me anytime. I'll see you soon."

Patricia hugged her. "We have a lot to work on tomorrow. Try to get some sleep tonight." She slipped a honey-colored stone into Stevie's hand.

"What's this?" Stevie rubbed the smooth rock.

"Amber. We use it for protection." Patricia closed Stevie's palm around it. "Keep it with you."

"Let's go." Ruth snapped her fingers. "I wasn't planning on being here this long. I need to feed my dogs before they eat my couch."

144

Randy and the women filed out of the living room toward the door. Stevie said good night to everyone, bringing an end to the most bizarre evening she'd ever spent.

"Don't worry." Dylan touched her shoulder. "I will keep you and Charlie safe." In the candlelight of the living room, his profile glowed. Like an angel. She touched her forehead. Maybe Alice's tea had been a little too strong.

"I'll get a guest room ready for you." Stevie started toward the stairs.

He shook his head. "There's no need. I won't be sleeping tonight. If she comes back, I'll be ready for her."

Knowing Dylan would be on guard all night eased some of her worries. "Thank you."

"It's my pleasure." He smiled. "Now you go get some sleep. I've got this covered."

chapter twenty

Stevie

Stevie woke at sunrise and sat straight up in her bed. Images of witches, pirates, and projectile cars flashed through her mind. She shook her head, banishing the absurd thoughts.

It had to have been a dream.

She stretched and slipped out of bed so she could get ready for Charlie's first day of school. She'd been dreading it, but at least she knew it was real. After a quick shower, she dressed in a white t-shirt and a pair of faded jeans.

On the way out of her bedroom, a ray of sunlight shone through the window, causing an unexpected sparkle to catch her eye. She took a step back to get a better look at the source of the glimmer. It took only a second for her to recognize the item and understand what its presence meant.

Breathless, Stevie crept toward her dresser and scooped the smooth oblong piece of amber into her trembling hand. As she closed her fist around the stone, she realized that everything that had happened the day before, everything she so desperately wanted to deny, was real. She slipped the protective talisman into her pocket and left the room.

Stevie walked into Charlie's room to wake him. The rising sun had not yet lit his bedroom because his blackout curtains were still drawn.

She padded across the floor to one of the windows and opened the thick navy blue curtains. As the morning light filled the room, she turned to wake her son. But he was not in his bed.

Seized with panic, she raced to the bathroom in the hall, hoping to find him there. But he wasn't.

She thought of Vanessa and the speeding car.

"Charlie!" She ran down the stairs in search of her son. "Charlie!"

"He's in here," Dylan answered from the kitchen.

Her frantic pace slowed. She took a deep breath, hoping to calm her racing heart, and smelled the unmistakable scent of fried eggs and fresh coffee.

In the kitchen, Charlie sat in his usual seat, his tablet close by. She smiled as she watched him shovel a forkful into his mouth. She took a closer look at his plate and noticed that both of his eggs had broken yolks that were cooked firm, just the way he liked them.

Dylan cracked another egg and dropped the contents into the sizzling pan.

"Wow! You didn't have to do all this." Stevie gestured to the meal.

"First day of school, right? He needs a good breakfast to start the day." Dylan pointed to the pan with a spatula. "This is brain food."

"For someone who didn't get any sleep last night, you sure are perky." Stevie poured herself a cup of coffee.

"I'm fine." He turned the egg over in the pan. "I'll grab a nap later. No big deal."

Stevie rested her coffee mug on the tile-topped table and walked over to Charlie's red backpack hanging on the laundry room door. She reached into her pocket and removed the amber stone Patricia had given her. Running her thumb across its smooth surface, she remembered its purpose. *Protection.* She slipped the pretty piece of fossilized tree resin into the front pocket of his pack and returned to the table.

Two pieces of crisp bread popped up from the toaster. Dylan loaded the eggs and toast onto two plates and placed them on the table for himself and Stevie.

"This is great, Dylan. Thank you." Stevie took a seat next to him.

It had been a long while since there had been three faces around her breakfast table. She liked the change, especially since she didn't have to do the cooking.

Stevie looked down at her plate. Her egg yolks were runny, just the way she liked them. She looked at Charlie's plate and then back at her own. She opened her mouth to speak but stopped. *Not in front of Charlie.*

Stevie gripped Charlie's hand as she walked through the open double doors of the elementary school and entered the bustling foyer. She passed one of her neighbors who also had a young son. Her red-rimmed eyes proved that she too was unprepared for the trauma of sending her child to school for the first time. Other parents, with older children in tow, laughed and smiled as they made their way through the corridor, giddy to be dropping their kids off for the day.

A pang of sadness coursed through Stevie as she listened to the voices of the excited children in the hall, greeting their friends and gleefully sharing their summer adventures. She hoped Charlie would be able to communicate well enough with his tablet, but more than anything, she wanted him to make some friends.

She noticed some of the other mothers leading their children to the regular kindergarten classrooms. Those rooms would have bright pictures of animals, letters, and numbers and a little rug for circle time. A cheerful teacher would be waiting to greet each and every happy, talkative little boy and girl. Stevie had many fond memories of her own kindergarten days, and she wished her son could also have that experience. She didn't know what to expect from Charlie's special class, but she was sure it would not be the same.

Stevie scolded herself. She shouldn't think about what Charlie would miss. She loved him exactly as he was. But sometimes, she couldn't help but wish his life were a little easier. She pressed her hand against the knot that had formed in her stomach. It overwhelmed her to consider all of the new challenges he would have to face on the first day of school, much less all of the challenges in the years to come.

Charlie tightened his grip on Stevie's hand as they moved through the crowded hallway. She had done her best to prepare him for going to school. She'd even taken him inside the building during the summer so he could see it all for himself. But there was nothing that she could have done to ready him for this flurry of sounds and movements.

She knew that, to Charlie, the people moving back and forth along the hallway would be a blur of shapes and colors. The loud echo of everyone talking at once would assault his sensitive ears. When he looked down at his feet as he walked, Stevie suspected that he was trying to block out the chaos.

She squeezed his hand. "Almost there."

They stopped just outside the door to his classroom. Stevie squatted and tried to meet Charlie's gaze, but he looked away.

"You're going to have a great first day of school." She forced an enthusiastic grin.

And I am going to get through this without crying.

They rounded the doorway into the classroom, and Stevie realized that she was not going to be able keep her promise to herself. The depressing room had bare walls constructed of putty-colored cinderblocks. A tall bookshelf partially blocked the only window, a tiny one near the ceiling. Charlie took a seat at the kid-sized table in the middle of the room and removed his tablet from his backpack.

"Hi!" chirped a young woman with blond hair. Stevie recognized her as Charlie's special education teacher, Sherri. They had met once last spring to decide on his educational plan and accommodations.

Stevie shook the teacher's hand. "Nice to see you again. I'm sure you remember that Charlie uses a tablet for communication. Also, I've packed extra snacks for him. They are in his backpack along with his lunch." Stevie tried to present a calm demeanor, but the words tumbled from her mouth as she attempted to give Charlie's new teacher all the information she thought she might need.

"Don't worry, Mrs. Lewis." Sherri offered an understanding smile to Stevie's nervous rambling. "I remember. It's all in Charlie's IEP. Also, I have a lot of experience working with children with ASD, so I'm very familiar with the GFCF diet."

She spoke in the alphabet soup language that had become all too familiar to Stevie since Charlie's diagnosis. Yet another secret society she hadn't asked to join.

Stevie glanced around the classroom. There were five children, including Charlie, as well as a teacher's assistant. Each child seemed to operate in his or her own orbit, not interacting with the other students at all.

The only girl in the class appeared to be a year or two older than Charlie. She stood in a corner, flicking her fingers in front of her eyes. One boy with a choppy haircut leaned against the wall, rubbing his palm along the bumpy texture of the painted cinderblocks and reciting lines from a cartoon that Stevie recognized as one of Charlie's favorites. Another child rolled a toy car along a tabletop while another spent his time opening and closing a cabinet door, squealing with delight each time he slammed it shut. A lump formed in Stevie's throat. Charlie did not belong in this class any more than he belonged in the regular kindergarten class.

"I've seen that look before." Sherri met her gaze. "I'll be evaluating the children over the next few days. If this isn't a good fit for Charlie, we'll make some changes. Everything is going to be okay."

Stevie stifled an eye roll. She hated it when people told her everything was going to be okay. How could anyone possibly know that? Did this teacher have a crystal ball that showed her the future?

To be fair, given the events of the previous day, Stevie could not entirely write that possibility off.

"Will Charlie be a bus rider or a car rider?" Sherri poised her pen over a clipboard that held a printout of her student list.

Stevie resisted the urge to say *broom rider*. That joke would require more explanation that she was willing to offer. "Car rider."

Stevie turned to hug Charlie goodbye but saw only his red backpack and tablet on the table. Instead of sitting alone, he stood beside the boy with the toy car. Charlie held a car of his own and rolled it along the table too, mimicking the actions of the other boy. It was the first time she had ever seen him play with another child. Though neither boy spoke, it certainly looked like it could be the beginning of a friendship. She planted a quick kiss on her son's head and left the classroom. She didn't want anyone to see the tears she could no longer fight.

Chapter twenty-one

Stevie

Stevie parked her red Prius on Ann Street in front of her mother's cottage and dropped her head onto the steering wheel. Leaving Charlie at school had been much harder than she'd expected. In addition to all the normal worries a mother might have on the first day of school, she also wrestled with the fact that an attempt had been made on his young life just the day before. Now, he was in a classroom with strangers, protected by the silly rock her mother had given her. She stepped along the walkway to the porch, eager now to begin her training and learn how to protect her son by any means at her disposal.

"Mom?" She let herself in through the front door.

"In the kitchen," Patricia called.

Her mother greeted her with a hug as soon as she entered the kitchen. She leaned back, getting a good look at Stevie's face. "Rough morning, huh?" She didn't wait for a reply. Instead, she hugged her daughter once again.

Patricia stepped back to the stove and slid an egg white omelet from the frying pan onto a plate. "Just making breakfast for your father."

Stevie wrinkled her nose at the bland fare. "He's never going to eat that."

"Oh, are you psychic now too?" Patricia laughed as she plucked a handful of red grapes from a bowl on the counter and added them to the plate. She held her hand over the unappealing white blob, and in an instant, the omelet turned yellow. "There, that's better."

Stevie's eyes grew wide with surprise. "Wow!"

"If you think that's impressive, you should see what Alice can do." Patricia wagged her finger. "She can make a garden salad look *and taste* just like a chocolate cake."

Stevie walked with Patricia to the den, where her father sat in his recliner watching the tropical update on the Weather Channel. On the screen, a young meteorologist pointed to a newly developed tropical storm in the mid-Atlantic and reminded her viewers that it was too soon to know where the system was headed or if it might strengthen into a hurricane.

Stevie smiled, relieved to see her father at home again, already looking healthier than he had before the heart attack. "Hey, Dad." She leaned down to hug him.

"Hi, sweetie. How did Charlie do this morning?"

"He was great. I think he even made a friend already."

"That's my boy!" Jim's voice boomed with pride as he took the plate Patricia held out to him. "This looks great, Pat. Thanks."

After a taking a bite of the omelet, he grinned up at Stevie. "I swear your mom has a gift. She's found a way to make all this heart healthy food taste good."

Stevie returned his grin, cheered by his happiness. Patricia tugged on her arm, and she remembered that she had work to do. "I've got to go, but enjoy your breakfast. I'll see you later, Dad."

"Bye, sweetie." Jim shoveled in another bite as the women left the room.

"Okay, I'm ready." Stevie put her hand on her hip. "How does this work?"

"You're not going to learn everything in a day, honey. It takes time to master these abilities. I'll teach you the basics today, but it will take years of practice to access your full abilities."

Stevie frowned, unable to hide her disappointment. "Can you at least teach me what I need to know to keep Charlie safe?"

"Let's go back to your place. We'll need privacy for this." Leaning through the kitchen doorway, she called out to Jim. "I'm going over to Stevie's. Alice will come by with your lunch around noon."

"All right. You girls have fun."

Patricia giggled. "And just like that, he's none the wiser."

They stood in Stevie's living room, the same room where her life had changed so dramatically the night before. There was no candle-light now, and the chairs were all in their usual places. Patricia closed the curtains on the front windows and removed the few breakable knickknacks from the room before she turned to Stevie.

"Put your phone over there." Patricia gestured to an end table. "We don't want any distractions."

"Okay, but I have to leave the ringer on in case the school calls." Stevie placed her phone on the table and returned to her mother.

"Ready?" Patricia's eyes widened with excitement.

Stevie nodded. "Definitely."

"Take a deep breath in through your nose. Then let it out slowly through your mouth." Patricia demonstrated the motions.

Stevie rolled her eyes. "Seriously?"

"Trust me, honey." Patricia smiled.

"Fine." Stevie inhaled a great breath, filling her lungs to capacity, and let it out in a slow exhale. She could not deny that it was relaxing, but she didn't understand what it had to do with magic.

"Again." Her mother closed her eyes and inhaled.

Stevie obeyed, managing an even greater breath the second time. Her shoulders dropped as the stress of the morning rolled away.

"Now, hold your hand in front of you like this." Patricia extended her right arm in front of her body. She held her hand palm up, slightly cupped.

Stevie copied her mother and held the position, waiting for further instruction that did not come. In the silence, she focused her attention on her own hand. She gasped when she felt a slight tingle in her fingertips.

"You're feeling your own energy now. Concentrate on that and push that tingling sensation down through your fingers and into your palm."

Stevie did as she was told, and the energy rushed to the center of her hand, which soon began to feel hot. Alarmed, she shot a wide-eyed glance to her mother, hoping for guidance.

"That's right. Now visualize a white light in your hand." Patricia stared at her own palm.

Once again, Stevie concentrated on her palm. A tiny white light emerged from her skin, flickering like a lit candlewick. It grew and grew, forming into a sphere with firm edges and resting in the air just above her hand.

"Now, hold the light there. Maintain your focus no matter what happens." Patricia circled Stevie. She paused in front of the bubble of light and gave it a gentle poke. The edge gave way under the pressure but regained its form when Patricia pulled her finger away. "Excellent!"

Stevie continued to hold the warm light, keeping her focus intense and unwavering.

"Now, let the light fly."

Stevie drew in a sharp breath as the ball of pale light obeyed her thoughts, lifted from her hand, and circled the room in a graceful dance. "It's beautiful."

"Yes, it is. Now keep your focus though. You must maintain control of your energy."

"Okay." The floating light mesmerized Stevie.

The sudden peal of the phone ringing shattered the peaceful quiet of the house.

Stevie blinked out of her stupor, overcome with the cold whitewash of fear. "That could be Charlie's teacher!"

The ball of energy popped like an overfilled balloon, bursting the bulb in the ceiling light. The phone rang a second time, and she rushed to answer it.

"Hello?" She tried to control her erratic breath. "Hello? Is anyone there?"

Her mother tapped her shoulder and spun her around. "There's no one on the line, dear."

"You tricked me?" Stevie slammed her phone on the table.

"It's all part of your training. Believe it or not, there will come a day when no distraction will be able to break your focus."

Stevie had her doubts, but she bit her tongue and kept them to herself. After seeing the ball of light burst, she didn't have a lot of confidence in her newfound ability. Maybe the next area of study would be easier for her.

"Do you ever use spells?" Stevie tilted her head, considering all the possibilities.

"Sometimes, though I usually prefer simple energy manipulation." Patricia formed the white ball in her palm again. "We tend to use spells for more complicated or permanent intentions. We'll study those on another day."

They worked into the afternoon, and Stevie gained more confidence with each new exercise.

"You're doing very well." Patricia gave Stevie an approving nod.

"Thanks." Stevie's smile faded into a frown. "But I still don't feel like I know enough to protect Charlie from Vanessa."

"You will soon, honey. You're incredibly powerful. I'm not sure any of us could have stopped that car like you did. And you did it without any training."

"I didn't know what I was doing at the time." Stevie dropped her gaze. "I just wanted that car to stop."

"It doesn't matter how you stopped it. The point is you did it." Patricia reached into her pocket and pulled out an amber stone similar to the one she had given to Stevie the night before. "This one is for you to keep."

"How did you know I gave the other one to Charlie?" Stevie arched her eyebrow.

"I don't have to be a witch to guess that. Any mother would have done the same thing."

"I suppose so." Stevie looked at her watch. "It's time to pick up Charlie. Do you want me to drop you off at your house?"

"If you don't mind, I'd love to go with you to get him."

❖ ❖ ❖ ❖

With Patricia in the passenger seat, Stevie drove out of the historic district and turned onto the two-lane highway that led to Charlie's school. A man in an old white pickup began to tailgate her car just a couple of miles from her destination. She pressed her lips together, in an effort to contain the angry words that threatened to spill out of her mouth. Already driving a little over the speed limit, she was afraid to go any faster.

Stevie shot a wary glance at her rearview mirror. The front of that truck was practically in her backseat. She gripped the steering wheel tighter, wishing she could tap her brake to get his attention. But she knew if she did, he would almost certainly ram into her car.

"What a jerk!" Stevie eyed the impatient man with disgust.

When she couldn't take it anymore, she envisioned one of the truck's front tires blowing out, forcing the pickup off the road. At the sound of tires squealing, Stevie looked in her rearview mirror to see the truck swerve off the road. The driver slammed a clenched fist down on his dashboard. Though she couldn't hear him, she had a good idea of what he was saying. She grinned with satisfaction, relieved to have him off her bumper.

"Stevie! You can't just run people off the road! Someone could have been hurt." Patricia twisted in her seat to look at the truck. "Besides, you shouldn't use your power like that. It's too important to waste on people like him."

"I'm sorry, Mom. I just couldn't help it."

"Do better next time." Patricia crossed her arms and gazed out the window.

Stevie bit her lip and stayed silent for the rest of the drive, ashamed by her behavior. She didn't enjoy being chastised by her mother either—certainly not at this point in her life.

They reached the elementary school a few minutes later. Patricia walked with Stevie to Charlie's classroom and greeted her grandson with a hug when she saw him. She paused to look around the dismal room, making no attempt to disguise her disdain.

"You must be Charlie's grandmother." Sherri smiled as she approached the women.

"Yes, I'm Patricia Guthrie." She extended her hand. "It's a bit gloomy in here." She gestured to the bare walls.

Stevie cringed, hoping her mother's bluntness had not offended the teacher.

Sherri nodded. "We have to minimize distractions in the autism classroom, so we're not able to put a lot of decorations on the walls."

"Would a painting of single scene, like a mural, be appropriate for the class?" Patricia asked.

"I suppose that would be all right. But it would have to be something relatively simple, preferably with pastel colors."

Patricia stepped over to the Sherri's desk, jotted something down on a piece of scrap paper, and handed it to the teacher. "Call my friend Lexi. I'm sure she'd be happy to help with a project like that."

"I will. Thanks." Sherri accepted the paper with a grateful smile.

"All right, Charlie, let's go." Stevie grabbed his backpack.

They stopped at a neighborhood playground on the way home. Charlie ran ahead of them, making a beeline for the sandbox, eager to pursue his favorite ritual of sifting sand through his fingers. Patricia and Stevie took seats on a bench nearby and watched him play in his own unique way.

The sound of harsh laughter cut through the quiet of their peaceful afternoon. Patricia and Stevie both looked up to see a group of teenage boys sauntering toward the playground. They were all dressed in oversized t-shirts and baggy jeans, which they wore too low on their hips. The six boys gathered around another bench near the sandbox.

The tallest one, an angry-looking young man with dirty hair that fell over his eyes, lit a cigarette and then blew out the smoke with a loud exhale. He narrowed his eyes as he watched Charlie continue to scoop up sand, only to let it fall through his fingers.

"Look at that." He pointed at Charlie. "I guess the short bus is dropping the *retards* off at the park now."

Stevie clenched her fists as the boys' cackling clanged like cymbals in her ears. The word "retard" burned in her mind as she struggled to keep herself composed. She glanced at Charlie, who seemed undaunted by the boy's cruel comment. She hoped with all of her heart that he hadn't heard it.

Just as Stevie stood to confront the raucous group, the tallest one threw back his head in a fresh new roar of laughter, his mouth gaping wide. At the very same moment, a low-flying seagull soared over and relieved himself, with pinpoint precision, on the boy's face.

Stevie jumped in surprise and covered her mouth to stifle a laugh. She whirled around to her mother and put her hands up. "I swear I had nothing to do with that, Mom!"

"I know you didn't." Patricia ruffled her skirt, a self-satisfied grin on her face.

Stevie watched as the cruel boy wiped the bird excrement from his face. His fickle friends began to snicker at him instead of Charlie.

"You did that?" Stevie put her hands on her hips, incredulous as she remembered the reprimand she'd received earlier.

"There are exceptions to every rule." Patricia smirked.

Chapter twenty-two

Stevie

On Thursday, Stevie dropped Charlie off at school for his second day and returned home feeling stronger than ever before. Training with her mother had been exhilarating, and Stevie was gaining confidence in her ability to keep Charlie safe. Her everyday life had taken on a dreamlike quality, a change she welcomed.

The doorbell chimed. When Stevie opened the door, her mother and Deborah waited on her porch.

"Hi, honey." Patricia crossed the threshold. Her gauzy dip-dyed skirt swished as she walked.

Deborah smiled. "Morning, dear." As usual, she carried her canvas knitting bag slung over her arm.

"I just brewed a pot of coffee. Can I fix you a cup?" Stevie motioned for them to come with her to the kitchen.

"I'd love some," Patricia said.

"Me too." Deborah trailed behind them down the hallway.

Stevie poured the coffee and placed a mug in front of each woman. Deborah pulled out her large knitting needles and began to add a new row of white yarn to her never-ending project.

"You're always working on that blanket. Is it for someone special?" Stevie pointed at the needlework. Given Deborah's fervency, she assumed it was a gift for a baby due very soon.

Deborah chuckled. "Actually, this is for all of us."

Stevie furrowed her brow in confusion. "I—I don't understand."

Deborah pulled her project from the canvas bag. Several moments passed as each knitted row emerged. The multicolor blanket was impossibly long, long enough to fill twenty large totes at least. Yet somehow, it fit neatly in just one bag. Stevie sat in wordless disbelief as she looked at the enormous creation made up of white, pink, green, and red yarn. It had no discernible pattern. Some of the sections of color were larger than others, and they all repeated in an inconsistent fashion. Though pink and white yarns were dominant, there were also thin sections of red and, occasionally, green throughout.

"Knitting is my form of meditation. I find that I can access my magic easier when my mind is clear." Deborah held up her needles, lifting the whole blanket. "Each color has a meaning, and each row was knitted with a clear intention."

Stevie nodded, though she wasn't certain she understood. The blanket was not at all like the white bubble of energy she had produced the day before.

"See how Deborah has used white yarn most recently? White is the color of protection. While she knits, she is working a spell to help keep us all safe." Patricia touched a long white section, running her finger along the knots.

"Just below the white section, you'll notice a few rows of pink." Her hands full, Deborah gestured with her chin. "I worked on those in the waiting room of the emergency department after your father's heart attack."

"Pink?" Stevie wrinkled her nose. "That's not exactly my dad's favorite color."

Patricia chuckled. "Well, it should be. It helped to save his life that day. Pink is the color of health and healing."

"What's the green for?"

Deborah tucked part of the cumbersome creation back into her bag. "Prosperity and success. That one comes in handy when one of our local businesses is struggling or if the fishermen have a run of bad luck."

"And the red?" Stevie pointed to a bold crimson line that stretched across the width of the blanket.

Deborah tapped the bright row with her finger. "That one is my favorite. It's the color of passion and love."

"Have you been using that on Lexi?" Stevie raised her eyebrow. "Because if you have, you might want to ease up a little."

Deborah laughed. "I assure you my daughter has no help from me on that front." She sipped her coffee and returned the mug to the table. "When I hear of a relationship in trouble, I'll knit a couple of rows of red for the couple. It will help bring back their spark if it's meant to be."

"She tried to help you and Sam when you first separated." Patricia wrapped both hands around her coffee mug. "But apparently, it didn't work."

"Or perhaps it simply had a delayed effect." Deborah threw a furtive glance at Stevie.

Stevie pursed her lips. Did Deborah know about her recent encounter with Sam? "I don't think it worked." She traced the polka dot pattern on her mug.

"It happens like that sometimes, Stevie. We can't force people to do things they don't want to do." Patricia sipped her coffee. "Magic isn't always foolproof."

Stevie stared at her mother, feeling the heat rise in her cheeks. "So, my son is protected by a rock and some white yarn, and now you tell me it's not foolproof?"

"Relax, honey." Patricia rested her mug on the table and touched Stevie's arm. "We have protected him with multiple spells. Besides, the threat will be gone soon anyway."

Stevie's eyebrow arched. "What do you mean?"

"The dark moon is this Saturday. We'll take away Vanessa's powers with a binding ritual then."

Deborah stole a sidelong glance at Patricia. "Have you discussed this plan with the others yet?"

"Didn't you try that before—unsuccessfully?" Stevie chewed on her lip.

"Yes, but we didn't have you or Dylan then. Our coven is more powerful now than ever before. This time, it will work." Patricia's expression remained impassive, unreadable.

"You haven't answered my question yet." Deborah lowered her arms, allowing her knitting to rest in her lap. "Have you discussed it with the others?"

Patricia shook her head and turned to face Deborah. "I will tell them about it soon. But there will be no discussion. We have to do this."

Saying nothing more, Deborah looked away.

Their exchange confused Stevie. "Am I missing something here? What's the problem with the binding ritual?"

"Don't you worry about it. This will work." Patricia patted her daughter's shoulder. "But you need to practice as much as possible between now and Saturday night."

"A binding ritual is the strongest magic we'll ever do." Deborah lifted a skein of black yarn from her bag. "It's only performed as a last resort, but Vanessa has proven to be too dangerous as a witch. We can't allow her to keep her powers."

Deborah began to knit the black yarn into her blanket, a jarring contrast to the lighter colors of her work.

Uneasy, Stevie shifted in her seat. "Why are you using the black yarn?"

Deborah did not respond. Her eyes were unfocused, her expression blank.

"She can't hear you right now." Patricia took a casual sip of her coffee. "Black is the most powerful color. It opens up deeper levels of the unconscious, so it will aid us in banishing Vanessa's powers. Deborah is now in a trance. She has begun to prepare for the binding ritual and will spend much of the next few days in that state."

Stevie stiffened, wondering if Deborah was going to camp out at her kitchen table until Saturday. "Is she staying here until the ritual?"

"No, honey." Patricia chuckled. "I'll help her come out of the trance when it's time to leave, and she can resume her work when she's at home."

Stevie noticed her mother's cup was empty. "More coffee?"

"Oh, don't get up, dear. I'll get it." But she didn't move from her chair.

A movement across the room caught Stevie's attention. She turned to see the glass carafe, half-full of hot liquid, float toward the table from the counter unassisted. It stopped moving and hovered just above Patricia's mug before tilting to pour the coffee.

"I don't know how you kept this a secret from me for so long." Stevie watched the decanter float back to the coffee maker. "It seems like I would have noticed household objects flying around."

"I rarely use magic at home. With you and your father around, it's too risky."

The doorbell chimed. Stevie left the kitchen to answer. When she swung it open, the greeting died on her lips. Randy stood before her, a rifle in hand. Her mouth went dry. She pointed to the weapon. "What's that for?"

Chapter twenty-three

Stevie

N o need to be alarmed. I just thought you could use some target practice." Randy grinned as he stepped into the house. In addition to the rifle, he carried a paper shopping bag filled with empty glass bottles.

"With a gun?"

"Oh, this is just a BB gun." Randy raised the rifle so she could get a better look at it. "You'll understand when we get out there."

Patricia strolled down the hallway toward the foyer. "Target practice is an excellent idea, Randy. Thank you."

Deborah trailed behind her. "Oh, that sounds like fun."

Stevie did a double take at the walking, talking, alert Deborah—a distinct change from the deep trance she'd been in only moments earlier.

"I'll be at home with your dad for the rest of the day, honey. Call if you need anything." Patricia took Deborah's arm. "Come on, Deb."

"Okay, bye." Stevie waved as they left, still mystified by Deborah's transformation. She shook her head and turned to Randy.

He raised his puffy white eyebrows at her. "Shall we get started?"

"I guess so." Stevie led him through the house and out the back door.

Randy grabbed one side of her patio table and jerked his head toward an ancient live oak tree at the far end of the backyard. "Let's move this over there."

Stevie gripped the opposite side, and together, they hauled it away from the house. Humming a tune she didn't recognize, Randy placed ten empty bottles in a line along the glass tabletop.

After he finished straightening the row of targets, he stepped back to survey his work. "Ready?"

Stevie sighed as she held out her hand to accept the gun from him. "I've never fired a rifle before. Got any tips before I give it a try?"

Randy laughed. "The gun is for me. It's just a prop in case anyone is looking."

Baffled, she glanced at the bottles and then back at the rifle. "Oh!" A mischievous grin danced on her lips, and she wiggled her fingers. "You want me to use magic."

"That's right. You need to focus on one of them. Try to knock it over." He raised the BB gun to his shoulder, pretending to aim at the row of glass targets.

Stevie took a deep breath to help clear her mind, just as her mother had taught her to do. To start, she focused on the bottle closest to the left side of the table. She extended her right arm and pointed her index finger in its direction.

"Oh no, put that arm down!" Randy chuckled as he lowered his gun. "How long do you think it will be before someone notices that strange things happen when you point at stuff?"

"Oh, right. I'm sorry. I didn't think of that." Her cheeks grew hot as she realized her rookie mistake. Her people had managed to keep their magic a secret for centuries. She could expose them all with one thoughtless misstep. She hadn't considered the all the various responsibilities that came with this gift.

Randy raised his gun to his shoulder once more. "Try again, Stevie."

She leveled her gaze at her target and summoned the powerful magic that flowed through her. It came easier now than it had just the day before, surging forth with a palpable increase in intensity. What had started as a tingle in her fingertips yesterday had grown into an incredible force that coursed through her entire body.

Stevie clenched her fists but kept her arms at her sides. She balled her powerful energy into an invisible bullet and fired toward her target. But the empty bottle didn't budge. Instead, a small hole tunneled through the old live oak tree, leaving a smoldering patch on its bark.

"Oh, no!" She clasped her hand over her mouth. "I didn't mean to do that!"

"That's why we're practicing. By the time we're done, your aim will be perfect." Randy transferred the rifle to his left hand and walked toward the wounded tree. He placed his right hand over the burned area. After a moment, he pulled his hand away and revealed healthy brown bark where the hole had been.

Stevie's eyes grew wide. "Wow."

Randy grinned. "I didn't become a doctor by chance. I'm a healer."

"How did you discover that you could do *that*?"

He looked up into the green treetop. "It was during the summer of 1944 when my little brother, Joshua—."

"Wait." She did the math in her head. "That would you make you—"

"Pretty damn old." Randy laughed.

Stevie blinked. "But you don't seem..." She stopped, struggling to find a way to finish her sentence without insulting him.

"It's the healer in me, Stevie. That's all." He shifted the gun to his other hand. "My brother, Joshua, had been sick with a fever for more than a week. He could no longer move either of his legs. Our family doctor said it was polio, and his paralysis would likely be permanent." He stared off into the distance. "My parents prayed over Joshua every day, but his legs remained motionless. I wasn't allowed to be in the same room with him because they were afraid that I would catch it too. But I couldn't stay away. I knew my little brother was lonely and scared."

Randy met Stevie's gaze. "One night, while everyone was sleeping, I went into his room to sit with him while he slept. I'm still not sure why I felt compelled to touch his legs; I just remember feeling like I needed to do it. So, I stood at the foot of his bed, with a hand on each of his ankles. That's when I felt the energy for the first time. It just zipped through my body and down through my arms and hands. I felt it pour out of me and into Joshua. He was still asleep, but I knew I had healed him. I suddenly felt very tired, so I went back to my own bed. I woke to the sound of my mother's joyful scream first thing in the morning. My brother had walked right out of his room and into the kitchen, looking for breakfast."

Stevie's mouth fell open. "Did anyone know that you were responsible for healing him?"

"Neither of my parents had this gift. I inherited mine from my maternal grandmother, who easily figured out what had happened with Joshua. I never said anything to my parents about what I'd done, so they went on to believe they were witnesses to a miracle. I suppose in a way they were right about that, though the miracle came to pass in a different manner than what they'd prayed for."

"You said it made you tired. Is that why you fall asleep so much?"

"Sometimes. But I take my naps for a number of reasons. There are times when I'm exhausted from doing a healing. Other times, I sleep because a vision is trying to come through."

Stevie raised her brows. "A vision?"

"I can see events happening in other places while they are occurring. I saw Vanessa buy a ticket for a flight to North Carolina, so we were able to prepare for her return. But don't get excited." He raised both hands like he would to calm a crowd. "I don't always see the important things. It's a frustrating gift actually. Most of the time, the information is useless. You wouldn't believe how many times I've had a vision of Ruth eating her dinner. Can't figure out for the life of me why I see that." He rubbed his neck. "That woman sure does love to eat shrimp and grits."

"Did you see what happened to Dylan's mother? Is that how you know it wasn't an accident?"

Randy frowned and lowered his gaze. "I did. I clearly saw Vanessa and Susan standing by the side of the road, just beyond the drawbridge. They waited there until Rebecca drove across it so they could toss her off."

He shook his head as if to clear the dark memories from his mind. "That was one of those rare occasions when my unusual gift was actually useful. Though I wasn't able to save Rebecca that night, I did see enough to know it wasn't an accident. I'm sure Vanessa and Susan would have continued with their plans for the rest of us if we hadn't stopped them."

A shiver zipped up Stevie's back. "My grandmother. She died that night also." Her heart thudded, faster and faster as the realization formed in her mind. "It wasn't really a stroke, was it? Did they kill her too?"

"That was a horrible night for all of us." Randy glanced away. "I can assure you though; Susan and Vanessa did not kill Rose."

She studied the old doctor for a long minute. *He's holding something back.* She clenched her jaw. Though the coven had just let her in on one of the biggest lies-by-omission in the history of the town, she had no doubt that there was much more to uncover. *Secrets piled upon secrets.*

She still had plenty of questions left to ask, but she decided not to push Randy any further on the subject. As a physician, he'd been a professional secret keeper for decades. Stevie thought she might have better luck getting Alice to talk.

Besides, there had been one question burning in her mind since she'd discovered her magical heritage, and Randy was the only one who could answer it. Despite her eagerness to ask it, she also feared his response. She wasn't sure she could handle another "no." She ran her hand through her hair, stalling. Right now, in this moment, anything was possible. But once she uttered her request, there would be no turning back.

She summoned her voice with the same force of will she'd used to draw on her magic. "Can you heal Charlie?"

Randy rested his arm around her shoulders. "I have thought about that since the day he stopped talking, Stevie."

She gulped. "Can you do it?"

He let his arm drop away and stepped in front of her to look into her eyes. "I'm not an expert on autism. In fact, in my fifty years of medical practice, I only saw two cases of it, and both of them were the year before I retired. It's much more common these days than it was back then." He paused for a moment. "Healing autism is not the same as chasing away a virus like polio or repairing a heart after an attack like I did for your dad. Its effects on the mind and body are still not fully understood."

Stevie stared down at her feet, unable to meet his compassionate gaze.

"It would not be safe for me to attempt to heal him. It's possible that I could do more harm than good, and that's something neither of us could live with."

A knot twisted in Stevie's stomach. "I understand." Randy was not the first doctor to say her son couldn't be cured, but he was the first witch to say so. It had been foolish to dream of recovery for Charlie. She pressed her hand against her aching chest. All of his specialists had said the autism diagnosis was permanent, but that hadn't stopped her from striving for more for her son.

"Just because I can't heal him doesn't mean that he won't get better. Look at how far he's come already. You've made good choices for him, Stevie. You've got to have confidence in that."

She pressed her lips together and nodded. She couldn't bring herself to speak, fearing the flood of tears that would come if she tried to do so. In her heart—the heart of a devoted mother—she'd harbored the dream that Charlie would somehow be the exception to the rule. The knowledge that even magic could not cure him was almost too much to bear. She remembered the despair she had endured when she'd first learned of his diagnosis. Somehow, this was worse.

Randy rested the gun on the grass. "Well, you can't give up now. It all boils down to hope. That's what will carry you through the difficult days, and it will force you to continue to do what's best for him." He reached for her hands and gave them a gentle squeeze. "It's not going to be easy, but it will be worth the effort."

Even in dark moments like this, Stevie was sure of one thing. She raised her chin. "I will never give up on him." She let go of Randy's hands. Autism was hard, but loving Charlie was easy.

"I've lived a long time, and I've seen a lot of heartbreak and loss. But I've also seen what boundless hope can do." He removed a small piece of paper from his pocket, unfolded it, and handed it to her.

She studied his handwritten words, aware of the emotion welling in her eyes. These were not the familiar tears of sorrow or grief or guilt. They were tears of acceptance as a great weight lifted from her shoulders. The peaceful sensation was so very different from the devastation she'd felt an instant earlier that she wondered if Randy had done something to heal her broken heart.

"It's from a poem written by Emily Dickinson." He recited the words that he'd scrawled on the page.

"Hope is the thing with feathers
That perches in the soul
And sings the tune without the words
And never stops—at all."

"How long have you been carrying this around?" She held up the scrap of paper.

"Just since this morning. I had a feeling this conversation was coming." The corners of his mouth turned up into a kind smile. "Are you ready for more target practice?" Randy lifted his rifle from the grass.

She wiped the tears from her cheeks and took in a deep breath. "Sure." Then she turned her focus back to the line of bottles on the table.

This is for Charlie. I need to master my magic for him. She curled her hands into fists as she aimed her energy at the target on the left and fired the invisible bullet. This time, she hit her mark, and the bottle flew off the table onto the soft grass below.

"Well done!" Randy pumped his fist.

Stevie repeated the same sequence nine more times, striking each one with precision.

"I'd say you've mastered target practice, Stevie." Randy lowered the gun to his side. "You're a quick learner."

"Thanks. I had a good teacher."

Together, they loaded the fallen bottles back into Randy's bag and moved the patio table back to its usual spot. Stevie walked with him to the side gate, more grateful than she had words to express.

"I may not have all the answers, but I bet that little fella of yours is going to surprise us all." Randy winked before he turned to walk away.

chapter twenty-four

Stevie

Stevie pulled into the driveway of Alice's modest cottage on Queen Street. She followed the walkway, lined with vibrant pansies in full bloom, to the front porch. Ruth and Alice sat in white rocking chairs, awaiting her arrival. Alice waved and smiled as she sipped her sweet tea. Ruth gripped a coffee mug in one hand and swatted away mosquitoes with the other.

"I'm so glad you could come by today, dear." Alice placed her glass on the table beside her.

"Thanks for inviting me."

"Can we go inside now? These bloodsucking parasites are eating me alive!" Ruth slapped her arm in an attempt to squash an ambitious mosquito. She missed, and the insect flew away.

Alice lifted a small spray bottle and offered it to Ruth. "I don't know why you won't just try my spray. It's very effective."

Ruth abandoned her coffee mug and perched on the edge of her seat with both hands poised, ready to strike the next bug that tried to feast on her. "I don't want to smell like lemon and eucalyptus all day, that's why." She growled and smacked her arm again.

"Suit yourself." Alice shrugged and returned the bottle to the table. "I guess we better get inside before Ruth hurts herself." She rose and walked toward the door.

Ruth stood, arms flailing in a futile fight against the hungry bugs. Her face turned crimson as sweat beaded on her forehead. "This is ridiculous!" She swatted one away from her face, just as another one landed on her neck. "Ouch!"

Alice and Stevie stared on as Ruth succumbed to a furious fit amid the swarm of buzzing insects, obscenities spewed forth from her like hot steam from a boiling kettle.

Stevie leaned closer to Alice. "Isn't there something we can do to help her?"

"Oh honey, Ruth is just as able as we are to get rid of mosquitoes—probably even more so given her talent with animals—but she can't focus her energy when she's this riled up." She shook her head. "It's a shame really. You'd think after all these years she would have learned that lesson."

"She has a talent with animals?" Stevie glanced back at the cloud of determined bloodsuckers that surrounded Ruth.

"Oh, yes. It's quite incredible actually. She can communicate with them. She could just politely ask those mosquitoes to leave her be. If she knew how to be polite, that is." Alice shook her head, though a grin ghosted her lips. "Bless her heart."

"Don't talk about me like I'm not here!" Ruth continued her violent dance.

"Oh dear." Alice clapped a hand over her mouth, trying to hide a chuckle as she watched her friend thrash and cuss. She walked back to the porch table and lifted her spray bottle, pointing the nozzle in Ruth's direction. She tapped the trigger once, and the attacking mosquitoes flew away.

With a huff, Ruth let her arms collapse to her sides. "Why'd you do that? I almost had 'em!"

"It looked to me like you were losing that battle." Alice spun around, turning her back on Ruth and opened the door.

Stevie touched Ruth's arm, worried about the old woman's labored breathing. "Are you okay?"

"She's fine, honey." Alice dismissed Stevie's concern with a wave and stepped inside her house. "Doesn't take much to send her over the edge."

Ruth muttered something under her breath as she smoothed her disheveled gray hair.

Stevie had never been inside Alice's house before, but she wasn't surprised by the décor. She walked into the living room, where lace doilies adorned almost every flat surface in sight and paintings of various flowers and herbs hung on the bright yellow walls. But she didn't expect to see a large portrait of Jesus hanging above the fireplace, however, and she paused to get a closer look.

Ruth wagged her bony finger toward the painting. "Didn't know that Alice was a Bible thumper, did you?"

"Well, it's just that—um—I didn't realize…"

"I'm guessing that you didn't know that a witch could also be a Christian." Alice arched an eyebrow.

Stevie shook her head. "No, I didn't."

"Honey, I haven't missed a Sunday morning service in my entire life." Alice approached the portrait of Jesus. "My parents were devoutly religious. As far as I know, neither of them possessed this gift we have. Or, if they did, they kept it a secret from me. My powers developed at a young age; I was only eight years old when it started."

"That must have been very confusing for you." As an adult, the transformation had been nothing short of shocking for Stevie. She blinked, unable to imagine how a small child would handle it.

"I think it's an easier adjustment when you're younger, before you have a chance to get stuck in the notion of how life is supposed to be." Alice rested her hand on the mantel. "It was pretty exciting actually. I didn't think there was anything wrong with it, or me for that matter. That is until Mama caught me." Her eyes lost their sparkle. "One day, I was playing in my bedroom with a doll. Sure, that sounds normal enough, but I was dancing my doll around with my powers. And my mother saw me." Alice looked at Jesus' face and took a deep breath. "I'd never seen her so angry. She called me a witch and slapped me so hard I fell to the floor."

Stevie flinched as though she'd taken the hit herself.

"Mama told me that witches were of the devil and God wouldn't love anyone practicing magic." Alice faced Stevie. "I didn't believe that. Why wouldn't God love me when he made me this way? I made the mistake of asking Mama that and earned myself another slap.

"I didn't use my powers again for several years, until your grandmother asked me about it in school one day. Before that, I didn't know that there were others like me." Alice's eyes sparkled once again. "Your grandmother showed me all the good that we could do with our magic."

Stevie smiled as she remembered her grandmother. "I'm glad you found each other."

"I know that I was born this way; it wasn't something that I chose to be." She touched the frame of the portrait. "However, I do choose to believe in Him, and it's a choice I make every day."

"Is Sunday school over yet?" Ruth mock yawned.

Alice chuckled. "Talk of eternal salvation tends to make Ruth uncomfortable." She cast one final adoring look at the picture of Jesus before she started toward the kitchen. "Are you hungry? I've got clam chowder simmering on the stove."

"It smells delicious." Stevie followed Alice to the back of the house.

"Help yourselves to the tea." Alice gestured to the pitcher of sweet iced tea resting on the round table by the window. After Ruth and Stevie poured themselves a glass, they each took seats at the table.

A tall, stainless steel pot sat on the old yellow stove. Alice lifted the lid and stirred the chowder one last time before filling three bowls. She joined Ruth and Stevie at the table.

"Dig in." Alice bowed her head for a moment, offering a silent prayer of gratitude for the meal before she ate.

Stevie stared at the food in front of her. Potatoes, clams, and bacon floated in a non-traditional flour and water based broth. Though it looked like regular "Down East" clam chowder, she remembered how Alice had drugged her with tea last time. Her stomach growled, begging her to eat, but her mind refused to let go of the memory.

When Alice lifted her head, Stevie grimaced. "So...there's nothing in here that will knock me out. Right?"

Alice laughed. "No, dear. That was a special circumstance. This is just plain old chowder."

Despite Alice's assurance, Stevie took a moment to examine the contents of her bowl before lifting a spoonful to her mouth.

"How is it, dear?" Alice sipped her tea.

Stevie loaded another spoonful. "It's perfect! It tastes just like my grandmother's chowder."

"It should. I used Rose's recipe."

Stevie remembered helping her grandmother in the kitchen. Together, they had perfected this very recipe. What a thrill it had been to stand on a chair in front of the stove and add the ground pepper to the savory mixture. She'd taken such pride in stirring it in with her grandmother's long-handled wooden spoon. That old spoon still hung on the wall of her own kitchen.

Grandma. Stevie still had questions about her sudden passing. She met Alice's gaze. "Can you tell me about the night she died?"

Ruth and Alice exchanged a worried look.

"Well, Patricia didn't tell us *not* to tell her." Ruth shrugged before shoveling another spoonful of chowder into her mouth.

"I just want to know the truth," Stevie said.

Alice placed her spoon next to her bowl and dabbed the corners of her mouth with a paper napkin. She let out a long breath. Resting her plump arm on the table, Alice leaned in. "You remember that the pirates took Charlotte, Catherine, and Hannah?"

Stevie nodded.

"Hannah eventually gave birth to Blackbeard's son here in Beaufort. Vanessa and Susan are descendants of Hannah and Blackbeard. Now, that alone is not a reason to distrust them. Some very honorable witches have come from that line."

"I knew Susan was bad news the minute I met her." Ruth gloated, her mouth full.

Alice sat back and lifted her spoon. "Susan chose to operate as a solitary witch and avoided our coven for many years."

"Solitary witch?" Stevie glanced from Alice to Ruth, eyes wide. "Are you saying that there are more of us?"

"Of course there are more of us. You can't walk down Front Street without crossing paths with a witch." Ruth drained the tea from her glass.

"We don't force anyone to join our coven. As long as they follow the rules, we let them be." Alice stirred her chowder before loading another spoonful.

Stevie fidgeted with the corner of her napkin. "Maybe you should fill me in on the rules. I'd hate to inadvertently break one of them."

"There are only two. It's really not that hard to keep up with." Ruth counted them off on her fingers. "Rule number one: harm no one. Rule number two: keep the secret."

179

"I think I can manage that." Stevie nodded, both relieved and confident.

"Susan came to us after Vanessa developed her powers. They both wanted to join the coven."

"The only reason they wanted to join the coven was to get close enough to destroy us." Ruth punctuated her statement by making a stabbing motion with her spoon.

Stevie stiffened. "How do you know that?"

"Dylan's mother, Rebecca, had an unusual gift," Alice said. "She had the ability to read minds. Once she met Susan and Vanessa, she immediately knew their intentions were dark."

Stevie shook her head, incredulous. *Read minds?*

"They wanted to eliminate the coven because we are responsible for enforcing the rules. Susan had always resented our power over her." Ruth waved her spoon as she spoke. "She didn't have a problem with the 'keep the secret' rule. It was the 'harm no one' part that pissed her off."

"Rebecca told us of their intentions, and, of course, Rose refused to allow them into the coven. Clearly, they decided to move forward with their plans to destroy us, and they chose Rebecca as their first victim." Alice sighed. "As soon as Rose heard what had happened, she called an emergency meeting of the coven."

Stevie's clam chowder grew cold as she listened to the story of that tragic night. "Was Dylan there?"

"No. He hadn't developed his powers at that point." Ruth dipped her spoon into her bowl.

"In order to prevent any more deaths, we had to act fast, so we decided to strip both Vanessa and Susan of their powers. The binding ceremonies had to be done separately, so we chose to bind Susan first. That went very well. But when we began to bind Vanessa's powers, Rose collapsed on the floor." Alice fell silent and shifted her gaze to the window.

Stevie swallowed hard as the unwanted image of her fallen grand-mother sprung into her mind. "I don't understand."

"Vanessa is extraordinarily powerful. To bind her magic, we had to put everything we had into the ceremony. Your grandmother had to channel all of that energy." Alice met Stevie's gaze once more. "It was just too much for her."

"Randy did everything he could to try to save her, but it was too late." Ruth's lips formed a tight line. "She died instantly."

Stevie considered her own power and tried to imagine that same force coming from several different witches at once. How could any-one manage that? "Wait." She held up her hand. "This is the same ceremony that my mother wants to do *again*?"

"Yep, it is." Ruth scowled as she set her spoon next to her bowl.

"We can't go through with it!" Stevie's fists clenched. "There's got to be another way."

"Well, we can't exactly call the police and have Vanessa arrested." Ruth leaned back and crossed her arms.

Alice shook her head. "Your mother is the reigning queen. We will do what she asks of us." Alice patted Stevie's hand. "You should have seen her that night. In the face of so much loss, she assumed her role as our leader with grace and dignity."

Ruth refilled her tea glass. "You should tell her about the rest of that night."

"We still had to figure out what to do with Susan and Vanessa, so Ruth and I went to Susan's house to look for them. By the time we got there, Vanessa had already taken off, and Susan was positively hysterical over the loss of her powers."

Ruth jerked her thumb toward her chest. "It was my idea to have her locked up."

"Yes, it was." Alice gave a quick nod. "Ruth and I cast a truth-tell-ing spell on Susan. Our activities that night left her without her magic and forced her to always tell the truth."

"That's when I loaded Susan into the car and drove her sorry ass straight to the hospital." Ruth smirked. "I told the doctor that she claimed to be a witch and was planning to kill people. I made it clear that she should be committed." She covered her mouth with the napkin, but the corners of her eyes still crinkled in amusement. "Of course, Susan only validated my story because she couldn't tell a lie. They eventually transferred her to the loony bin where she's been locked up and medicated ever since."

Alice winced and reached for Stevie's hand. "I'm sorry we had to keep all of this from you for so long."

Stevie sat in silence for a moment, once again astounded by the secrets her friends and family kept. How could she have been so oblivious to it all of these years? She pushed her bowl away. She had no appetite now.

"I know this is a lot to take in all at once. Dylan had a tough time processing it all too. He can help with some of your questions." Alice sipped her tea. "He's still staying at your house, right?"

"Yeah, but he hasn't told me anything." Stevie sighed.

Ruth smacked her hand against the table. "I bet I know exactly why that little rascal is being tight-lipped!"

Stevie's eyes darted to Ruth. "Is there more to the story?"

"There always is." Ruth leaned in, holding Stevie's gaze. "Dylan can…"

Alice cleared her throat and shot a warning glare at Ruth. "I think that's something Dylan should explain for himself. It's really not our place to discuss it."

"Aw, come on! I just want to see the look on her face when she finds out." Ruth stomped her foot like a petulant child. "I swear, Alice. You can suck the fun right out of anything!"

Chapter twenty-five

Stevie

Stevie reached the special education classroom a few minutes before the dismissal bell rang. The room was empty except for Charlie's teacher.

"Hi, Mrs. Lewis." Sherri tugged on the corner of a table, dragging it away from the back wall.

Stevie gestured to a row of empty chairs. "Where are all the children?"

"They're outside with my assistant." Sherri pulled on the opposite side of the table. "It's such a pretty day today. Fresh air and sunshine are as important as anything they'll learn in here."

Stevie gave a deep nod. "I couldn't agree more."

"Have you heard the news?" Sherri gave the table another tug, pulling it farther away from the wall. "Lexi is coming by tonight to start on the mural. She said she'll be able to do the whole thing over the weekend. That way, the kids will have a nice surprise when they return on Monday."

"That's great. Lexi is a talented artist. I'm sure you'll be pleased with her work."

"She wouldn't accept any payment from me. Can you believe that?"

Stevie tucked a stray hair behind her ear and met the teacher's baffled gaze. "That sounds exactly like Lexi."

"Since we have a moment…" Sherri stepped closer to Stevie and lowered her voice. "I'd like to talk to you about Charlie."

Stevie stiffened, bracing herself for bad news.

"Charlie is a great kid, but I don't think this class is the best fit for him." Sherri smiled. "I think he would do well in a traditional classroom. However, if you prefer, I can continue to work with him in here."

Stevie stood silent for a moment, absorbing the words she never thought she would hear. Mainstream Charlie? Could he function in a regular kindergarten classroom?

"He'd benefit socially from spending time with his typically developing peers. But there is still the concern about sensory overload. What do you think?" Sherri's eyebrows rose as she leaned forward.

"I—I'm not sure what to think." Stevie let her gaze drift around the dismal classroom. This was not what she wanted for her son. But the special education teachers understood his quirks, and his classmates didn't tease him for his differences. She raked a hand through her hair. "Will he be able to fit in with the kids in the regular class?"

Sherri shrugged. "We'll never know if he stays in here. It might not work out for him, but I think we should give it a try and see what happens."

"What if he has a meltdown?" Stevie's mouth went dry. "Will his new teacher know what to do?"

"I've found a wonderful teacher for him, and she's excited to work with Charlie. I'd like to give it a trial run next week to see how he likes it. We can keep the option open for him to return to my room if he gets overstimulated or upset. Of course, I'll check on him throughout the week to see how he's doing."

Stevie imagined Charlie in a regular classroom, picturing him playing alongside all of those happy, talkative five-year-olds. Her worries gave way to optimism. Friends. Giggles. Birthday parties. A lump formed in her throat. Could that happen for Charlie?

"Okay, let's give it a try."

Sherri beamed. "Excellent! We'll start on Monday. If it goes well, we'll write up a new IEP for Charlie."

The young students returned to the classroom. Stevie's lip quivered when she spotted her son. *He's come so far since the diagnosis.* She picked up his backpack and waved goodbye to Sherri. Hand in hand, Stevie and Charlie walked out of the school together.

She buckled him into his car seat and placed his tablet in his hand as she struggled to think of a way to ask him how he felt about changing classrooms. There was no way he could understand the importance of joining a regular kindergarten class, and the last thing she wanted to do was put any pressure on him. At this moment, she'd give anything to know what her son was thinking.

Dylan's mother had the ability to read minds.

Oh if only . . .

An onslaught of memories raced through Stevie's head, and she gripped the car door to brace herself against them. She remembered Dylan's sudden smile while she watched him reading a book on his back porch, the flash of anger she saw in his eyes after her night with Sam, and his pretend conversation with Charlie. He hadn't been pretending at all.

As the initial shock began to wear off, Stevie released her grip on the car door. She sunk down into the driver's seat, chest heaving with ragged breaths. The indulgent fantasies she'd had about Dylan flashed in her mind. The spicy warmth of his cologne. His broad chest. His lips. *His lips.* He'd heard it all. Her face grew hot with embarrassment and anger. How could she face him now, knowing he had heard all of her private thoughts about him? How could he have kept this from her?

Stevie pulled out of the school parking lot, determined to confront him.

chapter twenty-six

Stevie

On Friday afternoon, Stevie stood on her front porch waving goodbye to Charlie as Sam's truck pulled away from the curb. She'd wanted to cancel the weekend visit, but her mother, the queen, had insisted she go through with it. Randy, Ruth, and Alice had volunteered to keep an eye on him until the binding ceremony required their presence. She shook her head, unable to imagine the three senior members of the coven performing an inconspicuous stakeout at Sam's house. But then again, anything was possible at this point. She now lived in a world where even the laws of physics had been reduced to mere suggestions.

Magic, witches, and secrets.

So many secrets.

That's what bothered her the most. She could forgive those she loved for keeping her in the dark about the magic. She could even understand their need to cover up the true cause of her grandmother's death. But knowing Dylan had been reading her mind all along was just too much. She clenched her fists. He must have found her lusty thoughts amusing.

He's probably laughing at me right now. The anger flushed hot on her cheeks, and she spun around to enter the house, slamming the door behind her.

Stevie paced around her living room, planning her verbal assault on Dylan. He would be there soon for the nighttime protection detail, and she wanted to be ready.

The doorbell chimed, interrupting her thoughts. Still fuming, Stevie marched to the front of the house and threw open the door.

"I've never laughed at you, Stevie." Dylan shook his head, his eyes dark with regret.

She threw her hands up. "How could you keep this from me?"

"I'd be happy to explain it to you." Dylan waved the bottle of chilled chardonnay he held. "A peace offering?"

"All right. But this better be good." Still glaring, she stepped out of the way and allowed him to cross the threshold.

Dylan slipped by her, walked to the kitchen, and found the corkscrew in a drawer. Stevie crossed her arms, frowning at him while he opened the bottle of chardonnay and poured two glasses.

He pulled out a chair at the table. "Please, have a seat." He handed her a glass of wine.

"Start talking." She ground her teeth as she sat.

Dylan joined her at the table. He stared at the contents of his glass for a moment. "My powers developed in the middle of my mother's funeral."

Stevie's glare softened as she remembered the tragic events she and Dylan had endured together twelve years earlier. She listened as he continued.

"As the pastor delivered the eulogy, I suddenly began to hear the thoughts of those around me. I heard Patricia first, then Ruth and Alice. As more and more minds opened up to me, it soon became an unbearable cacophony in my head. I could hear everything that had happened with Susan and Vanessa, and I knew my mother's death was not an accident." He paused to take a breath and then a sip of wine. "At first, I thought I was hallucinating. It was just so unbelievable."

His gaze met hers. "After the funeral, I approached your mother and told her that I knew what had happened. She was incredibly kind to me. That night, on the very same day that we buried my mother, I joined the coven."

Stevie sipped her wine and returned the glass to the table. The thought of Dylan as a grieving teenager tugged at her heart. Developing his magic at such a difficult time must have been awful. She leaned back in her chair as sympathy dulled the edges of her anger.

"I'm not the first one of us to have this particular gift. And, as you clearly understand, no one wants someone else reading their thoughts." He paused and studied the condensation forming on his wine glass for a moment before he sighed. "So, long ago, some witches devised a method to block mind readers from gaining access to the other coven members' thoughts."

Whatever sympathy she'd felt for him evaporated. She sucked in a sharp breath through clenched teeth. "Are you kidding me? Not only have you been poking around in my brain without my knowledge, but I could have blocked you from doing it?" She slammed her fist on the table and stood up to pace the length of the kitchen counter. "How could you possibly think that I'd be okay with this?"

"You have every right to be upset, but please let me explain why we did it this way." Dylan rose from his seat.

"We?" Stevie whipped around to face him. "Are you saying that this was a *group* decision?"

"I only discussed it with Patricia. It's a matter of timing, Stevie. With Vanessa back in town, you need to be fully focused on developing your powers right now." He raised his hands as if to stall a charging bull. "You can't have your energy divided between blocking me and defending yourself against an attack. And, since we couldn't tell you how to block it, we decided it would be best if you didn't know that I could hear your thoughts. We didn't want you to feel self-conscious about it."

Stevie rolled her eyes and threw her head back. "Like I do right now?"

"I'm sorry, Stevie." Dylan stepped closer to her. "I know you're angry. If the situation were reversed, I'd feel the same way."

"But you've heard my private thoughts. If I'd wanted you to know about them, I would have said them out loud." Stevie set her hands on her hips.

"Would it help you to know that I've been thinking the same things?" Dylan's lips quirked into a sly smile.

"Not at all!" She blinked. "What? Wait—really?" Her cheeks grew hot as she processed Dylan's confession.

"Yes." He moved closer to her. "That was another issue that I planned to address after we took care of Vanessa."

"You should really just tell me how to block you. *Now.*" Stevie struggled to push new thoughts of Dylan far from her mind, but the very act of trying not to think about him brought forth even more embarrassing ideas.

"Okay, Stevie, please stop trying to fight this." Dylan kept his voice steady. "I will show you how to block me, but promise me you won't worry about this while we're doing the binding ritual tomorrow night. You'll need all of your focus for that."

"Fine." She gave a curt nod. "Now tell me."

Dylan opened his mouth to speak but stopped. He looked into Stevie's eyes and then his gaze shifted to her full lips. Her breath caught as he stepped forward and reached out to touch her cheek. "Just one minute more." He leaned in.

She knew what was coming, and she didn't stop him. She'd waited for this moment for far too long. Whatever remained of her anger washed away the minute his lips met hers.

Dylan's hand slipped from her cheek to her neck, his mouth pressed against hers. Stevie kissed him back, timid at first. But as her heart pounded faster, her inhibitions slipped away. She ran her hands through his hair and pulled him even closer. Lost in the moment, she let her thoughts run unrestrained.

Tenderness gave way to urgency. He wrapped his arms around her while she pressed her body against his. Exploring the muscles of his back, she clutched his broad shoulders hungrily. Dylan let out a low growl, responding to her touch. She wasn't sure where this would end, and, for the moment, she didn't care.

Time stopped. The world fell away. It was just the two of them now, locked in the kiss she'd dreamed of forever.

Breathless, Dylan cupped his hands around her face and pulled away, meeting her gaze with a smile. He leaned in again and brushed her lips with a soft peck.

"That wasn't fair." Stevie trembled.

He brushed a stray hair away from her face. "Can you blame me for wanting to hear your thoughts about our first kiss?"

The word *first* caught her off guard. *That means there will be others.*

Dylan's smiled broadened. "I sure hope so."

"I don't suppose you'd be willing to even the playing field just a little, maybe let me in on what you're thinking?" Stevie raised her eyebrows.

Dylan exhaled and took her hands in his. "I haven't stopped thinking about you since high school, Stevie."

Her jaw dropped. "I—I had no idea."

"I didn't know you felt the same way until my powers developed. By then it was too late." He rubbed his thumb along the back of her hand. "My father was already planning the move to London. I considered staying here, but I didn't want to leave him alone after my mother's death."

Stevie sighed and looked away.

"Now, do you still want to know how to block me from reading your thoughts?"

"Even more so now." She met his gaze again.

"Okay." He squeezed her hands before letting them go. "Close your eyes and visualize a wall of white light around your mind." He paused. "Can you see it yet?"

Stevie kept her eyes closed and stared at the brilliant white barrier she'd constructed out of nothing. "Yes. Is it working?"

Dylan fell silent as he listened for her thoughts. "Yes, it is. Keep in mind that it may be difficult for you to maintain the shield continuously at first, but soon, it will be second nature. With more practice, you'll be able to manage that along with anything else you want to do."

Stevie opened her eyes and blinked. She closed them again, checking to make sure the wall was still in place. It was…for now anyway. But keeping it in place required energy and focus. She looked forward to the day when she could manage the shield easily. Now, she understood why the coven had kept this a secret from her, but she still didn't agree that it was the best decision.

Dylan sighed. "I already miss hearing your thoughts."

"I guess you'll just have to ask me questions like a normal person." Stevie landed a playful swat against his chest.

He chuckled. "I suppose you're right."

Stevie stepped to the table and picked up their wine glasses. "Is it hard for you to hear all of the noise from everyone else's minds?"

"At first, it was overwhelming. In fact, it was similar to what Charlie experiences every day as he copes with sensory input. I eventually learned to filter unnecessary information and only focus on what I wanted to hear. Everything else just became background noise." He watched her walk toward the counter. "It helps that I have to be in fairly close proximity to hear it. If I need a break, I can always go off on my own for a while."

"Like Charlie does." Stevie refilled their glasses and returned to her seat. She traced the rim of her glass, deep in thought. "Tell me about him."

"He's a *really* smart kid, Stevie." Dylan joined her at the table. "The difference with him is not so much what he's thinking but *how* he's thinking it."

"What do you mean?"

"He thinks in pictures."

She considered Dylan's words. "Don't we all think in pictures?"

He sipped his wine. "Our thoughts are a combination of words and pictures. We may be able to see a memory or, in your case, a fantasy."

He grinned and waggled his eyebrows. Stevie punched his arm.

He clutched his arm in mock horror and then leaned back in his chair. "But along with that picture, we have an inner narrative describing it. We could explain it with words if someone asked us to. For the most part, Charlie just sees the picture."

Stevie's shoulders slumped. She finally knew how Charlie's mind worked, but she had no idea what to do with that information. She still didn't know how to help him.

Dylan reached for her hand. "Hey, this isn't necessarily a bad thing. It's just different. I think the words will come in time. He can understand most of what he hears, and he's already kicking a few new words around in his mind. He's really doing quite well."

Dylan's words comforted her, but it wasn't enough. With all of Charlie's challenges, Stevie had just one wish for him that outweighed all of the others. She bit her lip, uncertain if she should voice the question she so desperately wanted the answer to.

"You know, Charlie doesn't show much emotion, and he rarely smiles. It's impossible for me to know how he's feeling most of the time. He just has so many struggles in life..." She pulled her hand away and let it fall to her lap. "I have to know. Is he happy?"

"Oh, yes!" Dylan's eyes lit up. "Stevie, he *is* happy."

"Thank you." Overcome with joy, she threw her arms around Dylan and rode the waves of relief as they carried her away to a peace she'd lost long ago.

chapter twenty-seven

Stevie

"Hey, Stevie! Where are you?" Lexi called from Stevie's foyer on Saturday morning.

"In my room. I'll—uh—I'll be down in a minute." Stevie threw on her bathrobe and attempted to tie its belt with her shaky hands. She cast a wide-eyed glance at Dylan, who was perched, shirtless, on the edge of her bed. Behind him, the sheets lay in a twisted, wrinkled mess, and the white eyelet coverlet rested in a heap on the old wooden floor.

Dylan watched her panic with an amused grin. "I don't have to be a mind reader to know what you're thinking right now." He chuckled.

"Shhh!" She reached forward and grabbed his arm, pulling on it with all her might. He didn't budge. "You have to hide."

"Embarrassed?" Dylan found his shirt among the crumpled sheets and slipped it over his head.

"Not of you." Stevie's gaze darted around the room in search of a suitable hiding spot. "Lexi gets a little obsessive about my sex life. I'm just not ready to open that can of worms yet."

Stevie had gone from having no love life at all to sleeping with two different men in one week. If Lexi found out, she would never hear the end of it.

"Tonight's the night!" Lexi yelled up from the bottom of the stairs.

Stevie heard her best friend's footsteps on the stairs. Heart racing, she tugged on Dylan's arm again. "Come on. You can hide in the bathroom."

"Don't worry. I've got this." He stood and walked across the bedroom to an open window.

"No! I don't want you to get hurt."

Dylan offered a reassuring smile and slipped through the window. She watched in awe as he floated down through two stories of thin air and landed on his feet. He waved before he crossed the grassy lawn to his house.

Stevie exhaled sharply. She still had so much to learn about this new life. Each day brought new revelations and, of course, new secrets.

"Did you hear me?" Lexi now stood in the doorway of Stevie's bedroom. "The binding ritual is tonight!"

Stevie spun around to see her friend's excited smile. "Yes, I—I heard you."

"Don't tell me you're getting nervous about it." Lexi placed a hand on her hip and tilted her head like Stevie had just admitted to being afraid of the Easter bunny.

She nodded, grateful Lexi's question had nothing to do with the real reason she appeared unsettled. "I guess I am. All of this stuff is new to me."

"Now that we have you, this binding ritual will be a piece of cake." Lexi snapped her fingers.

Stevie swallowed, feeling the weight of this new responsibility on her shoulders. She still had so much to learn. How could her presence at the ritual be helpful at all? "I'm not so sure about that."

"How about we go get some lunch? It'll help get your mind off of this stuff for a while."

"Sounds good to me." Her stomach growled, and she remembered she'd skipped breakfast. She smiled at the memory of why.

Lexi glanced at the bathrobe, the untidy bed, and Stevie's messy hair before eyeing her with a sly grin. "While you're getting dressed, I'll go ask Dylan if he'd like to join us for lunch."

"Okay." Stevie turned away and started toward her bathroom so Lexi wouldn't see her blush at the mere mention of Dylan's name.

Lexi giggled as she waved toward the messy bed. "I'll bet he's worked up quite an appetite after all of *this*."

Stevie let out a long, loud groan. Apparently, everyone could keep a secret but her. She slammed the bathroom door.

Stevie, Dylan, and Lexi walked east on Front Street, heading toward Clawson's Restaurant. Like a typical late-summer Saturday, plenty of foot traffic bustled around the historic area. Stevie used the opportunity to scan passersby, looking for any indication that they too were witches. She furrowed her brow, unable to sense anything about anyone.

"I don't get it." She shook her head. "Ruth said you can't walk down Front Street without crossing paths with a witch. How can you tell?"

"I suppose I have an unfair advantage when it comes to that." Dylan chuckled.

"It's easy." Lexi waved her hand as if there was nothing to it. "You know how everyone has an aura?"

"Uh, no." Stevie tucked her hair behind her ear. "I mean, I guess I've heard about auras, but I thought they were just New Age stuff. Are you saying they're real?"

Lexi giggled. "Yes, they're real. And witches' auras tend to shimmer more than others. It's because of the extra energy we possess."

"Hmm." Stevie squinted at the nearby people, hoping for a glimmering clue, and sighed. "I'm not seeing anything like that."

"I don't see the aura that Lexi's talking about either. You may have a different method of identifying other witches. Some of us are able to feel the magical energy coming from others. I'm sure it will happen for you in time." Dylan patted her arm. "Remember, you're still pretty new to all of this."

"How about her?" Stevie nodded toward a young woman on the other side of the street. She wore a long, crinkled white tunic with elaborate embroidery along the neckline and sleeves. A clear, round crystal hung from the black cord around her neck. "She looks kind of witchy."

"Nope." Lexi shook her head. "I don't see any shimmer."

Dylan looked at the woman. "She likes to think of herself as a witch, but she's definitely not one of us."

"A wannabe." Lexi focused her attention on a middle-aged man walking toward them. "Now, that guy." She nodded in his direction. "He's one of us, but he probably doesn't even know it."

"Sometimes, the power develops so subtly, the witch doesn't even realize it's there." Dylan leaned in close to Stevie's ear. "He's never actually cast a spell, but things tend to work out for him. Right now, he's thinking how lucky he was to find a twenty-dollar bill in his jacket pocket this morning. He's short on cash this week, and he figures it was just a happy coincidence."

"Sounds like a good way to live. Can you see my energy too?" Stevie glanced at Lexi.

"Now I can. But I couldn't see it until the day you stopped Vanessa's attack on Charlie."

"The day my powers developed."

"Exactly." Lexi nodded.

"There's a strong one in that crowd up ahead." Dylan tilted his head forward. "Let's see if you can pick out the witch."

They approached a small group that had gathered on the sidewalk. The mayor and his wife had stopped to greet a few of the town residents while out for a walk. Stevie sized them both up. The short, round mayor stood by his tall, elegant wife. Her knee-length skirt, matching jacket, and high-heeled shoes spoke of fashion over functionality, while the mayor's casual khaki pants and polo shirt confirmed their mismatched pairing.

Aside from the mayor's wife's glittery diamonds, which graced her ears, neck, and hand, Stevie couldn't see anything shimmery about the couple. She pursed her lips and frowned, trying to discern something special about either of them.

She let her gaze drift among the residents who had gathered to greet the mayor. Nothing. There were no auras. No magical sensations whatsoever. She dropped her shoulders in defeat. "I'm not sure. Maybe the mayor's wife?"

"Nope." Lexi grinned. "It's the mayor."

"No way!" Stevie gasped.

The mayor looked up at them and nodded as if to confirm Lexi's statement before returning his attention to his gathered constituents.

Stevie, Lexi, and Dylan stepped around the group and continued down the sidewalk. Stevie gazed in wonderment as she walked, as if seeing her hometown for the first time. *The witches have always been here, but how had that remained a secret for so long?* She shook her head. If it hadn't been for her own initiation, she'd still be in the dark too. If she'd witnessed magic, glimpsed the impossible, she would have attributed it to a trick of the light or some other mundane thing. Just like anyone else.

As they neared the timber and glass entrance to Clawson's, Dylan grabbed Stevie's arm, forcing her to stop. Lexi bristled as well. For a moment, they were all silent. Stevie scanned the area, searching for the cause of the tension.

"Now there's a witch." He released his grip on Stevie's arm but stayed by her side.

Lexi let out a low hiss. "With a capital B."

Stevie followed their gaze and saw Vanessa crossing Front Street, heading straight for them.

"Stevie, go ahead and drop your shield," Dylan whispered. "Just in case."

Stevie lowered the white shield in her mind, freeing her focus and allowing Dylan access to her thoughts. Icy terror raced through her veins as the dark witch stepped closer. She drew in shallow breaths, unable to slow her rapid pulse.

"She won't risk exposing the secret here, right?" Lexi asked Dylan.

He did not look away from Vanessa. "Be prepared for anything."

"Of course."

I could hurl a car at her, just like she did to Charlie. We could finish this right now.

Dylan shook his head. "No. Not here. We'll do this the right way." He held his chin high. "Unless we're forced to do otherwise."

They stood together, watching and waiting. Vanessa took her time reaching them, oozing arrogance as she slinked closer. Her dark blue tank dress revealed her toned legs and clung to her curves. Stevie suspected that she was the kind of woman who attracted attention everywhere she went.

Stevie spotted a young mother pushing a stroller along the waterfront, and she became aware of all of the innocents nearby. If this encounter with Vanessa got out of control, exposing the secret would be the least of their worries. She couldn't allow any of these people to get hurt.

Dylan grasped her hand and offered a supportive squeeze before letting go.

Vanessa's high black heels found purchase on the sidewalk, and she greeted them with a forced smile.

"Hello, old friends." She met their gazes with unnerving confidence.

Stevie's heart raced even faster. She fought to maintain control as she remembered the silver sedan speeding toward Charlie. She locked on the image of his terrified face, his hands covering his ears. He'd been so helpless in that moment. Fear and pain ripped through her body. In an instant, those weaker emotions gave way to rage. The fire burned hot in her eyes, and she clenched her fists.

"What do you want?" Dylan's hatred for Vanessa singed each word.

"I thought we could have a truce." Vanessa batted her long eyelashes.

"You've got to be kidding." Lexi sneered. "Not a chance."

Vanessa leaned closer, and Dylan's jaw tightened. Stevie remained silent as she struggled to quell her anger, knowing that innocent people could be hurt if she lost control.

"The situation has become more complicated now that the newbie has joined your coven." Vanessa nodded toward Stevie. "Don't you think?"

"What did you expect? She's a direct descendant of Lucia. Of course she has powers." Lexi crossed her arms.

"Strange that her magic would show up now, after all these years." Vanessa eyed Stevie with suspicion.

Lexi stepped forward, drawing Vanessa's attention away from Dylan and Stevie. "You're crazy if you think we would even consider a truce with you." She propped her hand on her hip. "Speaking of crazy, how is your mother doing these days?"

Vanessa snarled. "We're not done with you yet."

"What a coincidence!" Lexi narrowed her eyes. "We're not done with you either."

Vanessa towered over Lexi. "Be careful. I no longer abide by your rules."

"As expected, you have nothing to say that's worth hearing." Dylan placed his hand on the small of Stevie's back, nudging her toward the restaurant's entrance. "We're leaving."

Stevie resisted his gentle push and stepped up to Vanessa. "Come near my son again, and I will kill you on the spot." She started to walk away but stopped short. "Oh, and I don't care who's watching."

"Be careful, newbie." Vanessa's lip curled. "We may be equal in power, but I've had years of practice."

"Let's go." Lexi's tugged on Stevie's arm.

Dylan whispered in her ear. "That's enough for now. We're done here." He wrapped his arm around her waist, easing her away from Vanessa, and guided her into the restaurant.

chapter twenty-eight

Stevie

Dylan had refused to leave Stevie's side since their encounter with Vanessa. They sat together in the wicker rockers on her front porch, watching the night sky grow darker as a handful of stars became visible in the absence of moonlight. The temperature had plummeted after sunset, and Stevie shivered.

"You're cold." Dylan covered her hand with his. "Let's go back inside."

"I'm okay." She folded her arms across her chest. "The others will be here soon. I want to wait for them."

Stevie had left her mental shield down in case Vanessa attempted a surprise attack before the ceremony, and she knew Dylan was listening to her unspoken worries. She had many concerns about the binding ritual. She was unsure what her role in it would be and uncertain that it would be successful this time. More than anything, she worried for her mother's safety.

"I know what really happened to my grandmother." Stevie stared out over the water. "How can we be sure that the same thing won't happen to my mom?"

Dylan took in a deep breath and rubbed his chin. "I won't lie to you, Stevie. The truth is, I don't know that we can be sure at all."

"But if it goes bad…" She couldn't bring herself to finish the statement aloud. *I'm not ready to lose my mom.* She squeezed her eyes shut, considering the worst-case scenario. *And if I did, I wouldn't have the courage to step up as queen like she did.*

"The circumstances are different this time though. They'll have our help, *and* we will only perform one ceremony tonight." He paused. "I think it may have been just too much for Rose to handle two bindings in one night."

"Alice said that the energy was too intense for my grandmother to manage. But my mom told me that having you and me there will help make this attempt successful." She gripped the arms of her chair as she faced Dylan. "Don't we bring more energy to the coven? Won't that make it even more dangerous?"

"We have to trust Patricia." He reached for her hand once again. "She wouldn't do this if she believed there was any other way to protect all of us. Vanessa must be stopped."

Lexi's excited giggle drifted toward them. An unintelligible grumble from Ruth soon followed. The sounds grew louder as the other coven members approached. Within a few moments, they had all joined Stevie and Dylan on the porch.

"I don't see why we had to walk." Ruth scowled. "Are you trying to kill me?"

Deborah shifted her oversized canvas bag from one hand to the other. "Walking is good for you, Ruth. It gets the blood flowing and helps with focus."

Patricia set her tote bag down and placed her hand on Stevie's shoulder. "Are you ready, honey?"

At her mother's touch, a knot formed in Stevie's throat. Without a word, she nodded and rose from her seat. She opened her door and gestured for the others to go inside.

Dylan approached Randy. "Have you had any visions today regarding Vanessa?"

"No." Randy shook his head. "Is there something specific that you're worried about?"

"Vanessa confronted us earlier, and I was able to hear her plans. She's going to be at the Maritime Museum tonight searching for the amulet."

Lexi eyes gleamed, and she laughed. "This is going to work out even better than we thought." She clasped her hands together in delight.

"My thoughts exactly." Dylan grinned.

Chapter twenty-nine

Stevie

Patricia stood in the foyer outside the entrance to the living room, issuing instructions and assigning tasks to her coven members. Stevie watched her, awestruck.

She looked regal in her black cotton dress with the amethyst crystal hanging from her neck. There was no glimmer of emotion in her eyes, no hint of concern on her face. In the bustle of activity surrounding her, she remained steadfast in her duty, resolute in her mission. Stevie found comfort in her mother's calm demeanor. Perhaps she knew what she was doing. Maybe Stevie's worries were unnecessary.

"Lexi, please clean the room for us." Patricia gestured toward the living room.

"It's clean, Mom." Stevie stole a glance at the living room just to be sure. "I just vacuumed and dusted in there yesterday."

"This is a different kind of clean." Patricia spun on her heel and walked to the kitchen. Alice, Randy, and Deborah accompanied her.

Ruth approached Dylan. "We're going to need something to sink it in. Got any ideas?"

"Yes. I'll be right back." He left the house.

Stevie watched Dylan leave, wondering what they planned to sink. Everyone was involved in some facet of the preparations except for her. She had a few foggy memories of the last time they had come together for magical work. But much of that night was still a blur to her, and she'd given up on trying to sort it all out.

She faced her formal living room and found Lexi holding a bundle of dried sage. The end of the bundle smoldered, and white smoke poured from it as Lexi walked along each wall of the room, pausing at the corners. The vapor swelled thicker and thicker until Lexi was nothing more than a dark shape within the murky haze.

"Hey, Stevie, could you open the door for me?" Lexi called.

"Uh, yeah, sure." Stevie hustled to open the front door.

"Watch this!"

Stevie watched, captivated as the white smoke swirled away from the walls of the living room. It began to concentrate in the center of the room, pooling several feet above the floor. Lexi beamed as her creation took form. The plume coalesced into a ball and throbbed like a beating heart.

Lexi pointed toward the front door. "Out!"

The thick sphere of smoke elongated into a snakelike shape and shot toward Stevie. She jumped out of its way, allowing the mysterious creature to zip past her and soar through the open doorway. It dissipated the instant it hit the cool night air.

"All clean!" Lexi rubbed her hands together. Now, just a thin tendril of smoke emanated from the bundle of dried sage. Lexi rested it on a thick clamshell, allowing it to burn itself out.

Before Stevie had a chance to close the door, Dylan returned carrying a small metal safe with a combination lock. He placed it on the hall floor, just outside of the living room, and turned to face Stevie with a soft smile.

He stroked her cheek with his fingers. "How are you holding up?"

"Despite the fact that things just keep getting weirder and weirder, I suppose I'm doing all right."

"Be ready. It's going to get even stranger before this night is done." He smiled wider, gave her a quick peck on the forehead, and walked down the hall toward the kitchen.

Deborah entered the living room carrying her overstuffed canvas bag, which she set on a chair near the doorway. Behind her, Lexi whistled as she pushed the furniture away from the center of the room and closer to the walls, leaving just one small table in the middle.

Stevie joined them in the living room and watched as Deborah removed a skein of black yarn from her bag. She tugged on the exposed end, extracted a piece about three feet long, and cut it away from the bundle. She placed the string on the table in the center of the room and returned to her bag. Next, she produced an old color photo of Vanessa, taken years before.

"I cut this out of Lexi's high school yearbook. It was the most recent picture of Vanessa I could find." Deborah laid the photo on the table. "But it'll suit our purposes just fine."

Stevie nodded as though she understood, but she wasn't sure what role the picture would play in the ritual.

Deborah removed four pillar candles of different colors from her bag and placed them on the small table while Lexi busied herself lighting the votive candles she'd scattered around the perimeter of the room. Ruth plodded in and waited near the wall as Alice delivered an ornately carved oak wand to the table.

Randy crossed the threshold with a broom in his hand. He left it propped by the doorway and then found a place to wait next to Ruth. Dylan soon joined them, carrying the small safe. He delivered it to the table and walked to Stevie's side. He stood close enough that his arm pressed against hers. Heat rose in her cheeks as she reveled in the electric sensation that came from his touch.

Patricia entered the room with a tiny burlap sack in the palm of her hand. In her other hand, she carried a black chalice filled with red wine. She placed it on the table and then stretched open the top of the sack. She tilted the small bag and poured a thin line of sea salt on the floor, casting a perfect circle that encompassed more than half of the room.

She stood in the center and met Stevie's gaze. "Honey, don't cross this salt line until I tell you to."

Patricia continued the preparations by placing the green pillar candle on the northern point of the circle. "This represents earth."

She placed the yellow one on the eastern point. "This symbolizes air."

Making her way to the southern point, she set down the red one. "Fire."

She positioned the blue candle last, on the western point. "Water."

Once the pillars were in place, all four lit at once, as if of their own accord.

Patricia took a final glance at her preparations. "We're ready."

chapter thirty

Vanessa

Vanessa planned her break-in at the Maritime Museum while lounging on a chaise on the deck of her extravagant yacht. From her location beside the outermost dock, she watched the dark night roll through Beaufort and settle on the town. There were few people on the streets now. Some had gone home for the day; others sought the company of friends in one of the local bars. Muted music carried through the cool evening air, advertising several different bands at play.

For a fleeting moment, Vanessa wondered what her life might have been like if she had chosen to stay in Beaufort. What if she hadn't remained loyal to Susan? She might have joined the coven and lived out her days in this small town, surrounded by people she'd known her entire life. It was difficult to compare such a simple existence with her current pampered reality. It didn't really matter anyway. She might have learned to live with the coven's rules, but she never could have allowed her mother's imprisonment to go unanswered.

She ran her finger along the arm of the chaise. She couldn't deny that she was motivated in part by revenge. The coven had taken her mother away from her, and they should pay for that crime. But more than that, she wanted to make her mother happy or, at least, somewhat less furious. Though they'd been apart for more than a decade, she still craved her mother's acceptance like a wolf craved raw flesh.

Susan had told her to go after the boy first, so that's what she'd done. She closed her eyes, remembering the terror on his face as the car barreled toward him.

Was it really necessary to involve him in this war?

Vanessa had no love for children, but she'd never considered hurting one before. Not seriously anyway. It had taken time for her to work up the nerve to carry out her mother's instructions. Even then, she'd struggled with the act of following through with her plan. When the car she'd set in motion stopped before it hit the boy, she hadn't been disappointed. Instead, an unexpected sensation had jolted her from her singular focus.

I was relieved.

Vanessa sighed. She had not yet told Susan about her unsuccessful attack, and she wasn't sure that she ever would.

Susan did not merely cast disapproving glances when Vanessa failed to produce what she wanted. There was no forgiveness for mistakes. A cold chill crawled up her spine at the thought of her mother's disgusted glares and hateful diatribes that had punctuated so many of her childhood memories.

Vanessa would be successful next time. She was sure of that. There was no room for mercy in this endeavor. Tonight, she would make her mother proud. For once.

Soon, she would have the necklace in her possession. Anticipation flowed through her veins, like a young child on Christmas Eve. She recalled the stories of the ancient amethyst amulet worn by the original queen of her people. With power like that, it could undo the binding spell that had crippled her mother. Once Susan's abilities returned, they would destroy the coven. Then they would be free to use their magic in any way they saw fit; no one would be able to bind their unstoppable power. She raised her chin. Her mother would be forever grateful for her efforts.

She wanted that life, and it would begin tonight.

For the last several evenings, she'd watched the activity at the Maritime Museum. There had been a flurry of media attention in the days following the discovery of Blackbeard's treasure. Now that some of the excitement had died down, most of the employees and volunteers left promptly at five o'clock, but there was one dedicated researcher who continued to stay later than the others.

He'll be easy enough to take care of.

The security measures in place at the museum wouldn't be a problem either. The town police drove by the building at regular intervals every night, and she'd already figured out their schedule. She anticipated no trouble overcoming the electronic alarm system or working around the armed guard who monitored the video cameras. A creature of habit, the guard left his post for a short dinner break every night at nine o'clock. Vanessa would time her entrance between the predictable police drive-bys and the guard's nightly cheeseburger run.

That was what passed for tight security in a small town with a nearly nonexistent crime rate. They might as well have sent Vanessa an engraved invitation asking her to stop by and take whatever she wanted.

chapter thirty-one

Stevie

At this time, I ask that you all lower your shields so that we may put our full focus on the task at hand." Inside the circle, Patricia held her chin high and her shoulders square.

Dylan bristled.

Stevie gave his hand a squeeze. "Are you okay?"

He leaned in close to her ear. "I'll be fine." He kept his voice low. "It's just that I enjoyed the quiet that came with being around people who could block my ability. When everyone lowered their mental shields, it got real loud for me." He tapped his temple. "In here."

"Oh." Stevie imagined the cacophony of thoughts he must be enduring at the moment. *What's that like?*

He heard her unspoken question and gave a slight nod toward Ruth. "She's wondering if it's too much to eat shrimp and grits for both lunch *and* dinner." He chuckled. "And she's already decided that it's perfectly acceptable."

Stevie considered Ruth's mundane ruminations and imagined that multiplied across all eight of the coven members. *That must be awful.*

Dylan waved away her concern. "It'll only last for a few minutes. I'll be fine. Once we join together in a shared intention, we'll all be thinking the same thing."

His grin faded. "Randy is worried for Patricia. Throughout history, our queens have made sacrifices for their people. He knows Patricia is no exception. But if something goes wrong tonight, he's ready to jump in and save her."

Stevie glanced at her mother and raised a hand to her chest.

He kept his lips to her ear. "You are a bundle of nerves. I can hear it all." He stroked her back. "You're going to have to let those worries go so you can focus."

Easier said than done.

Patricia cleared her throat. "The spell we cast tonight is the most powerful magic we will ever use. We do not take this process lightly. However, it has become necessary given the threat posed by Vanessa."

All eyes focused on Patricia.

"As you enter this circle, come with perfect trust. Know that the work we do now is for the benefit of all." Patricia lifted the carved wooden wand and walked toward the salt line. She bent down, touched the wand to the floor, and raised it up in a straight line above her own head. Drawing an invisible doorway, she moved the wand to the right before bringing it back down to touch the floor again.

Each member of the coven filed in, one by one. They formed a circle of their own within the confines of the salt line. Stevie entered last, and Patricia sealed the door by reversing her earlier movements with the wand.

Patricia returned her wand to the small table and lifted the black chalice filled with red wine. "Our goal tonight is clear. We will render Vanessa powerless for the sake of protecting our people." She took a sip from the cup and raised it high. "Drink with me from this cup so that we all may share the same intention."

The witches stood silent and somber in the candlelit room. They passed the chalice around the circle, taking sips of wine to secure their focus. Stevie's breath caught as she awaited her turn.

Dylan passed the cup to her, and she took a sip before handing it to Lexi. Her shoulders dropped as her worries dissipated. She had no doubt the wine had helped to hasten her relaxation. *Magic.*

She did not fight it.

Her breaths came deep and even as her focus narrowed. She envisioned Vanessa. A weak and powerless Vanessa.

chapter thirty-two

Vanessa

Vanessa strolled toward the rear entrance of the Maritime Museum, confident that the dark blanket of the moonless night kept her hidden from view. Of course, if anyone did happen to notice her, she knew how to deal with that. She smirked. *This heist will be a breeze.*

As she approached the door, she caught a glimpse of the security camera. She focused her energy on the lens, and in a flash, it shattered to pieces.

She stood outside the thick steel door, studying the electronic keypad above the knob. Rather than touch the buttons, she held her hand a few inches away, curved as though she were holding the dial of an old-fashioned combination lock. She twisted her hand to the right, then to the left, and back to the right. A green light flashed on the keypad. She opened the door and slipped inside, unseen.

Stepping forward, she entered a narrow hallway and faced another door with its own electronic keypad in place. She disarmed that alarm and opened the door to the lab.

White cabinets and drawers flanked each wall. A high counter in the back held various pieces of equipment and a laptop. Glass bottles filled with colorful solutions stood in a tidy row beneath the cabinets. All of it meaningless. She glanced around the lab in search of Blackbeard's treasure.

Vanessa spotted an array of artifacts on one of the stainless steel tables in the middle of the room. Her pulse quickened, and she strode straight to it, eager to get a closer look. She blinked, imagining the look on her mother's face when she presented her with the powerful amulet. She'd never been so close to making Susan proud.

She studied the items spread out on the worktable in front of her.

Freshly cleaned coins gleamed under the bright lights of the lab. An ornate gilded buckle and a silver mug sat next to a piece of black velvet dotted with what appeared to be tiny flecks of gold. A snuffbox inlaid with mother-of-pearl occupied the corner of the table.

Pretty, but not what she was looking for. She hadn't come to admire the acquisitions of a long-dead pirate. Her gaze shifted to the right-hand side of the table.

She ran her fingers along a small collection of jewelry. Bypassing the rings, she focused on the necklaces. There was one long chain of gold beads and, next to it, a shorter chain with a locket, but neither matched the description of Lucia's necklace. She turned back to the snuffbox and raised its delicate lid. *Empty.* She threw it down on the table.

She whirled around, seeking more artifacts. *This can't be all of it.* Surrounded by empty tables and pristine counters, she blinked and shook her head.

Again, she scanned the items on the first table as if the amulet might appear if she only looked more carefully. The proud mother she'd imagined began to fade away. The beaming smile that Vanessa had expected to see twisted into the disgusted glare she knew all too well.

"No, no, no! It has to be here." She slammed her hands down on the table, rattling the artifacts.

"Who the hell are you?" A deep voice demanded from behind her.

Vanessa spun to find a middle-aged man with red hair and a freckled face standing in the doorway. The researcher.

Her frustration transformed into rage. "Where is it?" She glared at him, fists clenched.

Chapter thirty-three

Stevie

Patricia placed the empty chalice on the table in the center of the salt circle. She raised the old photograph of Vanessa, holding it so that each member of the coven could see it.

She picked up the piece of black yarn and began to wrap it around the picture. "Your evil will not harm me. As I will, so shall it be."

Patricia passed the picture and the yarn to Deborah, who continued the spell. Each witch repeated Patricia's words and actions until the picture traveled all the way around the circle. When the black yarn completely covered the photograph, Patricia held it above her head and began to recite the rest of the spell.

> We banish you of this power,
> Right now, in this hour,
> We cast this spell to harm none,
> Our magic today cannot be undone.

The rest of the coven joined her and recited the spell three times in unison. Their energies converged, pulled together by an unseen force.

The initial tingle of energy began in Stevie's hands, but it soon coursed throughout her entire being. She remembered Vanessa, the silver car, and the terror on Charlie's face. For a fleeting second, the electric sensation within her burned hot like fire. Gripped with pain, she stiffened and forced her energy toward the center of the circle with all her might.

A surge of brilliant white light escaped from her body. It floated to the center of the circle, merging with the light generated by each of the other coven members and surged toward her mother.

Patricia continued to hold the photograph as she stood inside the rounded mass of energy, her own powerful magic converging with that of the others. She maintained her position until the light dimmed and went dark.

Without the aid of human hands, the lid of the old safe popped open. Solemn, Patricia placed the bound photograph inside. Once the lid slammed shut, the combination dial spun clockwise, locking the safe.

Patricia raised her chin. "It is done."

"It is done," the coven echoed in unison.

No one spoke for a moment as each recovered from the massive energy output. Stevie now understood the depth and strength of the magic involved in this process. And she could see why no one wanted to impose a sentence like this on one of their own kind.

Patricia walked once again to the edge of the salt circle and, using her wand, unsealed the invisible door so that the coven could exit through it. In silence, they filed out. Patricia was the last to leave, and as she crossed the magical threshold, the symbolic pillar candles extinguished themselves.

Stevie rubbed her hands together, satisfied and relieved. *We did it. It's over.* She blinked, trying to adjust her eyes to the scant light provided by the remaining votive candles.

A loud thud shattered the silence.

Stevie gasped and raced through the darkness to hit the switch on the wall. As light filled the room, she spun around to find her mother on the floor.

She clasped her hand over her mouth. Patricia had fallen on her side. Her eyes were closed, and all color had drained from her face, leaving behind a ghostly pallor.

Randy rushed to Patricia's side. Stevie joined him, following with rapid, unsteady steps.

She knelt down and placed a trembling hand on her mother's shoulder. "Mom?" Patricia did not respond. Stevie glanced at Randy. "Is she…" She could not finish her question.

Randy's brow furrowed as he checked Patricia's pulse. Without a word, he moved his hand to her forehead and held it there.

An eternity passed while Stevie waited for Randy work his magic. She held her breath.

"She's going to be okay. I think she just fainted." Randy pulled his hand away from Patricia. "She'll come around in a minute."

Dylan came to Stevie's side and wrapped his arm around her shoulder. She leaned into him and released the breath she'd been holding, but she could not bring herself to look away from her mother.

Patricia let out a low moan and slowly opened her eyes. She smiled at Randy and then she met her daughter's worried gaze. "I'm all right, honey."

Dylan knelt down beside Randy. "Is it okay if I lift her? I think she would be more comfortable on the sofa."

Patricia shook her head. "That won't be necessary. I'm really okay. I could use some help standing up though."

Dylan helped Patricia to her feet but stayed close by, his arms poised to catch her if she became unsteady. She waved with more assurances that she was fine.

Patricia cleared her throat and held her chin high, as if nothing had happened. "Okay, everyone, let's finish up here."

Randy went to work sweeping up the salt, and Lexi blew out the votive candles. The rest of the coven gathered near the doorway of the living room.

Patricia placed a hand on Dylan's shoulder. "Will you drop the safe in Taylor's Creek for us?"

"Of course. But first, if you don't mind, I've got a quick phone call to make." He retrieved his phone and dialed a number. "I'd like to report a break-in at the Maritime Museum," He winked at Stevie, a mischievous sparkle dancing in his eyes.

Lexi grinned and threw her arm around Stevie. "Want to go with me to watch her get busted?"

"Sure." While Stevie would enjoy the sight of Vanessa in handcuffs, more than anything, she wanted to make certain that the ritual had been successful.

Lexi turned to Ruth. "Would you like to come with us?"

"You go on ahead without me." She yawned and muttered curses under her breath. "I'm getting too old for this shit."

Chapter thirty-four

Vanessa

The heat rose in Vanessa's cheeks. "Where is it?"

"Who are you?" The researcher cocked his head. "What are you doing in here?"

"Tell me where the amethyst is." She tapped her long fingernail on the stainless steel worktable.

He shook his head. "I don't know what you're talking about. You need to leave. *Now*." He pointed at the door.

His lack of fear perplexed her. *He doesn't know who he's dealing with.*

"Where is the rest of the treasure?" Vanessa hissed through gritted teeth.

"This is all of it." He gestured toward the artifacts she had already examined. "There is no amethyst."

Vanessa spun around to face the trifling items again. They were all meaningless to her. Overcome with a blind rage, she gripped the edge of the table and tossed it onto its side. Coins and rings crashed down, scattering across the floor of the lab. The silver mug clinked twice on the cold, tile floor before falling still.

"Are you crazy?" The researcher lurched forward, his face flushed. "Get out of here!"

Vanessa stalked toward him. "You *will* tell me the truth."

Still several feet away from him, she raised her hand, her fingers bent as though she were clutching his neck. She drew on her energy and used it to squeeze his throat from a distance. One way or another, she *would* have that necklace tonight.

The man stared at Vanessa, baffled.

She continued to stalk toward him, clenching her outstretched hand tighter and tighter.

He did not raise his hand to his neck or gasp for air. He only stood there, watching her.

She searched her body for the familiar electric sensation, but her energy refused to cooperate with her will.

It can't be. She stared at the palms of her hands. Her magic was gone. She drew in a jagged breath. Not only did she not have the necklace, but now she was powerless.

"No!" Vanessa wailed as the realization set in.

With an all-encompassing fury, she stormed around the room and overturned the remaining tables. She raced to the counter and swept the collection of liquid filled bottles to the floor. Unfazed by the shattered glass and chemical concoctions that splattered at her feet, she turned to the researcher. *Someone has to pay for this.*

"Beaufort Police!" a man's voice boomed from the doorway behind her.

Vanessa stopped cold. She whirled around to see six uniformed officers stampeding into the room. Every one of them held a gun pointed at her.

Chapter thirty-five

Stevie

By the time Stevie, Dylan, and Lexi reached the Maritime Museum, three police cruisers had already arrived with sirens blaring. Their spinning red and blue lights cut through the night and flashed on the small crowd that had begun to gather on the other side of the street.

"She won't be in jail forever." Stevie crossed her arms while they waited for the police to bring Vanessa out.

Dylan gave a slight nod. "True, but it will give her time to cool off. I'd bet she's more than a little angry at us right now."

"She'll still be powerless when they finally let her out." Lexi grinned. "She's no threat to us anymore."

They watched as Vanessa exited the building in handcuffs, flanked by two officers who led her to a waiting police car. Her wild eyes pierced through the dark night until her venomous glare locked on them.

Stevie could not take her eyes off Vanessa. The woman who'd tried to kill her son was now in handcuffs and rendered harmless. She drew in a deep, even breath. With any luck, the dark witch would stay locked away for a long stretch. When her gaze settled on Vanessa's hate-filled stare, she couldn't help but smile, just a little.

After Dylan loaded the small safe onto his speedboat, he extended his hand to Stevie. She accepted it with a grateful nod and boarded the sleek vessel.

She pointed to the key already in the ignition. "You just leave your key there? What if someone decides to steal your boat?"

Dylan chuckled. "It wouldn't be hard for me to figure out who stole it. Besides, this is Beaufort. The crime rate is pretty low."

"I wouldn't be so sure about that. There was a break-in at the Maritime Museum, you know." Stevie grinned as she took a seat on the passenger's side.

Dylan untied the boat and twisted the key. He brought the powerful motor to life and eased away from the quiet waterfront, coasting through the dark water of Taylor's Creek.

Stevie scanned the area. There were no other boats out at the late hour, so they were free to go wherever they wanted without fear of encountering anyone else. "How far out should we drop the safe?"

"If we go too far out, we run the risk of it showing up on a fishing radar or a diver finding it. So, we'll keep it close." Dylan kept his gaze fixed on the black water.

Stevie sunk back into her chair and raised her head, looking skyward. "Is it really over?"

"Yes. You and Charlie are safe now." Dylan patted her knee. "When Vanessa is released from jail, I'll make sure she leaves town."

Stevie sighed with relief. "As happy as I am that she's no longer a threat, I have to admit I'll miss having you as a bodyguard." She gave him a sidelong glance and grinned.

"I should probably stay over again tonight." His voice was thick with mock concern. "You know, just to be on the safe side." He gave her a wink.

"Good idea. Better to be safe than sorry, right?" Stevie giggled.

When they reached the middle of Taylor's Creek, Dylan eased off the accelerator and let the boat drift. "This looks like a good spot to me."

He rose from his seat, lifted the heavy safe with ease, and dropped it over the side of the boat. Filled with the dark magic that once belonged to Vanessa, it plummeted to the sandy bottom of the channel.

chapter thirty-six

Susan

Susan sat on the worn couch in the ward's day room. She had heard nothing from Vanessa in several days, though she was sure her daughter should have retrieved the necklace by now. She changed the channel on the television to catch the local Sunday morning news and waited with growing annoyance as the commercials droned on.

A blond woman with a stiff hairstyle appeared on the television. She zipped through a short list of upcoming, unimportant reports before promising that the meteorologist would soon be on to discuss the approaching tropical storm. Susan rolled her eyes. She couldn't care less about that storm.

The newscaster transitioned to a breaking story out of Beaufort. A picture of the Maritime Museum appeared on the screen. Susan leaned forward, awaiting the details.

"The town of Beaufort is still reeling from the news that a break-in occurred at the Maritime Museum last night. The target of the attempted robbery was the newly recovered treasure found near Blackbeard's sunken flagship, the *Queen Anne's Revenge*."

A mug shot of Vanessa filled the screen. Susan sat, motionless, with her mouth hanging open. The woman in the televised photo bore little resemblance to the glamorous beauty she knew. Vanessa's bold green eyes were bloodshot, and smears of mascara blackened her face.

"Vanessa Moore, a native of Beaufort, is the only suspect in the crime. She was arrested at the scene late last night," the newscaster continued.

The town police chief appeared on the screen next, his eyes bright with excitement. "We still don't know how she managed to disable the security system at the museum, but I can assure you we will find out. This won't happen again." He looked into the camera. "We don't tolerate this kind of nonsense in our town. And we expect to see the perpetrator prosecuted to the fullest extent of the law."

Susan closed her gaping mouth and blinked. Only one event would explain her daughter's capture. The coven had gained enough strength to disable Vanessa as well. They'd bound her daughter's powers, just as they had bound hers so many years ago.

She fell back against the lumpy cushions of the worn couch and clenched her teeth. Vanessa had failed her. She'd blown her only opportunity of escape, along with any chance of recovering her magic. Now, she'd have to spend the rest of her life powerless, rotting away in an institution.

"Susan." The perky nurse approached, carrying a tiny paper pill cup. With a cheery smile, she waved it as though she were offering a martini. "It's time for your medicine."

Without a word, Susan extended her hand to accept the pills. She raised the paper cup to her lips and threw her head back with a sharp jerk. Instead of tucking the medications under her tongue, she swallowed them. All of them.

Chapter thirty-seven

Stevie

Stevie and Dylan sat on the edge of her dock with their feet dangling just above the water. A cool breeze flowed across the calm surface of Taylor's Creek, carrying a hint of autumn with it, but the warmth of the bright midday sun kept the chill at bay. The sky was cloudless in spite of the tropical storm churning off the coast.

Stevie swung her legs back and forth. "Have you seen the forecast?"

Dylan nodded. "Yeah, looks like it will make landfall here."

"It's not a real hurricane." Stevie gave a nonchalant wave of her hand. "We'll just get a little wind and rain. No big deal."

Without further discussion, they watched as boats of all sizes navigated the channel in front of them. Some were returning from the sea after early-morning fishing expeditions, and others carried families on outings to the pristine barrier islands. A group of kayakers coasted by, leaving Carrot Island in search of another adventure elsewhere.

"We've gone about this all wrong, you know." Dylan broke their comfortable silence.

Stevie dipped her chin and gave him a sideways glance. "What do you mean?"

"I'd like to take you out to dinner." His eyes twinkled.

"Like a date?" She gulped.

Dylan nodded. "Yeah. A date."

Stevie raked her hands through her hair as she decided how to best respond. She hadn't been divorced for long. Was it too soon to start dating? "I'm not sure that I'm ready for that yet."

Dylan tilted his head but did not speak.

"It's just that everyone knows me here, and they know me as Sam's wife." Her gaze dropped to the water. "It's a small town. People talk. I haven't dated since the divorce."

"I see." He watched a shrimp boat pass by. "You know, I understand exactly what it's like to live in a fishbowl."

"Yeah, but London is a huge city." Stevie faced him. "You don't know everyone there."

"True. But they know me. I'm hounded by the paparazzi just about every time I go out."

"Paparazzi? Oh, come on! Really?" Stevie raised her eyebrows as she imagined her lifelong friend passing through a sea of chaotic camera flashes. She knew he'd been successful, but she had no idea he'd attained celebrity status in his time away from Beaufort.

"I'm actually more anonymous here than I am in London. Being back home has been a nice change of pace for me."

She cringed. "I don't think I could live like that."

"You already do, though it's a little less flashy and aggressive here." Dylan looked into her eyes. "Are you really worried about what everyone will think, or are you worried about Sam?"

She glanced away, unable to face him. "I—uh—I'm not sure."

"Are you still in love with him?"

"Yes. I mean, n—no!" The heat rose in her cheeks. "I mean—I don't think that I'm in love with him anymore, but I can't deny that there is still an attachment there." She heaved a great sigh. "It's complicated, I guess."

Dylan remained quiet for a moment. "If you want to go back to him, I won't stand in your way."

"It's not that." Stevie bit her lip as she struggled to find the right words. "We were a family once. I think that's the part I'm having trouble letting go of."

"If you're not still in love with him, then it sounds to me like it's time to consider moving on with your life. Maybe you shouldn't worry so much about what everyone else thinks." He took her hand in his. "Besides, you need to give people a little bit of credit. Do you really think anyone is going to care if you go out on a date?"

"Sam will."

Dylan's lips pressed into a tight line. "I don't think there's anything we can do about that."

Stevie turned back to the water and closed her eyes. Though their split was legal and final, truly letting go of Sam posed another challenge altogether. She'd managed to avoid thinking about it, until now. She could move on with her life...move on with Dylan. But she couldn't bring herself to say it out loud. Not until she was sure.

Dylan's phone rang, and he released Stevie's hand to answer it. "I'm sorry." He glanced at the screen. "I have to take this."

"Go ahead." She welcomed the interruption.

Dylan pressed the speaker button. "Hello." He placed the phone on the dock between them so both he and Stevie could hear.

"Yeah, uh, hey, man. This is Officer Bobby Chadwick down at the jail." The young officer spoke with a thick High Tider brogue, a remnant of Elizabethan English still prevalent in the surrounding island communities.

"Thanks for calling me back." Dylan scratched his chin. "What's happening with Vanessa Moore?"

"She sure is somethin'!" Bobby's voice rose up from the speaker. "Been in here since last night and hasn't said a word to anyone except her lawyer."

"Do you know when she'll be arraigned?" Dylan stared down at his phone.

"She's scheduled to go before the judge in the mornin'."

"What has she been charged with?"

"Right now, she's got felony breakin' and enterin', but I wouldn't expect that one to stick since she's all lawyered up now. He might could get it down to misdemeanor trespass since she didn't actually steal anything."

"I see." Dylan frowned.

"Now, if she gets one of our local judges, he might take the offense more seriously. She could get some jail time." Bobby paused. "But if she gets one of them dingbatters—well, then she might get away with just a fine."

Stevie grinned when she heard the word "dingbatters." It was not a compliment.

"Be careful with her." Dylan leaned closer to his phone. "She might try to manipulate you. She'll be desperate to get out of that jail."

Bobby chuckled. "Don't worry about me. I've seen it all. I can handle anything she tries to pull."

"I'm glad to hear that. Thanks for the update, Bobby."

"Yep."

Dylan sighed as he returned his phone to his pocket.

"How long do you think they'll keep her locked up?" Stevie watched a seagull soar overhead.

"Probably not long. We'll know more after she sees the judge in the morning." Dylan's jaw tightened. "I'll be there as well, just in case they set her free."

"We knew they wouldn't keep her forever." She glanced at her watch. "I guess I should get back. Charlie will be home soon."

"I'll walk with you." Dylan stood and offered his hand to help her up.

They strolled back up the dock toward Front Street. Stevie's shoulders stiffened as she saw Sam's pickup truck come into view and park in front of her house. "Oh no, they're early!"

"Right now, we're just two old friends walking together. You don't have to tell him anything more than that for my benefit."

As they stepped into the street, Sam turned in their direction. His sunny smile disappeared as he emerged from his truck.

A knot twisted in Stevie's stomach. "Hi, Sam." She waved, resisting the urge to announce that she was just out for a walk with an old friend. *Nothing to see here. Nothing to label.*

"Hey." He slammed the door to his truck and folded his arms across his chest.

"Do you remember Dylan Kent from school?" She gestured toward Dylan in the most casual manner she could muster.

Sam's jealous glare was so intense, Stevie suspected she could read his mind as well as Dylan could.

"Yeah, I remember you." Sam thrust his chin up. "Don't you live in Europe or something now?"

Dylan relaxed his arms at his sides. "London, actually."

"When are you going back?"

"I haven't made plans to return yet." Dylan shrugged.

Charlie waited in the truck, playing a game on his tablet while the three adults suffered through an excruciating stretch of silence.

Dylan glanced at Stevie. "Guess I'll see you around." Before he left, he nodded in Sam's direction. "It's good to see you again."

Sam's face darkened as he watched Dylan return to his home. "He lives next door, huh? Well, I guess that's convenient."

Stevie pretended not to hear his remark as she turned her attention to Charlie. Sam lifted him out of the truck and placed him on the grass near the curb.

"I missed you so much, Charlie. Did you have a fun weekend?" Not expecting an answer, she spread her arms wide to offer him a hug.

Charlie dipped his chin down to his chest and raised it back up.

Stevie froze, afraid to speak or move for fear the magic of the moment would disappear forever. Did he really just nod his head?

Sam broke the silence. "Did you see that?"

Stevie, still at a loss for words, continued to focus her unblinking gaze on Charlie.

"Charlie, did you have a fun weekend?" Sam echoed Stevie's question.

Charlie repeated the motion. This time, Stevie could not doubt her perception. He'd nodded his head in reply. Something he'd never done before. It was communication. It was progress.

"He nodded!" Sam wrapped his arms around Stevie, lifted her off the ground, and twirled her in unabashed excitement.

"He did." Stevie untangled herself and dropped to her knees to hug her son. "He really did."

Chapter thirty-eight

Stevie

Stevie woke early on Monday morning with a new concern gnawing at her. Today, Charlie would spend at least part of his day in a regular classroom. There was no way to predict how he would handle the new arrangement. She was both excited that Charlie might have a more normal school experience and terrified that it might not work out for him. As much as she hated having him in the separate special education classroom, she could not deny that it provided a certain safety net for him.

She padded across the hall to check on Charlie, who was still sound asleep in the dark room. Tiptoeing closer to his bed, she reveled in the peaceful sight of her son at rest. He had no anxiety now. No worries, no fear. There was nothing that made him different from any other boy. When Charlie slept, they both enjoyed a much needed break from autism.

Stevie leaned over his bed, wanting to stroke his face or touch the soft blond curls that lay on his pillow. She decided against it, knowing her touch would wake him, and let him sleep for a while longer.

She began to walk back toward the door, and her bare foot landed on an unexpected Lincoln Log. Stevie clasped her hand over her mouth to keep from yelping out in pain.

Her eyes had adjusted to the lack of light in the bedroom, and she scanned the floor for other potential hazards. There were a handful of small logs scattered around the wooden floor and several toy cars that Charlie had lined up neatly in a row near the center of the room.

She continued to creep toward the door when an idea occurred to her. She spun around to look again at the out-of-place toys. A broad smile lit up her face as she glanced back at Charlie to make sure he was still sleeping.

She drew on her energy, allowing the electric surge to course through her body. Focusing on the Lincoln Log closest to her, she raised it up from the floor and floated it across the room where it landed in the toy bin without a sound. She continued the same process with the other toys until the room was tidy once more. With her hands on her hips, she held her chin high. Charlie's room was now clean, and she hadn't even had her first cup of coffee yet.

Stevie held Charlie's hand as they crossed the busy school parking lot. When they reached the front door, they found Lexi waiting for them. She beamed with excitement as she greeted them.

"Hi, guys!" Lexi waved.

Stevie raised her eyebrows. "What are you doing here?"

"I finished the classroom mural, and I wanted to be with you when you saw it for the first time." She bounced up on the balls of her feet.

Lexi joined them as they made their way to the special education classroom. There, they found the other four students standing in front of the new wall-sized mural. None were engaged in any of the unusual behaviors Stevie had witnessed before. Captivated by Lexi's artwork, they all stood in peaceful stillness, studying the art. Sherri, the teacher, grinned at the spectacle.

Stevie and Charlie approached the painted wall to get a better look. It was a perfect rendering of Carrot Island at sunset. Lexi had captured the pristine, natural beauty of the small island in soft shades of tan and green. In the foreground, a fishing boat entered the calm blue water of Taylor's Creek, coming home after a long day at sea. In the background, three wild horses walked along the island shore.

It was similar to Lexi's other paintings, but Stevie felt was drawn to this one more than any other she'd seen. She pressed her hand against her chest. "This is beautiful."

Charlie stepped closer. As if unable to resist the pull of the picture, he put both palms on the island's shoreline.

Sherri approached Stevie. "I'm not sure how I'll get everyone back to work, but it's worth it to see them all so calm and happy." She turned to Lexi. "You have an extraordinary gift. Thank you."

Hearing the word "gift," Stevie understood why the children were so affected by the mural.

She leaned over to Lexi. "Did you put a spell on it?"

Lexi just grinned in reply and flitted to her bag, which rested on the floor near the door. She pulled out a thin, paper-sized canvas with the same picture on it.

She carried it over to Charlie, who was still staring at the mural. "I understand that you'll be in a different classroom today. I'd like you to have this copy." She held the canvas out to him. "You can keep it in your backpack and look at it when you're feeling yucky."

Stevie watched, awestruck, as Lexi interacted with Charlie. She understood him so much better than most people, and her gift would surely help him through the transition to the regular classroom.

Charlie reached out to accept the small canvas. His eyes flicked up to meet Lexi's, and a smile tugged at the corners of his mouth. He slipped the picture into his backpack.

Stevie blinked back the grateful tears that welled in her eyes. A nod, a smile, fleeting eye contact—all unimportant things for the average child—but for Charlie, they were triumphs of immeasurable importance.

The teacher's assistant ushered the children back to the tables to begin the school day. Though the magic of the mural had not cured any of the children, they were all much more at ease than Stevie had seen them before.

Stevie hugged Lexi. "Thank you."

"Charlie, I think it's time for us to go meet your new teacher. She's very excited to have you in her class." Sherri squatted down to Charlie's eye level, though he did not look up from his tablet to meet her gaze. "Remember, if you need a break, you can come back here for a while if you want to." She took his hand and led him out the door.

Lexi and Stevie followed them a few doors down the hall to a kindergarten classroom. They waited outside the door until Charlie's new teacher, a middle-aged woman with cropped chestnut-brown hair, noticed them.

She greeted them and then bent down to Charlie's level to introduce herself. "Hi. My name is Mrs. Garner. I'm your new kindergarten teacher, and I'm very happy to meet you."

Stevie caught Charlie peering into the classroom, watching the activity of the other students. One corner of the room was set up like a play kitchen, with several children standing nearby giggling as they prepared pretend food. Another corner of the room housed three stocked bookshelves. There, one girl sat on a shaggy rug, absorbed in a picture book. Other children were scattered among the small tables drawing with crayons.

There were many more children in this classroom than the one he had just come from. With more students came a lot more movement and chatter. Stevie held her breath, awaiting her son's reaction.

Charlie took a hesitant step back from the door, shoulders rigid. Stevie glanced back into the classroom. To her, twenty small children playing in relative quiet was an impressive sight. But she knew for Charlie it was chaos.

"I should get back to my class." Sherri stepped away from them. "Let me know if you need anything."

Mrs. Garner spoke to Charlie again. "Whenever you need a break, just show me this picture, and I'll take you back to Miss Sherri's class." She handed him a laminated photo of the special education classroom. "Now, you can go explore the room if you like."

Stevie knelt down to give Charlie a quick hug. "Don't forget the picture Lexi gave you. It will help." She smiled to mask her own apprehension. "I'll be here to pick you up right after school."

She watched him enter the classroom and head straight for the bookshelves. He took a seat on the floor next to a little girl with ebony hair and enormous brown eyes. Charlie did not respond as the girl chatted away. Instead, he pulled Lexi's painting out of his backpack and stared at it for a moment. His shoulders relaxed, and he selected a familiar book from the shelf and began to read.

"My other students will be happy to have Charlie in the class. Kids this age have no prejudices." Mrs. Garner nodded toward the room. "The girls are especially social and tend to be very helpful when they notice someone having a difficult time."

Lexi clasped her hands together. "I think he's doing well."

"He is." Mrs. Garner smiled as she faced Stevie. "My son has autism too. He's grown now, but I understand what you're going through." She paused for a moment, tilting her head. "It seems we have something else in common too."

Lexi put her hand on Stevie's shoulder. "She's new."

Stevie paused, taking a moment to catch up. "Oh, right—that." She nodded. "Yep, I'm new."

"Well, welcome to the club!"

Lexi linked arms with Stevie. "We should probably get going and let Charlie get settled in."

Stevie cast a glance back at Charlie, in the regular classroom, with all those other kids. She couldn't leave him yet.

Mrs. Garner spoke in a mock conspiratorial whisper. "Would you like for me to call you after school and let you know how his day was?"

"Would you?" Stevie leaned in, wide-eyed. "Oh, that would be fantastic. Thank you so much."

"It's no trouble. Remember, I get it." Mrs. Garner winked.

Stevie exhaled as relief washed over her. She hadn't realized how tense she'd been until her muscles began to relax. A renewed sense of hope eased into her heart. It was a fragile yet precious gift that brought with it a delicate bliss. Her eyes glistened as she stole one more glance at her son before leaving.

Chapter thirty-nine

Vanessa

Vanessa's attorney had brought a suit for her court appearance on Monday. It was simple and modest, nothing at all like the sexy, form-fitting dresses she preferred. She slipped into the structured navy blue skirt and matching jacket and glanced down, taking in the sight of herself in the atrocious outfit. Her curves had vanished beneath the heavy, lined fabric. She cast a wary glance at the plain, low heels he'd selected for her and shook her head.

It was agonizing enough to have to suffer through the loss of her powers, sentenced to live out her days as a flightless bird. The additional insult of spending two nights in the Carteret County Jail had been almost more than she could bear. And now, to endure the humiliation of not only appearing in court but also going in looking like this...

She crammed her feet into the ugly shoes and stomped across the concrete floor of her cell, consumed with hatred for the coven. They had destroyed her, broken her into a million little pieces. And yet they paraded around town as if they were righteous and chosen. Why should she have to follow their rules? Why were they above reproach?

Her attorney had assured her that she would be free today. He'd been confident that her punishment would consist only of a hefty fine and perhaps restitution for the damage she'd caused, both of which she was prepared to pay. If he were somehow unable to get the charge lowered to a misdemeanor, she would be allowed out on bail while awaiting trial. Either way, Vanessa intended to leave Beaufort today.

But she wanted to do it without attending the hearing.

She continued her furious pacing across the short length of her cage, considering her limited options. Between the frumpy suit and the lack of sleep, she didn't feel very seductive, but she could put on an act if she had to. The coven had not stolen all of her gifts. In fact, she possessed a unique skill set that had nothing to do with magic at all. She smirked. It was worth a try.

Vanessa waited for what seemed like hours for an officer to come to take her to the courtroom. When one stopped at her cell, she studied him. She'd seen him before.

He was younger than she was. Naïve, perhaps? His youth and lack of a wedding band set him apart from her usual targets, but that wouldn't stop her.

He stepped toward her door. "It's time for your court appearance, Ms. Moore."

She smiled as she approached the bars that stood between them. His gaze slipped to her hips, which she swayed back and forth as she walked. Surely, he knew she was out of her element here, nothing at all like the usual array of drunks, thieves, and hookers that he usually encountered in the jail.

"Hello." Vanessa watched him push his key into the lock as though it were the most fascinating thing she'd ever witnessed.

"Ma'am, it's gettin' close to time for your arraignment hearing," He swung the cell door open. "I'm gonna take you on over to the courthouse now."

"What's your name?" She slid her finger along one of the steel bars, holding his gaze.

He tapped his nametag. "Bobby Chadwick." He said his full name as though it were one word instead of two.

"Bobby." She slinked closer to him. "I would do *anything* to get out of this mess."

He held onto the open door and stared down at his feet for a long moment. Wide-eyed, he looked up to face her. "Anything?"

"Absolutely." She licked her lips.

Bobby scratched his head. "Well then, I reckon you can make it through your arraignment with that kind of determination."

Undeterred, Vanessa continued her coy act. "I think you know what I mean."

He gave a deep nod. "Yes, ma'am, I do know what you mean. My mama warned me about women like you." He wagged his finger at her. "You're one of them cougars, right?"

"Cougar!" Vanessa reeled back as though he'd slapped her.

"Yeah. You're the *older* woman, and I'm the *younger* man." Bobby pointed to Vanessa and then himself as if to eliminate any confusion on the topic.

"I know what a cougar is, you idiot!"

"I reckon you do, ma'am." Bobby stifled a chuckle.

Vanessa dug her nails into her palms, tightening her fists. She couldn't a recall a time when a man had ever rejected her advances. She certainly had not expected it from this bumpkin.

"I'm sorry, ma'am. I didn't mean to offend you." He dipped his head in a deep nod. "My mama also told me it was proper to always respect my *elders.*"

Vanessa growled through clenched teeth. "Just stop talking."

An amused grin stretched across the officer's face as he removed the handcuffs from his belt. "Let's get these bracelets on you so we can go. You don't want to be late for court."

The proceedings went as Vanessa's attorney had said they would. She was free to leave after paying restitution and a fine for misdemeanor trespassing.

Vanessa could have walked the few blocks back to her yacht, but she opted to call for a taxi instead. She didn't want to be seen in that awful suit by any more people than were absolutely necessary. When the taxi reached the dock, she tossed a handful of cash to the driver and hustled toward her boat.

After she stripped out of the suit and left it in a heap on the floor, she took a long shower, washing away the filth of the jail and the rejection of the young officer.

Wearing a more flattering dress and high heels, Vanessa prepared to get as far away from Beaufort as possible. She would figure out what to do with the yacht later. She grabbed her black leather bag and left the cabin.

But when she stepped outside, she froze. Dylan stood on the deck with his arms crossed, waiting for her.

"Going somewhere?" Dylan's voice oozed sarcasm.

Vanessa curled her lips into a sneer. "I'm leaving."

"Good. I'm here to make sure you do that."

Attempting to ignore her unwelcome visitor, she tightened her grip on her bag and began to walk toward the dock with quick, purposeful steps. How dare he show up here? After all they'd put her through. The heat of seething anger flushed through her entire body. She stopped, midstride, unable to contain her wrath.

She spun around to face Dylan. "Are you satisfied now? You and that coven of yours have destroyed me as well as my mother." She stalked toward him. "You all think you're so much better than the rest of us, but look at what you have done."

"You and Susan destroyed yourselves." Dylan snorted in disgust. "Are you complaining because we protected ourselves, or are you upset that we let you live?"

"There is no reason to live now. Not like this."

"I would be more than happy to end your miserable existence for you."

"You can't do anything to me." Vanessa shook her head "You are bound by the laws of that ridiculous coven."

"The rules keep us from turning into monsters like you and your mother." He let his arms drop to his sides. "Besides, I rather like the idea of you suffering for the rest of your life."

Vanessa averted her gaze. "I don't intend to suffer." It was a lie. She knew it, and he knew it. She'd already witnessed what the loss of power had done to her mother.

"You are a murderer, and yet the coven you despise so much has spared your life. You should be grateful."

"I didn't kill *anyone*." Vanessa remembered the night Susan had caused Rebecca's car to go off the bridge. She'd been there, but she had not assisted her mother in the murder.

Dylan glared at her for a long moment. "It doesn't matter whether you did it or not. You were there. You didn't stop her." He set his jaw. "As far as I'm concerned, you're just as guilty."

"Whatever." Vanessa gave a dismissive wave.

"If you *ever* come back here, I won't be so generous. Are we clear?"

Vanessa gulped. He'd kill her. Of that, she had no doubt. "I have no intention of returning." She raised her chin and stepped off the yacht without looking back. She planned to visit her mother one last time, return to California, and assume a new alias. Beaufort had become a past she'd never revisit. A bitter memory she'd just as soon forget.

She slid into the driver's seat of her black BMW and eased out of the parking space for her final trip down Front Street.

chapter forty

Stevie

Stevie parked her car in front of her parents' house, and her father waved a greeting from his perch on the front porch steps. Wearing old gray sweatpants and his favorite Big Rock Blue Marlin Tournament t-shirt, he busied himself tying and retying his sneakers.

"Hey, Dad." She pointed to his shoelaces. "Whatcha doin'?"

"Hi, Stephanie." He patted his tennis shoes. "I'm just getting ready to go for a walk. Doc says I have to get in thirty minutes of exercise *every day*." He scrunched up his face.

"It's good for you, Dad."

"I know. I know." He stood up. "I'm doing my best to follow all of his rules."

Stevie smiled and hugged him. "I know it's not easy. But I'm glad you're doing it. We want to keep you with us for a long time."

"I wouldn't mind sticking around for a while myself." He patted his chest. "Your mom's in the kitchen with Deborah." He shook his head in melodramatic exasperation. "Seemed like a good time for me to get out for my walk."

"Can't say that I blame you." Stevie let herself into the house.

As she made her way to the kitchen, she heard her mother and Deborah talking. "You need to ask them first!"

"Now, where's the fun in that?" Deborah laughed. "Besides, it's much easier to get forgiveness than permission."

"She'll be furious, and you know it."

"I'm not forcing anyone to do anything that they don't want to do. I'm just helping to open their eyes to what's right in front of them." Deborah paused. "If it's meant to be, it will be—with my help, of course."

Stevie rounded the corner into the kitchen and found Deborah sitting at the table working on her never-ending knitting project. She had just begun a new row of red.

"I hope that's not for me." Stevie pointed to the crimson knots that grew more numerous with each click of the knitting needles. *I already have my hands full at the moment.*

Patricia stood by the sink with a cup of steaming coffee in her hand. "No, honey." Grim-faced, she shook her head. "But trust me when I tell you that you don't want to know who it's for."

"Oh, come on. It won't be that bad." Deborah didn't bother to look up from her knitting.

Patricia opened her mouth to speak but stopped. She turned her attention to Stevie. "Are you ready for the storm? They're saying it'll be here tomorrow."

"Pretty much. I still have to make an extra loaf of bread to keep on hand in case we lose power and I can't bake for a couple of days."

"Good thing you're making it yourself." Deborah's needles clicked as she spoke. "I stopped by the grocery store this morning and all the bread, milk, and eggs were already sold out."

Stevie snorted. "I'll never understand that. It's like everybody's preparing for some sort of French toast emergency."

"What about water and batteries?" Patricia nodded to her pantry door. "I have plenty of extras if you need some."

"We'll be fine, Mom. I still have a lot of supplies left over from last month's hurricane." She leaned against the counter. "Besides, this one is just a tropical storm. No big deal."

Patricia took another sip of her coffee. "Why don't you and Charlie ride the storm out here?"

"Thanks, but I think Charlie will be more comfortable at home. He'll probably want to get in his hideout if the storm gets too loud." Stevie opened a cabinet door and selected a mug. "Really, Mom, we'll be okay."

"All right. But if you change your mind, the offer still stands."

Deborah glanced up from her knitting. "Did Charlie start in his new class today?"

"Yes." Stevie beamed with pride as she poured her coffee. "His new teacher is wonderful. She's one of us too."

"Oh, really? How nice." Deborah raised her eyebrows. "Anyone we know?"

"Her last name is Garner." Stevie wrapped both hands around her mug, enjoying the warmth it provided.

"Those Garners are good people." Patricia smiled. "They've always preferred to practice alone, but they've never caused any trouble."

Stevie remembered how Mrs. Garner detected that she was a witch. "Mom, how come I can't tell when someone has powers? It seems like everyone else can do it."

"Not everyone can, but I'm pretty sure you'll get the hang of it at some point." Patricia patted Stevie's arm. "You're just getting started. There's still a lot to learn."

"Like spell casting, moon phases, herbs, intuition..." Deborah rattled off the list while she knitted.

"And, of course, the histories," Patricia added, her tone matter-of-fact. "We've kept a thorough genealogical record of all the Beaufort families since the days of Hannah, Catherine, and Charlotte."

Stevie heaved a sigh. She knew there would be more to this witch stuff than merely moving objects with her mind, but she had no idea there would be so much to learn.

"And don't forget the Historic Society." Deborah's line of red yarn stretched across the full length of the blanket, so she started a new row.

"That's right. You'll need to learn the bylaws so you can take over for me when I retire."

"The Historic Society is real?" Stevie threw her head back and stared at the ceiling. "But I thought it was just a front for the coven." On top of everything else, she had to learn about that too?

"I'm afraid so, dear." Patricia nodded.

Stevie groaned. "I think I understand why so many of us prefer to be solitary practitioners."

"That's not an option for you, honey." Patricia poured more coffee into Stevie's mug. "One day, you'll be the queen. We've got to get you ready for it."

chapter forty-one

Stevie

Charlie placed his red backpack on a chair by the kitchen table and took a seat to await his afternoon snack. His face remained expressionless as he picked up his tablet and played a game.

Stevie peered at him as countless questions about his day trotted through her mind. He offered no clues about his transition to the new class. He wasn't crying, but he wasn't smiling either. She pursed her lips, wishing he could share his thoughts with her.

She plucked an apple from the fruit basket and placed it on a cutting board. Though she craved details about Charlie's experience, she knew she'd have to keep her inquiries simple. "Did you enjoy being in Mrs. Garner's class today?"

He set his tablet down. After a long moment, he dipped his chin and raised it back up again.

Stevie bit her lip, stifling a delighted squeal. She didn't want to startle Charlie but reining in her glee proved challenging. Nodding his head and having a successful day in a mainstream classroom didn't happen all the time. Forcing nonchalance, she settled herself. "Oh, good. I'm glad to hear it."

She cut the apple into slices and delivered them to Charlie on a small plate. He gobbled up the snack and then ran upstairs to his room.

Stevie had no doubt that he'd retreated to his hideout to decompress after all of the extra sensory input he'd experienced in the new classroom. She decided to let him stay up there until dinnertime if he wanted.

Her phone rang, and an unfamiliar number displayed on the caller ID. Stevie answered it on the first ring, hoping for the call she'd been waiting for.

"Hi, Stevie. It's Maura Garner. How are you?" Her cheerful voice chimed through the phone.

"I'm fine." Stevie drew in a deep breath. "How did it go?"

"He did really well." She paused for a moment. "He needed to take three breaks, which was to be expected. The good thing is that he remembered to ask for them, just the way I told him to. I've seen other children on the spectrum get so overwhelmed that they just melt down instead."

Stevie listened as the teacher described Charlie's day in exactly the sort of detail she wanted. He'd spent time reading and coloring and had even sat with the other children during circle time. It had been far more successful than she'd allowed herself to imagine.

"His speech therapist was curious about why he doesn't use the communication apps on his tablet. She says it's unusual for children his age to type their responses," Mrs. Garner said.

"I'm afraid I don't have an answer for that. We tried to get him to use those apps, but for reasons known only to Charlie, he doesn't like them." Stevie picked up the plate from the table and set it in the sink. "It's a little frustrating for me because he has only a few responses that he can type right now."

"I know this is easier said than done, but try not to worry about it. More words will come in time. My son didn't utter a word until he was six years old, and even then, he would only recite lines from television shows."

Stevie stared through her kitchen window. "It's great that he learned to speak." She'd give anything to hear Charlie's voice, even if he was only repeating someone else's words.

"Yes, but it was tough to hear him talk like that. They weren't his words, you know. Eventually though, he developed functional language. Now we can't get him to shut up." Mrs. Garner chuckled.

"How wonderful." Maybe the same thing would happen for Charlie. She placed her hand on her chest, feeling the steady thrum of her hopeful heartbeat. *Maybe.*

"My son attends the community college. He still lives at home with me, but I think he'll be able to get a place of his own someday."

"Wow." Stevie mouthed the word, but her voice failed her. She remained quiet for a moment. *College? Independent living?* These were lofty dreams she'd never dared to envision for her son. Until now.

"Charlie is very bright." Mrs. Garner's voice broke through the silence. "He's also very young. Anything is possible. Remember that."

Chapter forty-two

Vanessa

Vanessa arrived at the psychiatric hospital early Monday afternoon, prepared to confess her failure to retrieve the amulet. With a trembling hand, she signed the visitor registry. She winced, imagining the verbal assault that was about to come her way. After this, her mother would never want to see her again.

An orderly pointed her toward Susan's room. "She's in there. She hasn't come out all day."

Vanessa nodded and made her way toward her mother's closed door. She stood outside for a moment, unsure how to proceed. She took in a deep breath, bracing herself, and issued a timid knock.

"What?" Susan's voice called from the other side of the door.

Vanessa grabbed the door handle, giving it a slow turn before she pushed the door open and entered the room. "It's me, Mother."

Susan sat in a chair beside the narrow bed. "They let you out of jail?"

Her words lacked their usual sharp edges. Vanessa suspected that she had quelled her rage with pharmaceuticals once again. "I didn't realize you knew about that."

Susan glared at her daughter. "Of course I know. Your mugshot was on the news."

Vanessa cringed. She had not seen that particular photograph, but she knew it couldn't have been flattering. "I'm sorry I failed."

Susan scoffed. "I should have known better than to expect anything else from you." Her contempt for her only child seared through her drugged haze.

"The coven bound my powers. There was nothing I could do." Vanessa extended her hands, palms up. "I only came here today to say goodbye. I'm leaving for Los Angeles tonight."

"You can't leave now. You have to go back and find that necklace." Susan leaned forward in her chair. "Without it, we'll both be powerless forever."

Vanessa stepped closer to Susan. "But Mother, it was not with the treasure. For all we know, it's still sitting on the ocean floor."

"No, I've been thinking about this." She tapped a finger to her lip, pausing as if to recall an idea that was just out of reach. "The coven *must* have it. How else would they have been able to maintain control for all of these centuries?"

Vanessa rubbed her forehead. Maybe her mother really was crazy after all. They only knew about the amulet from stories and rumors passed down through the generations of their family. The damned thing might not even exist.

She glanced at her watch. "I have to get to the airport. I don't want to miss my flight."

"You would leave me here? All alone?" Susan's lip quivered, though not a single tear fell.

Never once had she felt like her mother wanted her. All her life, she'd tried in vain to gain her approval, her attention, her love. She gazed through the bars in the window. Now, after all of her failures, Susan had asked her to stay.

She couldn't walk away. Not now.

"What would you have me do, Mother?"

"Just get the necklace so we can restore our powers." Susan waved her hand as if it were a simple request. "Patricia is a direct descendant of Lucia. I bet she has it somewhere. Or maybe Stevie has it…"

"Dylan will kill me if he sees me in Beaufort again."

The corners of Susan's mouth pulled up. "Not if you kill him first."

"I don't stand a chance against any of them without my powers."

"Surely even you can figure something out."

Vanessa sighed, unable to ignore the venom in Susan's words. She wanted to please her mother even more than she wanted her own powers back. But she had no idea how to procure a magical amulet that may or may not exist.

"You'll have to be creative, that's all." Susan sunk back in her chair. "Everyone has a weakness. Find theirs and exploit it." From the safety of her hospital room, Susan possessed all of the answers. "Besides, it's not like you have anything left to lose."

Vanessa grimaced as her mother's last statement hit its mark. It was the truth. "All right, Mother. I'll try again."

Vanessa drove back to Beaufort, this time obeying speed limits and all applicable traffic laws. Her mind raced with fruitless, impossible plans. Each new idea presented its own set of potential complications she knew she could not overcome.

"Everyone has a weakness," Susan had said.

That may be true, but not everyone is as powerful as Stevie and Patricia.

Even as a new, unpracticed witch, Stevie had been able to stop a speeding car in only a second. How was that even possible?

Because the boy is her weakness.

A plan began to take shape in her mind. She knew exactly how to get Stevie to divulge the location of the necklace. It wouldn't be easy. She pressed her lips together in a tight line. Not for her. Not for the boy.

But it had to be done.

chapter forty-three

Stevie

Stevie brought Charlie home early on Tuesday afternoon as the region prepared for the tropical storm's impact. He scampered inside the house right away, but she remained on the porch. An eerie calm permeated the air, an unnatural quiet that both humans and animals recognized. No seagulls flew over Taylor's Creek on this day.

As the system whirled just off the coast of North Carolina, it drew in and devoured every cloud within reach, leaving the sky over Beaufort a deceptively pale blue. But it didn't fool Stevie. She'd been through these storms more times than she could count. With a sharp pivot, she marched into her house. She had work to do.

Stevie clicked on the television to see if there'd been any changes to the storm's track. Loud, dramatic music trumpeted through the opening of the forecast, proclaiming the channel's superior ability to predict the weather. A portly weatherman appeared on the screen with excitement oozing from his pores. He stood before the Weather Command 3000 backdrop, which was nothing more than an oversized picture of a collection of high-tech electronics surrounded by a fake window frame.

"The storm has gained strength and speed over the warm waters of the Gulf Stream. With maximum sustained winds of eighty miles an hour, the National Weather Service upgraded the system to a category one hurricane." He delivered the last words one at a time, each given its own space in which to reside.

Stevie blinked and crossed her arms. This would be worse than she'd expected.

The screen now showed a different radar picture, one taken of the storm just a few hours earlier. The system appeared as a circular mass of white clouds over the Atlantic Ocean. Though it was organized enough to demonstrate a cyclonic rotation, it lacked the defined edges that were visible with a more powerful storm.

"Now I'm going to show you what has happened to the system in the last few hours." The radar picture began to move. "Watch this!"

Stevie stared at her television, observing the system's rapid transformation from tropical storm to hurricane. She'd never seen one strengthen so fast. The nearly shapeless blob of clouds swirled around and around as it inched closer to the North Carolina coast. Its edges sharpened until it formed a perfect circle, and the hazy center of the system opened up to reveal the telltale eye.

The meteorologist played the transformation again, like a color commentator watching the instant replay of a Super Bowl touchdown. "Just look at that!" He pointed to the ever-tightening hole in the clouds at the center of the storm. "That's the eye right there." He paused. "This is a fast-moving storm. We expect the eye to make landfall somewhere between Morehead City and Beaufort near ten o'clock tonight. The outer bands will begin to arrive within the hour."

A direct hit. Stevie swallowed hard and clicked off the television.

She stepped out onto her front porch and scanned her lawn for forgotten toys that would become projectiles in the high winds. Satisfied that the front yard was clear, she hauled each of her white wicker rocking chairs into the living room before passing through the house to the back door.

"Hi!" Dylan greeted her as she stepped outside. He had already flipped her patio table over and pushed it up against the house. He grabbed the thick rope hanging out of his jeans and tied the table to the porch railing.

"Thanks." She flashed him a smile and then pushed a chair toward the railing.

"My pleasure." He looped another stretch of rope, securing the remaining furniture.

She scanned the back yard for any potential projectiles. "The new forecast says it's hurricane strength now." Spotting a toy car in the grass, she bent over and snatched it up.

"Yeah, I saw that. It's been a while since I've been through one of these, but I think I'm ready." He tugged on a knot, tightening it.

"Do you want to ride it out with me and Charlie?"

A sudden gust of wind blew through the yard. They both glanced up to the sky to see the first storm clouds rolling in, well ahead of the eye of the hurricane. The angry purple forms raced across the atmosphere, heralding the imminent arrival of far worse conditions.

"Sounds good to me." Dylan tucked a leftover strand of rope into his back pocket. "I'm just going to put the cover on my boat, and I'll be right back."

Stevie went back inside and pulled out the box of hurricane supplies she kept stored in her laundry room. She left one battery-operated lantern in the kitchen and another in the den before heading upstairs to leave flashlights on the nightstands in the bedrooms.

Stopping in Charlie's room, she found that he had tucked himself inside his hideout, unwinding from his school day and preparing himself for the coming storm. She gave him a small flashlight to hold on to. "Dylan will be here soon. He's going to ride out the storm with us."

Charlie's shoulders relaxed. Stevie guessed that he appreciated having someone around who understood him so well.

"I'm here, Stevie," Dylan called from downstairs.

She turned back to Charlie. "We'll be downstairs if you want to join us." She ruffled her son's curls before turning to leave.

Stevie joined Dylan in the kitchen and began preparing dinner. She wanted to be sure to have the pork chops fried before the storm knocked out the electricity. Working in silence, she mixed a breading of rice and tapioca flours and added a few tablespoons of ground flaxseed.

She stepped to the sink to rinse her hands and peered through the window at the darkening sky. "It's coming in fast."

"That sounded ominous." Dylan opened the refrigerator and pulled a cucumber from the crisper. "The hurricane you had here last month was stronger than this one. Why are you so worried?"

"That hurricane just brushed past us; it never made landfall. This one is expected to be a direct hit." Realizing her words tumbled from her mouth too fast, she paused and took a breath to steady herself. "It's still just a category one though. I'm sure we'll be fine." Her hands trembled as she gathered the spices to add to her breading.

Dylan ran a sharp knife through the cucumber. When the blade struck the cutting board, Stevie jumped and dropped a pork chop into her flour mixture, hurling a rush of white powder across her countertop.

She pursed her lips, frustrated with herself. Where had all of this anxiety come from? Hurricanes were as much a part of coastal living as salt water was. She'd been through far worse storms than this. What was so different this time around?

Charlie entered the kitchen and found a spot at the table. He sat in silence for a few minutes, watching Stevie coat the pork chops in the flour mixture as the oil heated in a cast-iron pan.

Her dismal mood worsened as the haze of the hurricane's outer bands overtook the Beaufort sky. Though the sun had not yet set, it was almost as black as midnight outside. Gusting breezes had grown into a steady wind, swaying thick tree branches and creating choppy whitecaps on the typically calm waters of Taylor's Creek.

Without discussion, Stevie and Dylan finished preparing the meal while Charlie fiddled with his tablet. When Stevie lifted the last pork chop from the frying pan, Dylan plated their dinner and delivered it to the table. In the silence, her mind wandered to catastrophic storm surges, toppled trees, and devastating winds.

Stevie tilted a pitcher over her glass only to slosh sweet tea onto the counter. Muttering under her breath, she wiped up the mess and carried her drink to the table. Ice clinked against the glass as it wobbled in her shaking hand.

She crossed the kitchen once more to grab the silverware, and as she opened the drawer, Dylan brushed her arm. She hadn't seen him follow her from the table, and she jumped at the unexpected touch.

"Are you okay?" His brow furrowed as he leaned close. "You seem really out of sorts."

"I can't explain it." She shrugged "I just have a very strange feeling about tonight."

"You've been under a lot of stress. It's understandable that you'd be anxious."

Stevie gave a curt nod as if to acknowledge the accuracy of his assumption, but she knew stress didn't explain this overwhelming bout of nervousness. "I'm glad you're here though. That helps." She selected forks and knives from the drawer and closed it.

They joined Charlie at the table. Stevie tried to let her worries go as she shared stories of previous hurricanes—ones she experienced as a child as well as the hurricane parties she attended as a young adult. With each tale, she reminded herself that each of those storms had come and gone without incident, just as this one would.

The wind howled, and the light over the table flickered as the conversation between Stevie and Dylan went on. When they finished eating, he cleared the table and cleaned the kitchen while Stevie pulled several small votive candles from a cabinet.

"I'll go ahead and put these out." Stevie bristled as the lights flickered again. "Looks like we'll need them soon."

She busied herself scattering candles around the first floor of the house, and she lit a few so they would be glowing when the lights went off. The activity did nothing to ease her nagging sense that something terrible was about to happen. She rattled off a checklist in her mind. Food. Water. Candles. Batteries. She had everything she needed to ride out the storm. *We're prepared for the worst.*

But she didn't feel ready at all.

Chapter forty-four

Stevie

Stevie and Dylan settled in the den with Charlie. She had picked up a new box of Lincoln Logs as a distraction for Charlie, and he'd already begun to build a house with it. The new set held enough logs and directions for creating a small village, but he ignored the colorful instruction sheet and set out to make one of his own unique creations.

Though Charlie preferred to keep his Lincoln Log masterpieces in his room, Stevie had insisted he stay downstairs as the storm's intensity increased. She watched him stack one log on top of another and resisted the urge to hold on to him. *It's silly to be this nervous.* With two witches in the house, they could stave off any danger the hurricane presented.

The rain pounded sideways against the house, like a persistent onslaught of metal pellets attacking the old wooden structure. The wind howled, hurling leaves from the live oak trees in every direction. Stevie winced at the racket, but Charlie remained calm. She wondered if the steady white noise of the heavy rain drowned out all of the other storm sounds that usually bothered him.

The lights flickered one last time before they went out. Stevie jumped up and switched on the lantern so Charlie could continue his work.

Dylan looked up from the novel he'd been reading. "I never noticed that before."

"What?"

"There's no thunder and lightning during hurricanes." He closed the book and set it on the coffee table. "Right, Charlie?"

Charlie continued playing, but Dylan tilted his head to the side and frowned. "Oh, I'm sorry." He turned to Stevie. "I meant to say that it's a *rare* occurrence." He glanced back at Charlie, who appeared to be focused on his Lincoln Log masterpiece. "Is that better?"

Charlie nodded without pausing his cabin construction.

Dylan grinned. "Smart kid."

It was well past Charlie's bedtime, but Stevie didn't mind allowing him to stay up later than usual given the circumstances. She intended to let him play right there in the den until he fell asleep on his own. Even then, she would keep him close, just in case. Jittery, she tapped her hand on her knee as she watched him. In spite of her attempts to relax, she'd only grown more unsettled as the storm wailed outside.

"Did you say something?" Deep creases appeared on Dylan's forehead.

"No." Stevie mirrored his confused expression. "What's wrong?"

Dylan rose to his feet and crossed the room to look out the window. He peered into the darkness and cocked his head, listening to something she couldn't hear.

He whirled around. "She's here!"

266

Stevie's eyes darted from Dylan to Charlie, and she jumped to her feet. Just as she reached for her son, the back door crashed open. Charlie jerked his head up as the unexpected noise jolted him from his construction project.

Before any of them had a chance to move, Vanessa burst into the den. Soaked tendrils of her long black hair clung to her face. Hatred darkened her eyes as her lips contorted into a wicked sneer.

Stevie's thoughts flew faster than the howling wind. She had to get Charlie to safety. Her heart thundered in her chest.

"Charlie, vacuum!" Stevie's gaze remained locked on Vanessa as her son stood and started to run from the den.

As he raced by her, Vanessa reached out to grab him, but Dylan threw her against the wall with an unseen force.

Charlie kept running. Stevie listened to his footsteps pound down the hall. *Don't stop.* When the rapid patter of his feet faded up the stairs, she knew he was heading to his hideout.

She glared at Vanessa. Now she knew the reason for the fear that had gnawed at her all night. It had never been the storm. Somehow, she had sensed the danger that stood before her now.

Dylan clenched his teeth. "I told you there would be no second chances if you came back!"

Vanessa stood tall, her expression impassive. Without a word, she slipped her hand into the pocket of her rain jacket.

Stevie's gaze darted to Dylan as he lurched forward. *He must have heard her thoughts.* She jerked her head back to Vanessa.

"No!" He jumped in front of Stevie, shielding her with his own body.

When Vanessa whipped a handgun from her pocket, Stevie realized too late why Dylan had leapt in front of her. Unable to draw a steady breath, she tried to summon her magic, focus her thoughts. But she couldn't do it. She could only see the glint of steel in the dark witch's hand.

In one swift movement, Vanessa leveled the weapon straight at Dylan's chest and fired. He slumped in a heap at Stevie's feet.

"Dylan!" The thunderous report clanged in Stevie's ears as she dropped to his side and placed her shaking hand over the wound in his chest, trying to stop the gush of blood. "No, no, no…" She wanted to hold him, to save him, but she had to stay alert. The next bullet would come for her and then…Charlie. She pulled her hand away and tightened it into a fist.

Stevie stood to face their attacker.

"He was irrelevant." Vanessa waved the gun as she spoke. "He always has been."

A rage she had never known before ripped through Stevie's body. Her muscles tensed as she drew on her power. She had no idea if her new abilities could outweigh the danger of the gun, but she was willing to die to keep Charlie safe. She focused her energy on the steely gray weapon.

In an instant, the gun flew out of Vanessa's hand and crashed to the wooden floor with a thud. Stevie soared over Dylan's body, hurling herself at their attacker.

She tackled her and took her down. Vanessa's arms flailed as she used her long fingernails like claws, seeking purchase on Stevie's skin. Stevie grasped for the dark witch's throat but stopped cold as Vanessa's nails tore deep gashes along the side of her face. Her skin ripped, flooding her with shock and pain, and she fell back.

Vanessa scrambled to her feet and raced toward the gun.

Stevie refocused and lunged once more, throwing the dark witch away from the weapon. She clutched a handful of black hair and pulled Vanessa to her feet. Determined to protect her child, she slammed the other woman's head against the wall.

Stevie bent over to retrieve the gun, but Vanessa kicked her in the side as she reached for it. Agony seared through her chest as her ribs cracked. She collapsed on the floor, breathless.

Vanessa grabbed the weapon and aimed it at Stevie, but she did not fire. Instead, she ran from the den and down the narrow hall. Her footsteps thudded on the stairs.

Charlie!

chapter forty-five

Stevie

Stevie's gaze fell on Dylan as she struggled to pull herself up from the floor. A stain of bright red blood expanded across his shirt. His breaths puffed out, strained and shallow.

As much as she wanted to, she could not help him now. Charlie needed her, and she knew Dylan would want her to save her son before anything else.

She stood, hunched over, grimacing from the jolts of pain coming from her broken ribs. She had to stop Vanessa before she found Charlie.

As she stumbled out of the room, she lowered her shield, freeing her focus to fight Vanessa. If there was any chance that Dylan could still hear her thoughts, she wanted to make sure he knew that he was not alone.

Don't let go. I'll come back for you.

Stevie gripped the railing and bit her lip to silence her gasps as she climbed the steps. Guided by the faint flickers from the candles she'd set out before the storm, she pushed through her pain to get to Charlie. No sound came from his room—no noises at all, in fact. Praying he was still hidden, she marched on.

It grew darker as she neared the upstairs landing, and she wished she'd thought to leave candles up here too. She pulled herself up onto the final step and headed straight for Charlie's room.

The sound of her own pounding heart rang heavy in her ears. As she crept into the absolute darkness of her son's bedroom, she felt her way along the wall, inching closer to his nightstand. She touched the corner of the small table and slid her hand along its surface until she bumped against the flashlight she'd left there before the storm. She snatched it up and clutched it to her chest.

A low moan came from close by. Stevie clicked on the flashlight and light filled the room.

She gasped at the sight. Charlie stood motionless near the foot of his bed. He held his arms straight out in front of him, palms facing forward. Just a few feet away, Vanessa lay slumped on the floor, dazed. A circular cell composed of nothing more than mere Lincoln Logs imprisoned her.

Stevie's jaw dropped. *He did this?*

Her stunned gaze traveled from him, to Vanessa, to the table in the back of the room that had once held his log village. The table was empty.

Yes, Charlie did this. She glanced back at him. Bursting with pride and relief, Stevie realized that he'd protected himself. She wanted to reach for him, to hold him. But she held back. His new gift would be difficult enough to manage, and a distraction was the last thing he needed.

Vanessa pushed herself up from the floor and swiped at the flimsy stacks of toy logs, expecting them to give way. Wide-eyed and furious, she stumbled back when they refused to topple.

Shaking off her own shock, Stevie stepped forward and grabbed the gun that lay on the floor just outside of the wooden prison. Wincing from the effort, she pressed her hand tight against her shattered ribs.

Vanessa sneered at her through the fixed logs that comprised her magical cell. "Let me out of here!"

Stevie held her chin high, ignoring the pain that exploded throughout her body. She didn't want to shoot Vanessa in front of Charlie, but she had to end the threat somehow and get back to Dylan.

She tracked Vanessa's seething glare as the dark witch's attention shifted to Charlie.

His face was like stone, and he stared straight on, unblinking. Her son's focus appeared unshakable.

But Stevie knew better.

Vanessa gripped the toy logs, turning her knuckles white. "I said let me out of here!" She attempted to shake the unyielding bars of her prison once more. "Ah!" She began to prowl within her cell. Stalking, watching. A caged beast ready to strike.

A sheen of sweat formed on their prisoner's brow. She bared her teeth and lunged at the bars, shattering the quiet with a feral scream.

At the sound of Vanessa's shriek, Charlie clasped his hands over his ears. The cell collapsed, sending hundreds of Lincoln Logs raining down, clattering against the old wooden floor.

Vanessa bolted out of the room and raced down the stairs. Stevie chased her, but her injuries slowed her pace. She pressed on, in spite of the pain.

"Stay in your room, Charlie!" She fought her way down the stairs, each step rattling the cracked bones in her chest. Stevie gripped the gun tighter, prepared to use it. Vanessa would not terrorize her family again.

Vanessa threw open the door and fled across the street toward the private docks. By the time Stevie made it onto the porch, Vanessa was nearing the end of Dylan's dock.

Stevie struggled to catch her breath, even as each gasp tore at her broken ribs. She reached for the porch railing to steady herself, knowing she would never be able to catch Vanessa now. The wind whipped her hair, slapping tendrils across her face.

Through the pouring rain, she watched the woman's dark form pull the cover from Dylan's boat.

I can't let her get away!

Stevie raised the gun to fire, but her hands shook so hard she couldn't make the shot.

Remembering her target practice with Randy, she formulated a plan. She was still unsure of her own power and not certain if she was strong enough to accomplish what she needed to do.

But she had to try.

In the darkness, Stevie could no longer see Vanessa, but she could hear the mighty roar of the boat's engine as it fired it up. The sound began to diminish as the vessel raced out of Taylor's Creek, heading toward the inlet. She placed the gun on the porch railing.

Stevie stood tall, ignoring the trauma of her wounds as she drew in as deep of a breath as she could.

There was only one way to keep Charlie safe.

Harm no one.

She pressed her lips together. This was the only way.

She focused not on Vanessa but on the only sound that rang through the night—the engine. She called on every bit of energy she had. The round, white mass swelled in the palm of her hand. When the heat from its energy became unbearable, Stevie fired it at her target.

Her energy shot through the air, lighting up the night in a bolt of unparalleled brightness, and plunged into the speedboat with the swiftness of a hunter's dagger. A fiery explosion flashed on the water, sending countless pieces of fiberglass in every direction.

Stevie stumbled back, slack-jawed, shocked by her own strength. She watched the flames lick up from the wreckage, burning the remains of the boat...and Vanessa.

She turned away, unwilling to face what she had just done. Her stomach clenched. She'd never dreamed she would end anyone's life. *But I had to.*

She shook away the remorse. She had to get to Dylan.

Stevie retrieved the gun from the railing and cast a final glance at the flaming mass in the water before she rushed back inside.

Dylan hadn't moved since she last saw him. She dropped to her knees, placed the gun on the floor, and cradled his face in her hands. He huffed out weak, inconsistent breaths.

"Stay with me!" Her gaze dropped to the ocean of crimson blood that stretched across his shirt. He was slipping away.

Hot tears pooled in her eyes. She knew what she wanted now. She didn't care what anyone else thought. She didn't care what Sam thought. She wanted Dylan.

Chapter forty-six

Stevie

Randy burst through the front door. "Stevie?"

"In here!" She kept her hand pressed against the gaping wound in Dylan's chest, trying to slow his blood loss.

Randy rushed in, rainwater dripping from his clothes. His gaze darted around the room. "Where's Charlie? Is he okay?"

"He's in his room. He's not hurt, but I'm sure he's terrified." Stevie squeezed her eyes shut for a moment. "I need to tell him we're safe now."

"Safe? Where's Vanessa?" Randy knelt over Dylan's body. "I had a vision, but I only saw you two get hurt."

Stevie hung her head. "I—I killed her."

He nodded and focused on Dylan's injury. Holding his weathered hand above the bloody wound, he said nothing as he willed the bullet back out of the hole. When it reached the surface of Dylan's skin, he plucked it out as if he were picking a grape from a vine. He placed the mangled metal on the floor.

Remaining silent, he rested his palm against Dylan's chest. When he lifted his arm, smooth skin appeared where the wound had been.

"Is he going to be okay?" Stevie pressed her fist to her lips.

"Yes, just give him a few minutes to come around." Randy studied the gashes on her cheek. "Now, let me take care of you."

"I need to get to Charlie." Stevie stumbled as she tried to stand. She gasped and clutched at her ribs.

Randy put his hands on her shoulders, holding her in place. "It will just take a minute. Broken bones and cuts are even easier to fix than bullet holes."

Stevie sighed her agreement and waited as Randy worked his magic. The instant he touched her shattered ribs, relief washed over her. The pain dissipated, replaced with the strange tingling sensation of bones knitting back together. In a matter of seconds, her ribs had completely healed. She inhaled a deep, desperate breath, reveling in the absence of pain. She would never take breathing for granted again.

Randy looked to the deep cuts on her face. "Looks like you were attacked by a wild animal."

"It sure felt like it at the time." Stevie shuddered.

Randy's white eyebrows knitted together. "I can take care of them."

When he cupped her face, Stevie's skin stretched back together as, one by one, each of the four deep gashes closed. Unexpected warmth grew in her cheek and burrowed down through the layers of her flesh.

Randy stepped back and grinned, pleased with his work. Stevie reached up to touch her cheek, surprised by its smooth texture. Even without a mirror, she knew her scars were healed. No sign of Vanessa's attack remained.

"Thank you, Randy. I don't know what we would have done without you." She choked up, a knot of unshed pain lodging in her throat. "Dylan would have died if it weren't for you."

Randy wrapped her in a hug. "You're safe now, Stevie."

She pulled away, realizing he was soaked from head to toe. "How did you manage to get here in the storm?"

He rubbed his neck. "The Buick had a harder time of it than I did. Going to need a new windshield for sure, maybe a new transmission."

"I'm sorry…"

"Don't worry about it. Between my mechanic and my magic, I'm sure I'll get it working again." He pointed down at the gun. "Would you like me to take care of that for you?"

"Yes, please. I need to go get Charlie." She passed him the weapon and stepped toward the stairs. When Dylan groaned, she whirled around and rushed back to his side.

His eyes fluttered open but were slow to focus. Stevie cast a worried glance at Randy. "Is that normal?"

"Honey, none of this is *normal*." He shook his head. "But yes, it'll take him a moment to process what has happened. He's okay."

Dylan lifted his head and glanced down at the bloodstains on his shirt. He brought his hand to his chest and patted it. "Thanks, Doc." He pulled himself up from the floor. Good as new.

He reached for Stevie and wrapped his arms around her. "I heard you."

"I meant it." She smiled as she met his gaze, lost for the moment in his eyes.

He leaned in, inching closer until he pressed his lips against hers, saying with a kiss everything they both felt, everything that would have to go unspoken for now.

Dylan pulled back and released her from his embrace. "Go get Charlie."

Stevie rushed out of the den, pausing only to scoop up a flashlight on her way out. Still unsure of how she was going to explain everything, she sprinted up the stairs to her son's bedroom.

She shined the flashlight beam into the room, expecting to see the scattered pile of Lincoln Logs on the floor. Instead, she found all of Charlie's creations on their usual table in the back of the room, as if nothing had happened.

Magic.

She spun around to face the wall and reached for the secret switch that opened the door to the hidden room. Her head ached with memories of the night her powers manifested. Now, she knew, Charlie endured the same.

She cracked the door open. "Charlie, it's just me."

She eased into the small room and sat on the floor next to him. She clicked off the flashlight and leaned against the wall, letting out a heavy sigh.

"We're safe now." She wrapped her arm around him. "She won't ever come back."

Stevie closed her eyes as he relaxed into her. Moments like this were rare with Charlie, and she gladly accepted the weight of her little boy as he rested against her body. She sat in silence for a while, savoring the sensation of being so close to him.

Everyday life was challenging enough to navigate with Charlie's limited communication skills. How could they begin to work through *this*? He'd have questions that he couldn't ask, and she'd have answers that she couldn't share.

Deciding to start at the beginning, Stevie opened her eyes. "We have a lot to talk about, Charlie." She stroked his blond curls.

She gave him an abbreviated, child-friendly version of the coven's history. She left out the details of how Blackbeard's DNA became involved, and she omitted the stories of the murders committed by the dark witches. In a few years, when Charlie was older, she would go into more detail.

Stevie couldn't avoid explaining Vanessa's attack. She spoke of the encounter with simple honesty, reminding Charlie often that they were no longer in any danger. "It's over. We're safe." She squeezed him tighter. "You're safe."

She continued, weaving an image of happy magic—a special gift that he had to use judiciously, and never in the presence of others. *Was it enough? Did he understand?* As smart as Charlie was, he was still only five years old. She wasn't sure that he would have the self-control to limit his magical activities. She raised her hand to her chest. As if autism weren't enough of a challenge, she now had to worry that he might accidentally expose them all.

With reluctance, she released her hold on him. "Shall we go check on Dylan?"

They emerged from the hideout together, and Stevie clicked on the flashlight again. She shined the beam on Charlie's collection of Lincoln Log buildings.

"You did a great job putting everything back together." She smiled.

Charlie's gaze flicked to his mother's face and then back to the floor.

"Magic," he said. It was barely more than a whisper.

Stevie froze, unable to breathe. Her legs wobbled beneath her, and she dropped to her knees.

She cupped his cheeks, listening to his solitary word echo in her mind. The joy of the moment exceeded anything she'd dared to imagine through the long years of his excruciating silence. *Magic.* The very best kind of magic.

She wrapped her arms around her son, overcome with gratitude and love and hope.

Especially hope.

chapter forty-seven

Stevie

Stevie stood on her front porch and gazed over the water as the sun rose on a new day. The storm was over, but it had left its mark. Leaves and branches carpeted her yard, and a restaurant sign lay mangled in a puddle on Front Street.

But these damages were fixable.

The night before, she'd stood on this very spot and blown up a speedboat—with Vanessa on it. Other than the absence of Dylan's boat, there was no evidence of the fiery spectacle that had occurred on Taylor's Creek. With its glassy surface, the water had erased her sin. She glanced up, studying a lone white cloud as it floated by. If only she could forget as easily as the water had.

"Good morning, beautiful." Shirtless, Dylan stepped onto the porch behind her and slipped his arms around her waist. "Did you sleep at all last night?"

Stevie shook her head. "No."

"Still thinking about Vanessa?"

"I killed her, Dylan." She scrunched her face, pained. "It would be bad enough if it had happened while she was here, but I did it when she was running away. I don't know how I can live with myself."

"She came after Charlie twice, and she shot me. We both saw the look in her eyes. She would have come back. You know she would have. It was self-defense." He stroked her arms. "I'm sure the coven will see it that way too."

Stevie swallowed hard. "Do you think they'll bind my power?"

Dylan was quiet for a moment. "Your mother is a reasonable person. I'm sure she'll understand that your actions were necessary." He spun her around and looked into her eyes. "Honestly, Stevie, I would have done the same thing. I think any of us would have."

Stevie rested her head on Dylan's bare chest and hid in the warmth of his embrace, grateful for his support.

"Good morning, kids," Randy called from the doorway. "Is the coffee on yet?"

"Not yet, Randy. I'm sorry. The power's still out." Stevie slipped out of Dylan's arms and faced the doctor.

Randy burst into a hearty chuckle. Dylan joined in with a laugh of his own.

Stevie tilted her head and cast a confused glance at both of them. "What's so funny?"

"You can stop speeding cars and blow up boats, but it never occurred to you that you could power up the coffee maker without electricity?" Randy stretched out his arms, amused and bewildered.

Hot embarrassment crept into Stevie's cheeks. She'd wanted a cup of hot coffee since before the sun had come up. There'd been plenty of time to figure out how to get the coffee maker going.

"Well, let me fix that right now." She stomped back into her house, heading straight for the kitchen.

Stevie held tight to Charlie's hand as they walked the short distance to her mother's house. Many of the town's residents were working hard to clear the storm debris from their yards. Stevie smiled and waved as she passed her neighbors.

Charlie had not spoken another word since the night before, but Stevie was confident more would come in time. She gave his hand a squeeze, dreaming of all that he might say someday.

When Patricia opened the door, her gaze dropped to Charlie. Her eyes lit up, and she clasped a hand over her mouth before uttering a word. Stevie recognized the pride in her mother's expression.

She looked to Stevie, seeking confirmation. Stevie smiled and nodded.

Patricia bent down to Charlie's level. "I'm so happy to see you! The power came back on a while ago, and Grandpa is watching TV in the den. Why don't you join him?" She leaned in closer to him. "Remember to be a good boy. No magic in front of Grandpa."

She beamed as she watched her grandson walk into the house. "He's so young. I think he might be our youngest yet."

Stevie stood, rigid, on the porch. She had so many things to tell her mother, but she had no idea where to start.

"Well, don't just stand there, Stevie. Come on in!" Patricia stepped back and motioned for her to follow.

"Mom, I have to tell you something." She waited as her mother stepped outside and closed the door.

Patricia listened as she relayed the story of Vanessa's attack and Charlie's newly developed powers. She nodded even as Stevie stumbled through the account of Vanessa's demise.

"Well, it's not an ideal outcome, but I understand why you did it. You were protecting Charlie." Patricia hugged her.

Stevie pulled back. "But I broke the rules."

"There are exceptions to every rule." Patricia winked. "Now, let's put this behind us. It's over now."

Stevie's shoulders relaxed, unburdened by her confession. "There's something else, Mom."

"Oh?" Patricia raised an eyebrow.

"Charlie spoke."

"He did? What did he say?" Patricia clapped her hands together and hugged Stevie again.

Buoyed by the memory, Stevie smiled. "He said 'magic.'"

Patricia laughed. "That's my favorite word!"

Chapter forty-eight

Susan

Susan sat alone on the worn couch in the day room, waiting for the news program to start. She'd heard the wind and rain from the hurricane the night before, but the hospital's sturdy structure had kept the disturbances to a minimum.

The show began with the promise of a shocking discovery on Atlantic Beach, near Fort Macon State Park. Video footage showed hundreds of tires washed ashore on the sandy beach.

What a mess.

The newscaster began her report. "Crystal Coast beaches are littered with tires today due to the turbulent water conditions brought on by the hurricane. These tires were once part of a decades-old artificial reef located several miles offshore. It's a familiar sight on our beaches following a big storm, but this time, something else washed ashore along with those tires."

The screen displayed video of an emergency medical technician closing the doors on an ambulance. Red lights flashed, and the siren blared as it hurried out of view.

"A young woman was found among the tires on the beach. She'd suffered horrible burns and lost consciousness shortly after beachgoers discovered her. At this time, we do not know her identity or how she came to sustain such extensive injuries. We'll bring you updates as the story develops."

Already bored, Susan turned away from the television and searched the day room for a nurse. It was time for her morning medications.

About the Author

Chrissy Lessey is a beach bum with a deep appreciation for good jokes, strong coffee, and salt air. She lives on the beautiful Crystal Coast of North Carolina where she finds endless opportunities to procrastinate and daydream. A long-time fan of rock music, Chrissy married a talented drummer. She still loves listening to him play—as long as it's not in the house. Together, they have two energetic children and an ill-mannered dog.

She enjoys connecting with her fans both in person and online. Visit ChrissyLessey.com or follow her on Facebook, Twitter, and Instagram to stay up-to-date on her latest book news and upcoming appearances.

praise for the crystal coast series

"*The Coven* is atmospheric, intriguing, and at times deeply moving. With terrific characters, a vivid setting, and plot that clips along smartly, this book is a great read. A series to dive into!"

-Paula Brackston,
New York Times Bestselling Author of *The Witch's Daughter*

"Very well-written, easy to read and engaging. I was surprised by how much I cared about the characters. For me, this demonstrates Lessey's ability to cross genre boundaries and engage ALL readers."

-Steph Post,
author of *Lightwood*

"Lessey's story is both heartwarming and surprisingly believable."

-C.H. Armstrong,
author of *The Edge of Nowhere*

"I devoured this book in one sitting! *The Coven* opens the reader's mind to the magic all around us. Ms. Lessey's beautiful account of the lengths a mother will go to for her child is splattered with a family's age-old quest for revenge, a touch of romance, and a loving account of a small town community's bond and commitment to each other. Fans of Nora Roberts' light paranormal stories (Cousins O'Dwyer Trilogy, Three Sisters Island Trilogy) will love *The Coven*."

-Jessica Calla,
author of The Sheridan Hall Series and *The Love Square*

"It's *Practical Magic* meets *Steel Magnolias*."

-Chanda Platania,
Neuse Regional Library

"Chrissy Lessey doesn't disappoint with her fast-paced, easy-to-read, enjoyable witch story. I loved the setting and the relationship between Stevie and her son Charlie, who has autism. The connection of the witches to the famous pirate Blackbeard is a great twist."

-Teri Harman,
author of The Moonlight Trilogy

"*The Coven* is extraordinary for two reasons. First, it is a well-written story with fully developed characters. The story draws you in and doesn't let go. The second reason I love *The Coven* is the way the author treats her autistic character. Too often, these depictions wind up being caricatures of autism. Chrissy Lessey manages to avoid this by presenting a realistic character who is multifaceted and engaging. My heartfelt thanks for that."

-Josh Leone,
author of The Calling Tower Saga

Made in the USA
Middletown, DE
16 July 2018